The CALLING of DAN MATTHEWS

Harold Bell Wright
Author of *The Shepherd of the Hills*

The CALLING *of* DAN MATTHEWS

PELICAN PUBLISHING COMPANY
Gretna 2002

Copyright © 1909
By Harold Bell Wright and Elsberg W. Reynolds

Copyright © 1995
By Pelican Publishing Company, Inc.

First hardcover edition, August 1909
First Pelican paperback edition, March 1995
Second paperback printing, September 2002

---

*The word "Pelican" and the depiction of a pelican
are trademarks of Pelican Publishing Company, Inc.,
and are registered in the U.S. Patent and Trademark Office.*

Library of Congress Cataloging-in-Publication Data

Wright, Harold Bell, 1872-1944.
  The calling of Dan Matthews / by Harold Bell Wright. — 1st
Pelican pbk. ed.
    p. cm.
  ISBN 1-56554-048-4
  1. City and town life—Ozark Mountains Region—Fiction.
2. Clergy—Ozark Mountains Region—Fiction. I. Title.
PS3545.R45C3 1994
813'.4—dc20   93-41972
                                                        CIP

Printed in Canada

Published by Pelican Publishing Company, Inc.
1000 Burmaster Street, Gretna, Louisiana 70053

CONTENTS

CONTENTS

The CALLING *of* DAN MATTHEWS

The
Calling of Dan Matthews

CHAPTER I.

THE HOME OF THE ALLY

"And because the town of this story is what it is, there came to dwell in it a Spirit—a strange, mysterious power—playful, vicious, deadly; a Something to be at once feared and courted; to be denied—yet confessed in the denial; a deadly enemy, a welcome friend, an all-powerful Ally."

HIS story began in the Ozark Mountains. It follows the trail that is nobody knows how old. But mostly this story happened in Corinth, a town of the middle class in a Middle Western state.

There is nothing peculiar about Corinth. The story might have happened just as well in any other place, for the only distinguishing feature about this town is its utter lack of any distinguishing feature whatever. In all the essential elements of its life, so far as this story goes, Corinth is exactly like every other village, town or city in the land. This, indeed, is why the story happened in this particular place.

Years ago, when the railroad first climbed the

backbone of the Ozarks, it found Corinth already located on the summit. Even before the war, this county-seat town was a place of no little importance, and many a good tale might be told of those exciting days when the woods were full of guerrillas and bushwhackers, and the village was raided first by one side, then by the other. Many a good tale *is* told, indeed; for the fathers and mothers of Corinth love to talk of the war times, and to point out in Old Town the bullet-marked buildings and the scenes of many thrilling events.

But the sons and daughters of the passing generation, with their sons and daughters, like better to talk of the great things that are going to be— when the proposed shoe-factory comes, the talked-of mills are established, the dreamed-of electric line is built out from the city, or the Capitalist from Somewhere-else arrives to invest in vacant lots, thereon to build new hotels and business blocks.

The Doctor says that in the whole history of Corinth there are only two events. The first was the coming of the railroad; the second was the death of the Doctor's good friend, the Statesman.

The railroad did not actually enter Corinth. It stopped at the front gate. But with Judge Strong's assistance the fathers and mothers recognized their "golden opportunity" and took the step which the eloquent Judge assured them would result in a "glorious future." They left the beautiful, well-drained site chosen by those who cleared the wilderness, and stretched themselves out along the mud-flat on either side of the sacred right-of-way—that same mud-flat being, incidentally, the property of the patriotic Judge.

Thus Corinth took the railroad to her heart, literally. The depot, the yards, the red section-house and the water-tank are all in the very center of the town. Every train while stopping for water (and they all stop) blocks two of the three principal streets. And when, after waiting in the rain or snow until his patience is nearly exhausted, the humble Corinthian goes to the only remaining crossing, he always gets there just in time to meet a long freight backing onto the siding. Nowhere in the whole place can one escape the screaming whistle, clanging bell, and crashing drawbar. Day and night the rumble of the heavy trains jars and disturbs the peacefulness of the little village.

But the railroad did something for Corinth; not too much, but something. It did more for Judge Strong. For a time the town grew rapidly. Fulfillment of the Judge's prophecies seemed immediate and certain. Then, as mysteriously as they had come, the boom days departed. The mills, factories and shops that were going to be, established themselves elsewhere. The sound of the builder's hammer was no longer heard. The Doctor says that Judge Strong had come to believe in his own prediction, or at least, fearing that his prophecy might prove true, refused to part with more land except at prices that would be justified only in a great metropolis.

Neighboring towns that were born when Corinth was middle-aged, flourished and have become cities

15

of importance. The country round about has grown rich and prosperous. Each year more and heavier trains thunder past on their way to and from the great city by the distant river, stopping only to take water. But in this swiftly moving stream of life Corinth is caught in an eddy. Her small world has come to swing in a very small circle—it can scarcely be said to swing at all. The very children stop growing when they become men and women, and are content to dream the dreams their fathers' fathers dreamed, even as they live in the houses the fathers of their fathers built. Only the trees that line the unpaved streets have grown—grown and grown until overhead their great tops touch to shut out the sky with an arch of green, and their mighty trunks crowd contemptuously aside the old sidewalks, with their decayed and broken boards.

Old Town, a mile away, is given over to the negroes. The few buildings that remain are fallen into ruin, save as they are patched up by their dusky tenants. And on the hill, the old Academy with its broken windows, crumbling walls, and fallen chimneys, stands a pitiful witness of an honor and dignity that is gone.

Poor Corinth! So are gone the days of her true glory—the glory of her usefulness, while the days of her promised honor and power are not yet fulfilled.

And because the town of this story is what it is, there came to dwell in it a Spirit—a strange, mysterious power—playful, vicious, deadly; a Something to be at once feared and courted; to be denied

16

—yet confessed in the denial; a dreaded enemy, a welcome friend, an all-powerful Ally.

But, for Corinth, the humiliation of her material failure is forgotten in her pride of a finer success. The shame of commercial and civic obscurity is lost in the light of national recognition. And that self-respect and pride of place, without which neither man nor town can look the world in the face, is saved to her by the Statesman.

Born in Corinth, a graduate of the old Academy, town clerk, mayor, county clerk, state senator, congressman, his zeal in advocating a much discussed issue of his day, won for him national notice, and for his town everlasting fame.

In this man unusual talents were combined with rare integrity of purpose and purity of life. Politics to him meant a way whereby he might serve his fellows. However much men differed as to the value of the measures for which he fought, no one ever doubted his belief in them or questioned his reasons for fighting. It was not at all strange that such a man should have won the respect and friendship of the truly great. But with all the honors that came to him, the Statesman's heart never turned from the little Ozark town, and it was here among those who knew him best that his influence for good was greatest and that he was most loved and honored. Thus all that the railroad failed to do for Corinth the Statesman did in a larger, finer way.

Then the Statesman died.

It was the Old Town Corinth of the brick

Academy days, that inspired the erection of a monument to his memory. But it was the Corinth of the
newer railroad days that made this monument of
cast-iron; and under the cast-iron, life-sized, portrait
figure of the dead statesman, this newer Corinth
placed in cast-iron letters a quotation from one of his
famous speeches upon an issue of his day.

The Doctor argues in language most vigorous that
the broken sidewalks, the permitted insolence of the
railroad, the presence and power of that Spirit, the
Ally, and many other things and conditions in
Corinth, with the lack of as many other things and
conditions, are all due to the influence of what he
calls "that hideous, cast-iron monstrosity." By this
it will be seen that the Doctor is something of a
philosopher.

The monument stands on the corner where Holmes
Street ends in Strong Avenue. On the opposite
corner the Doctor lives with Martha, his wife. It
is a modest home for there are no children and the
Doctor is not rich. The house is white with old-
fashioned green shutters, and over the porch climbs
a mass of vines. The steps are worn very thin and
the ends of the floor-boards are rotted badly by the
moisture of the growing vines. But the Doctor
says he'll "be damned" if he'll pull down such a fine
old vine to put in new boards, and that those will
last anyway longer than either he or Martha. By
this it will be seen that the Doctor is something of
a poet.

On the rear of the lot is the wood-shed and stable;
and on the east, along the fence in front, and down

the Holmes Street side, are the Doctor's roses—the admiration and despair of every flower-growing housewife in town.

Full fifty years of the Doctor's professional life have been spent in active practice in Corinth and in the country round about. He declares himself worn out now and good for nothing, save to meddle in the affairs of his neighbors, to cultivate his roses, and—when the days are bright—to go fishing. For the rest, he sits in his chair on the porch and watches the world go by.

"Old Doctors and old dogs," he growls, "how equally useless we are, and yet how much—how much we could tell if only we dared speak!"

He is big, is the Doctor—big and fat and old. He knows every soul in Corinth, particularly the children; indeed he helped most of them to come to Corinth. He is acquainted as well with every dog and cat, and horse and cow, knowing their every trick and habit, from the old brindle milker that unlatches his front gate to feed on the lawn, to the bull pup that pinches his legs when he calls on old Granny Brown. For miles around, every road, lane, by-path, shortcut and trail, is a familiar way to him. His practice, he declares, has well-nigh ruined him financially, and totally wrecked his temper. He can curse a man and cry over a baby; and he would go as far and work as hard for the illiterate and penniless backwoodsman in his cabin home as for the president of the Bank of Corinth or even Judge Strong himself.

No one ever thinks of the Doctor as loving anyone

or anything, and that is because he is so big and rough on the outside: but every one in trouble goes to him, and that is because he is so big and kind on the inside. It is a common saying that in cases of trying illness or serious accident a patient would rather "hear the Doctor cuss, than listen to the parson pray." Other physicians there are in Corinth, but every one understands when his neighbor says: "The Doctor." Nor does anyone ever, ever call him "Doc"!

After all, who knows the people of a community so well as the physician who lives among them? To the world the Doctor's patients were laborers, bankers, dressmakers, scrub-women, farmers, servants, teachers, preachers; to the Doctor they were men and women. Others knew their occupations—he knew their lives. The preachers knew what they professed—he knew what they practiced. Society saw them dressed up—he saw them—in bed. Why, the Doctor has spent more hours in the homes of his neighbors than ever he passed under his own roof, and there is not a skeleton closet in the whole town to which he has not the key.

On Strong Avenue, across from the monument, is a tiny four-roomed cottage. In the time of this story it wanted paint badly, and was not in the best of repair. But the place was neat and clean, with a big lilac bush just inside the gate, giving it an air of home-like privacy; and on the side directly opposite the Doctor's a fair-sized, well-kept garden, giving it an air of honest thrift. Here the widow Mulhall lived with her crippled son, Denny. Denny was to have been educated for the priesthood, but the accident that left him such a hopeless cripple shattered that dream; and after the death of his father, who was killed while discharging his duties as the town marshal, there was no money to buy even a book.

When there was anything for her to do, Deborah worked out by the day. Denny, in spite of his poor, misshapen body, tended the garden, raising such vegetables as no one else in all Corinth could— or would, raise. From early morning until late evening the lad dragged himself about among the growing things, and the only objects to mar the beauty of his garden, were Denny himself, and the great rock that crops out in the very center of the little field.

"It is altogether too bad that the rock should be there," the neighbors would say as they occasionally stopped to look over the fence or to order their vegetables for dinner. And Denny would answer with his knowing smile, "Oh, I don't know! It would be bad, I'll own, if it should ever take to rollin' 'round like. But it lays quiet enough. And do you see, I've planted them vines around it to make it a bit soft lookin'. And there's a nice little niche on yon side, that does very well for a seat now and then, when I have to rest."

Sometimes, when the Doctor looks at the monument—the cast-iron image of his old friend, in its cast-iron attitude, forever delivering that speech on an issue as dead today as an edict of one of the Pharaohs—he laughs, and sometimes, even as he laughs, he curses.

But when, in the days of the story, the Doctor would look across the street to where Denny, with his poor, twisted body, useless, swinging arm, and dragging leg, worked away so cheerily in his garden, the old physician, philosopher, and poet, declared that he felt like singing hymns of praise.

And it all began with a fishing trip.

CHAPTER II.

A REVELATION.

"And because of these things, to the keen old physician and student of life, the boy was a revelation of that best part of himself—that best part of the race."

I T happened on the Doctor's first trip to the Ozarks.

Martha says that everything with the Doctor begins and ends with fishing. Martha has a way of saying such things as that. In this case she is more than half right for the Doctor does so begin and end most things.

Whenever there were grave cases to think out, knotty problems to solve, or important decisions to make, it was his habit to steal away to a shady nook by the side of some quiet, familiar stream. And he confidently asserts that to this practice more than to anything else he owes his professional success, and his reputation for sound, thoughtful judgment on all matters of moment.

"And why not?" he will argue when in the mood. "It is your impulsive, erratic, thoughtless fellow who goes smashing, trashing and banging about the field and woods with dogs and gun. Your true thinker slips quietly away with rod and line, and while his hook is down in the deep, still waters, or his fly is dancing over the foaming rapids and swiftly swirling eddies, his mind searches the true depths of the matter and every possible phase of the question passes before him."

For years the Doctor had heard much of the fishing to be had in the more unsettled parts of the Ozarks, but with his growing practice he could find leisure for no more than an occasional visit to nearby streams. But about the time that Martha began telling him that he was too old to stay out all day on the wet bank of a river, and Dr. Harry had come to relieve him of the heavier and more burdensome part of his practice, a railroad pushed its way across the mountain wilderness. The first season after the road was finished the Doctor went to cast his hook in new waters.

In all these after years those days so full of mystic beauty have lived in the old man's memory, the brightest days of all his life. For it was there he met the Boy—there in the Ozark hills, with their great ridges clothed from base to crest with trees all quivering and nodding in the summer breeze, with their quiet valleys, their cool hollows and lovely glades, and their deep and solemn woods. And the streams! Those Ozark streams! The Doctor wonders often if there can flow anywhere else such waters as run through that land of dreams.

The Doctor left the train at a little station where the railroad crosses White River, and two days later he was fishing near the mouth of Fall Creek. It was late in the afternoon. The Boy was passing on his way home from a point farther up the stream. Not more than twelve, but tall and strong for his age, he came along the rough path at the foot of the bluff with the easy movement and grace of a young deer. He checked a moment when he saw the Doctor, as a creature of the forest would pause at first sight of a human being. Then he came on again, his manner and bearing showing frank interest, and the clear, sunny face of him flushing a bit at the presence of a stranger.

"Hello," said the Doctor, with gruff kindness, "any luck?"

The boy's quick smile showed a set of teeth—the most perfect the physician had ever seen, and his young voice was tuned to the music of the woods, as he answered, "I have caught no fish, sir."

By these words and the light in his brown eyes the philosopher knew him instantly for a true fisherman. He noted wonderingly that the lad's speech was not the rude dialect of the backwoods, while he marveled at the depth of wisdom in one so young. How incidental after all is the catching of fish, to the one who fishes with true understanding. The boy's answer was both an explanation and a question. It explained that he did not go fishing for fish alone; and it asked of the stranger a declaration of his standing—why did he go fishing? What did he mean by fisherman's luck?

The Doctor deliberated over his reply, while slowly drawing in his line to examine the bait. Meanwhile the boy stood quietly by regarding him with a wide, questioning look. The man realized that much depended upon his next word.

Then the lad's youth betrayed him into eagerness.

"Have you been farther up the river just around the bend, where the giant cottonwoods are, and the bluffs with the pines above, and the willows along the shore? Oh, but it's fine there! Much better than this."

He had given the stranger his chance. If the Doctor was to be admitted into this boy's world he must now prove his right to citizenship. Looking straight into the boy's brown eyes, the older fisherman asked, "A better place to catch fish?"

He laughed aloud—a clear, clean, boyish laugh of understanding, and throwing himself to the ground with the easy air of one entirely at home, returned, "No, sir, a better place to fish." So it was settled, each understanding the other.

An hour later when the shadow of the mountain came over the water, the boy sprang to his feet with an exclamation, "It's time that I was going, mother likes for me to be home for supper. I can just make it."

But the Doctor was loth to let him go. "Where do you live?" he asked. "Is it far?"

"Oh, no, only about six miles, but the trail is rough until you strike the top of Wolf Ridge."

"Humph! You can't walk six miles before dark."

"My horse is only a little way up the creek," he answered, "or at least he should be." Putting his fingers to his lips he blew a shrill whistle, which echoed and re-echoed from shore to shore along the river, and was answered by a loud neigh from somewhere in the ravine through which Fall Creek reaches the larger stream. Again the boy whistled, and a black pony came trotting out of the brush, the bridle hanging from the saddle horn. "Tramp and I can make it all right, can't we old fellow?" said the boy, patting the glossy neck, as the little horse rubbed a soft muzzle against his young master's shoulder.

While his companion was making ready for his ride the Doctor selected four of the largest of his catch—black bass they were—beauties. "Here," he said, when the lad was mounted, "take these along."

He accepted graciously without hesitation, and by this the Doctor knew that their fellowship was firmly established. "Oh, thank you! Mother is so fond of bass, and so are father and all of us. This is plenty for a good meal." Then, with another smile, "Mother likes to fish, too; she taught me."

The Doctor looked at him wistfully as he gathered up the reins, then burst forth eagerly with, "Look here, why can't you come back tomorrow? We'll have a bully time. What do you say?"

He lowered his hand. "Oh, I would like to." Then for a moment he considered, gravely, saying at last, "I think I can meet you here day after tomorrow. I am quite sure father and mother will be glad for me to come when I tell them about you."

Was ever a fat old Doctor so flattered? It was not so much the boy's words as his gracious manner and the meaning he unconsciously put into his exquisitely toned voice.

He had turned his pony's head when the old man shouted after him once more. "Hold on, wait a moment, you have not told me your name. I am Dr. Oldham from Corinth. I am staying at the Thompson's down the river."

"My name is Daniel Howitt Matthews," he answered. "My home is the old Matthews place on the ridge above Mutton Hollow."

Then he rode away up the winding Fall Creek trail.

The Doctor spent the whole of the next day near the spot where he had met the boy, fearing lest the lad might come again and not find him. He even went a mile or so up the little creek half expecting to meet his young friend, wondering at himself the while, that he could not break the spell the lad had cast over him. Who was he? He had told the Doctor his name, but that did not satisfy. Nor, indeed, did the question itself ask what the old man really wished to know. The words persistently shaped themselves—*What* is he? To this the physician's brain made answer clearly enough—a boy, a backwoods boy, with unusual beauty and strength of body, and uncommon fineness of mind; yet with all this, a boy.

But that something that sits in judgment upon the findings of our brain, and, in lofty disregard of us, accepts or rejects our most profound conclusions, refused this answer. It was too superficial. It was not, in short, an answer. It did not in any way explain the strange power that this lad had exerted over the Doctor.

"Me," he said to himself, "a hard old man calloused by years of professional contact with mankind and consequent knowledge of their general cussedness! Huh! I have helped too many hundreds of children into this world, and have carried too many of them through the measles, whooping-cough, chicken-pox and the like to be so moved by a mere boy."

The Thompsons could have told him about the lad and his people, but the Doctor instinctively shrank from asking them. He felt that he did not care to be told about the boy—that in truth no one could tell him about the boy, because he already knew the lad as well as he knew himself. Indeed the feeling that he already knew the boy was what troubled the Doctor; more, that he had always lived with him; but that he had never before met him face to face. He felt as a blind man might feel if, after living all his life in closest intimacy with someone, he were suddenly to receive his sight and, for the first time, actually look upon his companion's face.

In the years that have passed since that day the Doctor has learned that the lad was to him, not so much a mystery as a revelation—the revelation of an unspoken ideal, of a truth that he had always known but never fully confessed even to himself, and that lies at last too deeply buried beneath the accumulated rubbish of his life to be of any use to him or to others. In the boy he met this hidden, secret, unacknowledged part of himself, that he knows to be the truest, most precious and most sacred part, and that he has always persistently ignored even while always conscious that he can no more escape it than he can escape his own life. In short, Dan Matthews is to the Doctor that which the old man feels he ought to have been; that which he might have been, but never now can be.

It was still early in the forenoon of the following day when the Doctor heard a cheery hail, and the boy came riding out of the brush of the little ravine to meet his friend who was waiting on the river bank. As the lad sprang lightly to the ground, and, with quick fingers, took some things from the saddle, loosed the girths and removed the pony's bridle, the physician watched him with a slight feeling of— was it envy or regret? "You are early," he said.

The boy laughed. "I would have come earlier if I could." Then, dismissing the little horse, he turned eagerly, "Have you been there yet—to that place up the river?"

"Indeed I have not," said the Doctor. "I have been waiting for you to show me."

He was delighted at this, and very soon was leading the way along the foot of the bluff to his favorite fishing ground.

It is too much to attempt the telling of that day: how they lay on the ground beneath the giant-limbed cottonwoods, and listened to the waters going past; how they talked of the wild woodland life about them, of flower and tree, and moss and vine, and the creatures that nested and denned and lived therein; how they caught a goodly catch of bass and perch, and the Doctor, pulling off his boots, waded in the water like another boy, while the hills echoed with their laughter; and how, when they had their lunch on a great rock, an eagle watched hungrily from his perch on a dead pine, high up on the top of the bluff.

When the shadow of the mountain was come once more and in answer to the boy's whistle the black pony had trotted from the brush to be made ready for the evening ride, the Doctor again watched his young companion wistfully.

When he was ready, the boy said, "Father and mother asked me to tell you, sir, that they—that we would be glad to have you come to see us before you leave the hills." Seeing the surprise and hesitation of the Doctor, he continued with fine tact, "You see I told them all about you, and they would like to know you too. Won't you come? I'm sure you would like my father and mother, and we would be so glad to have you. I'll drive over after you to-morrow if you'll come."

Would he *go!* Why the Doctor would have gone to China, or Africa, or where would he not have gone, if the boy had asked him.

That visit to the Matthews' place was the beginning of a friendship that has never been broken. Every year since, the Doctor has gone to them for several weeks and always with increasing delight. Among the many households that, in his professional career, he has been privileged to know intimately, this home stands like a beautiful temple in a world of shacks and hovels. But it was not until the philosopher had heard from Mrs. Matthews the story of Dad Howitt that he understood the reason. In the characters of Young Matt and Sammy, in their home life and in their children, the physician found the teaching of the old Shepherd of the Hills bearing its legitimate fruit. Most clearly did he find it in Dan—the first born of this true mating of a man and woman who had never been touched by those forces in our civilization which so dwarf and cripple the race, but who had been taught to find in their natural environment those things that alone have the power to truly refine and glorify life.

Understanding this, the Doctor understood Dan. The boy was well born; he was natural. He was what a man-child ought to be. He did not carry the handicap that most of us stagger under so early in the race. And because of these things, to the keen old physician and student of life, the boy was a revelation of that best part of himself—that best part of the race. With the years this feeling of the Doctor's toward the boy has grown even as their fellowship. But Dan has never understood: how indeed could he?

It was always Dan who met the Doctor at the little wilderness station, and who said the last good-bye when the visit was over. Always they were together, roaming about the hills, on fishing trips to the river, exploring the country for new delights, or revisiting their familiar haunts. Dan seemed, in his quiet way, to claim his old friend by right of discovery and the others laughingly yielded, giving the Doctor—as Young Matt, the father, put it—"a third interest in the boy."

And so, with the companionship of the yearly visits, and frequent letters in the intervening months, the Doctor watched the development of his young friend, and dreamed of the part that Dan would play in life when he became a man. And often as he watched the boy there was, on the face of the old physician, that look of half envy, half regret.

In addition to his training at the little country school, Dan's mother was his constant teacher, passing on to her son as only a mother could, the truths she had received from her old master, the Shepherd. But when the time came for more advanced intellectual training the choice of a college was left to their friend. The Doctor hesitated. He shrank from sending the lad out into the world. He foolishly could not bear the thought of that splendid nature coming in touch with the filth of life as he knew it. "You can see," he argued gruffly, "what it has done for me."

But Sammy answered, "Why, Doctor, what is the boy for?" And Young Matt, looking away over Garber where an express train thundered over the trestles and around the curves, said in his slow way, "The brush is about all cleared, Doctor. The wilderness is going fast. The boy must live in his own age and do his own work." When their friend urged that they develop or sell the mine in the cave on Dewey Bald, and go with the boy, they both shook their heads emphatically, saying, "No, Doctor, we belong to the hills."

When the boy finally left his mountain home for a school in the distant city, he had grown to be a man to fill the heart of every lover of his race with pride. With his father's powerful frame and close-knit muscles, and the healthy life of the woods and hills leaping in his veins, his splendid body and physical strength were refined and dominated by the mind and spirit of his mother. His shaggy, red-brown hair was like his father's but his eyes were his mother's eyes, with that same trick of expression, that wide questioning gaze, that seemed to demand every vital truth in whatever came under his consideration. He had, too, his mother's quick way of grasping your thoughts almost before you yourself were fully conscious of them, with that same saving sense of humor that made Sammy Lane the life and sunshine of the countryside.

"Big Dan," the people of the hills had come to call him and "Big Dan" they called him in the school. For, in the young life of the schools, as in the country, there is a spirit that names men with names that fit.

Secretly the Doctor had hoped that Dan would choose the profession so dear to him. What an ideal physician he would make, with that clean, powerful, well balanced nature; and above all with that love for his race, and his passion to serve mankind that was the dominant note in his character. The boy would be the kind of a physician that the old Doctor had hoped to be. So he planned and dreamed for Dan as he had planned and dreamed for himself, thinking to see the dreams that he had failed to live, realized in the boy.

It was a severe shock to the Doctor when that letter came telling him of Dan's choice of a profession. For the first time the boy had disappointed him, disappointed him bitterly.

Seizing his fishing tackle the old man fled to the nearest stream. And there gazing into the deep, still waters, where he had cast his hook, he came to understand. It was that same dominant note in the boy's life, that inborn passion to serve, that fixed principle in his character that his life must be of the greatest possible worth to the world, that had led him to make his choice. With that instinct born in him, coming from the influence of the old Shepherd upon his father and mother, the boy could no more escape it than he could change the color of his brown eyes.

"But," said the Doctor to his cork, that floated on the surface in a patch of shadow, "what does he know about it, what does he really know? He's been reading history—that's what's the matter with him. He sees things as they were, not as they are. He should have come to me, I could have—" Just then the cork went under. The Doctor had a bite. "I could have told him," repeated the fisherman softly, "I—" The cork bobbed up again—it was only a nibble. "He'll find out the truth of course. He's that kind. But when he finds it!" The cork bobbed again—"He'll need me, he'll need me bad!" The cork went under for good this time. Zip—and the Doctor had a big one!

With fresh bait and his hook once more well down toward the bottom the Doctor saw the whole thing clearly, and so planned a way by which, as he put it, he might, when Dan needed him, *"stand by."*

CHAPTER III.

A GREAT DAY IN CORINTH.

"'Talk of the responsibilities of age; humph! They are nothing compared to the responsibilities of youth. There's Dan, now—'"

CORINTH was in the midst of a street fair. The neighboring city held a street fair that year, therefore Corinth. All that the city does Corinth imitates, thereby with a beautiful rural simplicity thinking herself metropolitan, just as those who take their styles from the metropolis feel themselves well dressed. The very Corinthian clerks and grocery boys, lounging behind their counters and in the doorways, the lawyer's understudy with his feet on the window sill, the mechanic's apprentice, the high school youths and the local sporting fraternity—all imitated their city kind and talked smartly about the country "rubes" who came to town; never once dreaming that they themselves, when they "go to town," are as much a mark for the like wit of their city brothers. So Corinth was in the midst of a street fair.

On every vacant lot in the down town section were pens, and stalls, and cages, wherein grunted, squealed, neighed, bellowed, bleated, cackled and crowed, exhibits from the neighboring farms. In the town hall or opera house (it was both) there

36

were long tables covered with almost everything that grows on a farm, or is canned, baked, preserved, pickled or stitched by farmers' wives. The "Art Exhibit," product mainly of Corinth, had its place on the stage. Upon either side of the main street were booths containing the exhibits of the local merchants; farm machinery, buggies, wagons, harness and the like being most conspicuous. The chief distinction between the town and country exhibits were that the farmer displayed his goods to be looked at, the merchant his to be sold. It was the merchants who promoted the fair.

In a vacant store room the Memorial Church was holding its annual bazaar. On different corners other churches were serving chicken dinners, or ice cream, or in sundry ways were actively engaged for the conversion of the erring farmer's cash to the coffers of the village sanctuaries. In this way the promoters of the fair were encouraged by the churches. From every window, door, arch, pole, post, corner, gable, peak, cupola—fluttered, streamed and waved, decorations—banners mostly, bearing advertisements of the enterprising merchants and of the equally enterprising churches.

Afternoons there would be a baseball game between town and country teams, foot races, horseback riding, a greased pig to catch, a greased pole to climb and other entertainments too exciting to think about, too attractive to be resisted.

From the far backwoods districts, from the hills, from the creek bottoms and the river, the people came to crowd about the pens, and stalls and tables;

to admire their own and their neighbors' products and possessions, that they had seen many times before in their neighbors' homes and fields. They visited on the street corners. They tramped up and down past the booths. They yelled themselves hoarse at the games and entertainments, and in the intoxication of their pleasures bought ice cream, chicken dinners and various other things of the churches, and much goods of the merchants who promoted the fair.

The Doctor was up that day at least a full hour before his regular time. At breakfast Martha looked him over suspiciously, and when he folded his napkin after eating only half his customary meal she remarked dryly, "It's three hours yet till train time, Doctor."

Without answer the Doctor went out on the porch.

Already the country people, dressed in their holiday garb, bright-faced, eager for the long looked for pleasures, were coming in for the fair. Many of them catching sight of the physician hailed him gaily, shouting good natured remarks in addition to their salutations, and laughing loudly at whatever he replied.

It may be that the good Lord had made days as fine as that day, but the Doctor could not remember them. His roses so filled the air with fragrance, the grass in the front yard was so fresh and clean, the flowers along the walk so bright and dainty, and the great maples, that make a green arch of the street, so cool and mysterious in their leafy depths, that his old heart fairly ached with the beauty of it. The Doctor was all poet that day. Dan was coming!

It had worked out just as the Doctor had planned it on that fishing trip some three months before. At first Martha was suspicious when he broached the subject. Mostly Martha is suspicious when her husband offers suggestions touching certain matters, but the wise old philosopher knew what strings to pull, and so it all came out as he had planned. Sammy had written him expressing her gladness, that her boy in the beginning of his work was to be with the friend whose counsel and advice they valued so highly. The Doctor had growled over the letter, promising himself that he would "stand by" when the boy needed him, but that was all he or an angel from heaven could do now. And the Doctor had written Dan at length about Corinth, but never a word about his thoughts regarding the boy's choice, or his fears for the outcome.

"There are some things," he reflected, "that every man must find out for himself. To some kinds of people the finding out doesn't matter much. To other kinds, it is well for them if there are those who love them to stand by." Dan was the kind to whom the finding out would mean a great deal, so the Doctor would "stand by."

There on his vine covered porch that morning, the old man's thoughts went back to that day when the boy first came to him on the river bank, and to all the bright days of Dan's boyhood and youth that he had passed with the lad in the hills. "His life—" said he, talking to himself, as he has a way of doing—"His life is like this day, fresh and clean and—" He looked across the street to the monument that stood a cold, lifeless mask in a world of living joy and beauty; from the monument he turned to Denny's garden. "And," he finished, "full of possibilities."

"Whatever are you muttering about now?" said Martha, who had followed him out after finishing her breakfast.

"I was wishing," said the Doctor, "that I—that it would be always morning, that there was no such thing as afternoon, and evening and night."

His wife replied sweetly, "For a man of your age, you do say the most idiotic things! Won't you ever get old enough to think seriously?"

"But what could be more serious, my dear? If it were morning I would always be beginning my life work, and never giving it up. I would be always looking forward to the success of my dreams, and never back to the failures of my poor attempts."

"You haven't failed in everything, John," protested Martha in softer tones.

"If it were morning," the philosopher continued, with a smile, "I would always be making love to the best and prettiest girl in the state."

Martha tossed her head and the ghost of an old blush crept into her wrinkled cheeks. "There's no fool like an old fool," she quoted with a spark of her girlhood fire.

"But a young fool gets so much more out of his foolishness," the man retorted. "Talk of the responsibilities of age; humph! They are nothing compared to the responsibilities of youth. There's Dan now—" He looked again toward the monument.

"My goodness me, yes!" ejaculated Martha. "And I've got a week's work to do before I even begin to get dinner. You go right off this minute and kill three of those young roosters—three, mind you."

"But, my dear, he will only be here for dinner."

"Never you mind, the dinner's my business. Kill three, I tell you. I've cooked for preachers before. I hope to the Lord he'll start you to thinking of your eternal future, 'stead of mooning about the past." She bustled away to turn the little home upside down and to prepare dinner sufficient for six.

When the Doctor had killed the three roosters, and had fussed about until his wife ordered him out of the kitchen, he took his hat and stick and started down town, though it was still a good hour until train time. As he opened the front gate Denny called a cheery greeting from his garden across the street, and the old man went over for a word with the crippled boy.

"It's mighty fine you're lookin' this mornin', Doctor," said Denny pausing in his work, and seating himself on the big rock. "Is it the ten-forty he's comin' on?"

The Doctor tried to appear unconcerned. He looked at his watch with elaborately assumed carelessness as he answered: "I believe it's ten-forty; and how are you feeling this morning, Denny?"

The lad lifted his helpless left arm across his lap.

"Oh I'm fine, thank you kindly, Doctor. Mother's fine too, and my garden's doing pretty good for me." He glanced about. "The early things are all gone, of course, but the others are doing well. Oh, we'll get along; I told mother this morning the Blessed Virgin hadn't forgotten us yet. I'll bet them potatoes grew an inch some nights this summer. And look what a day it is for the fair, and the preacher a comin' too."

The Doctor looked at his watch again, and Denny continued: "We're all so pleased at his comin'. People haven't talked of anything else for a month now, that and the fair of course. Things in this town will liven up now, sure. Seems to me I can feel it—yes sir, I can. Something's goin' to happen, sure."

"Humph," grunted the Doctor, "I rather feel that way myself." Then, "I expect you two will be great friends, Denny."

The poor little fellow nearly twisted himself off the rock. "Oh Doctor, really why I—the minister'll have no time for the likes of me. And is he really goin' to live at Mrs. Morgan's there?" He nodded his head toward the house next to his garden.

"That's his room," the other answered, pointing to the corner window. "He'll be right handy to us both."

Denny gazed at the window with the look of a worshiper. "Oh now, isn't that fine, isn't it grand! That's such a nice room, Doctor, it has such a fine view of the monument."

"Yes," the Doctor interrupted, "the monument

and your garden." And then he left abruptly lest he should foolishly try to explain to the bewildered and embarrassed Denny what he meant.

It seemed to the Doctor that nearly every one he met on the well-filled street that morning, had a smile for him, while many stopped to pass a word about the coming of Dan. When he reached the depot the agent hailed him with, "Good morning, Doctor; looking for your preacher?"

"*My* preacher!" The old physician glared at the man in the cap, and turned his back with a few energetic remarks, while two or three loafers joined in the laugh, and a couple of traveling men who were pacing the platform with bored expressions on their faces, turned to stare at him curiously. At the other end of the platform was a group of women, active members of the Memorial Ladies' Aid who had left their posts of duty at the bazaar, to have a first look at the new pastor. The old Elder, Nathan Jordan, with Charity, his daughter, was just coming up.

"Good morning, good morning, Doctor," said Nathan grasping his friend's hand as if he had not seen him for years. "Well I see we're all here." He turned proudly about as the group of women came forward, with an air of importance, the Doctor thought, as though the occasion required their presence. "Reckon our boy'll be here all right," Nathan continued.

"*Our* boy!" The Doctor caught a naughty word between his teeth—a feat he rarely accomplished.

The ladies all looked sweetly interested. One of

43

them putting her arm lovingly about Charity cooed: "So nice of you to come, dear." She had remarked to another a moment before, "that a fire wouldn't 'keep the girl away from the depot that morning."

The Doctor felt distinctly the subtle, invisible presence of the Ally, and it was well that someone just then saw the smoke from the coming train two or three miles away, around the curve beyond the pumping station.

The negro porter from the hotel opposite the depot, came bumping across the rails, with the grips belonging to the two traveling men, in his little cart; the local expressman rattled up with a trunk in his shaky old wagon; and the sweet-faced daughter of the division track superintendent hurried out of the red section-house with a bundle of big envelopes in her hand. The platform was crowded with all kinds of people, carrying a great variety of bundles, baskets and handbags, asking all manner of questions, going to and from all sorts of places. The train drew rapidly nearer.

The Doctor's old heart was thumping painfully. He forgot the people, he forgot Corinth, he forgot everything but the boy who had come to him that day on the river bank.

Swiftly the long train with clanging bell and snorting engine came up to the depot. The conductor swung easily to the platform, and, watch in hand, walked quickly to the office. Porters and trainmen tumbled off, and with a long hiss of escaping air and a steady puff-puff, the train stopped.

In the bustle and confusion of crowding passengers getting on and off, tearful good-byes and joyful greetings, banging trunks, rattling trucks, hissing steam, the doctor watched. Then he saw him, his handsome head towering above the pushing, jostling crowd. The Doctor could not get to him, and with difficulty restrained a shout. But Dan with his back to them all pushed his way to an open window of the car he had just left, where a woman's face turned to him in earnest conversation.

"There he is," said the Doctor, "that tall fellow by the window there."

At his words the physician heard an exclamation, and, glancing back, saw the women staring eagerly, while Charity's face wore a look of painful doubt and disappointment. The Elder's countenance was stern and frowning.

"Seems mightily interested," said one, suggestively.

"What a pretty face," added another, also suggestively.

The Doctor spoke quickly, "Why that's—" Then he stopped with an expression on his face that came very near being a malicious grin.

The conductor, watch again in hand, shouted, the porters stepped aboard, the bell rang, the engineer, with his long oil-can, swung to his cab, slowly the heavy train began to gather headway. As it went Dan walked along the platform beside that open window, until he could no longer keep pace with the moving car. Then with a final wave of his hand he stood looking after the train, seemingly unconscious of everything but that one who was being carried so quickly beyond his sight.

He was standing so when his old friend grasped his arm. He turned with a start. "Doctor!"

What a handsome fellow he was, with his father's great body, powerful limbs and shaggy red-brown hair; and his mother's eyes and mouth, and her spirit ruling within him, making you feel that he was clean through and through. It was no wonder people stood around looking at him. The Doctor felt again that old, mysterious spell, that feeling that the boy was a revelation to him of something he had always known, the living embodiment of a truth never acknowledged. And his heart swelled with pride as he turned to lead Dan up to Elder Jordan and his company.

The church ladies, old in experience with preachers, seemed strangely embarrassed. This one was somehow so different from those they had known before, but their eyes were full of admiration. Charity's voice trembled as she bade him welcome. Nathaniel's manner was that of a judge. Dan himself, was as calm and self possessed as if he and the Doctor were alone on the bank of some river, far from church and church people. But the Doctor thought that the boy flinched a bit when he introduced him as Reverend Matthews. Perhaps, though, it was merely the Doctor's fancy. The old man felt too, even as he presented Dan to his people, that there had come between himself and the boy a something that was never there before, and it troubled him not a little. But perhaps this, too, was but a fancy.

At any rate the old man must have been somewhat excited for when the introductions were over, and the company was leaving the depot, he managed to steer Dan into collision with a young woman who was standing nearby. She was carrying a small grip, having evidently arrived on the same train that brought the minister. It was no joke for anyone into whom Big Dan bumped, and a look of indignation flashed on the girl's face. But the indignant look vanished quickly in a smile as the big fellow stood, hat in hand, offering the most abject apology for what he called *his* rudeness.

The Doctor noted a fine face, a strong graceful figure, and an air of wholesomeness and health that was most refreshing. But he thought that Dan took more time than was necessary for his apology.

When she had assured the young fellow several times that it was nothing, she asked: "Can you tell me, please, the way to Dr. Abbott's office?"

Dr. Abbott! The Doctor's own office—Dr. Harry's and his now. He looked the young woman over curiously, while Dan was saying: "I'm sorry, but I cannot. I am a stranger here, but my friend—"

The older man interrupted gruffly with the necessary directions and the information that Dr. Abbott was out of town, and would not be back until four o'clock. "Will you then direct me to a hotel?" she asked. The Doctor pointed across the track. Then he got Dan away.

The church ladies, with Charity and her father, were already on their way back to the place where the bazaar was doing business. Half way down the block the Doctor and Dan were checked by a crowd. There seemed to be some excitement ahead. But in the pause, Dan turned to look back toward the young woman who had arrived in Corinth on the same train that had brought him. She was coming slowly down the street toward them.

Again the thought flashed through the Doctor's mind that the boy had taken more time than was necessary for his apology.

CHAPTER IV.

WHO ARE THEY?

"And the old man pointed out to Dan his room across the way—the room that looked out upon the garden and the monument."

JUD HARDY, who lives at Windy Cove on the river some eighteen miles "back" from Corinth, had been looking forward to Fair time for months. Not that Jud had either things to exhibit or money to buy things exhibited. For while Jud professed to own, and ostensibly to cultivate a forty, he gained his living mostly by occasional "spells of work" on the farms of his neighbors. In lieu of products of his hand or fields for exhibition at the annual fair, Jud invariably makes an exhibition of himself, never failing thus to contribute his full share to the "other amusements," announced on the circulars and in the Daily Corinthian, as "too numerous to mention."

The citizens of the Windy Cove country have a saying that when Jud is sober and in a good humor and has money, he is a fairly good fellow, if he is not crossed in any way. The meat of which saying is in the well known fact, that Jud is never in a good humor when he is not sober, that he is never sober when he has money; and that with the exception of three or four kindred spirits, whose admiration for the bad man is equalled only by their fear of him, no one has ever been able to devise a way to avoid crossing him when he is in his normal condition.

With three of the kindred spirits, Jud arrived in Corinth that day, with the earliest of the visitors, and the quartette proceeded, at once, to warm up after their long ride. By ten o'clock they were well warmed. Just as the ten-forty train was slowing up at the depot, Jud began his exhibition. It took place at the post office where the crowd was greatest, because of the incoming mail. Stationing himself near the door, the man from Windy Cove blocked the way for everyone who wanted to pass either in or out of the building. For the women and young girls he stepped aside with elaborate, drunken politeness and maudlin, complimentary remarks. For the men who brushed him he had a scowling curse and a muttered threat. Meanwhile, his followers nearby looked on in tipsy admiration and " 'lowed that there was bound to be somethin' doin', for Jud was sure a-huntin' trouble."

Then came one who politely asked Jud to move. He was an inoffensive little man, with a big star on his breast, and a big walking stick in his hand—the town marshal. Jud saw an opportunity to give an exhibition worth while. There were a few opening remarks—mostly profane—and then the representative of the law lay in a huddled heap on the floor, while the man from the river rushed from the building into the street.

The passing crowd stopped instantly. Scattered individuals from every side came running to push their way into the mass of men and women, until for a block on either side of the thoroughfare there was a solid wall of breathless humanity. Between these walls strolled Jud, roaring his opinion and defiance of every one in general, and the citizens of Corinth in particular.

It could not last long, of course. There were many men in the crowd who did not fear to challenge Jud, but there was that inevitable hesitation, while each man was muttering to his neighbor that this thing ought to be stopped, and they were waiting to see if someone else would not start first to stop it.

Nearly the length of the block, Jud made his triumphant way; then, at the corner where the crowd was not so dense, he saw a figure starting across the street.

"Hey there," he roared, "get back there where you belong! What th' hell do you mean? Don't you see the procession's a comin'?"

It was Denny. He had left his garden to go to the butcher's for a bit of meat for dinner. The crippled lad had just rounded the corner, and, forced to give all his attention to his own halting steps, did not grasp the situation but continued his dragging way across the path of the drunken and enraged bully. The ruffian, seeing the lad ignore his loud commands, strode heavily forward with menacing fists, heaping foul epithets upon the head of the helpless Irish boy.

The crowd gasped.

"Oh, why does someone not do something!" moaned a woman. A girl screamed.

Several men started, but before they could force their way through the press, the people saw a stranger, a well-dressed young giant, spring from the sidewalk, and run toward the two figures in the middle of the street. But Dan had not arrived upon the scene soon enough. Almost as he left the pavement the blow fell, and Denny lay still—a crumpled, pitiful heap in the dirt.

Jud, flushed with this second triumph, turned to face the approaching stranger.

"Come on, you pink-eyed dude! I've got some fer you too. Come git your medicine, you—"

Dan was coming—coming so quickly that Jud's curses had not left his lips when the big fellow reached him. With one clean, swinging blow the man from Windy Cove was lifted fairly off the ground to fall several feet away from his senseless victim.

There was an excited yell from the crowd. But Jud, lean, loose-jointed and hard of sinew, had the physical toughness of his kind. Almost instantly he was on his feet again, reaching for his hip pocket with a familiar movement. And there was a wild scramble as those in front sought cover in the rear.

"Look out! Look out!"—came from the crowd.

But the mountain bred Dan needed no warning. With a leap, cat-like in its quickness, he was again upon the other. There was a short struggle, a sharp report, a wrenching twist, a smashing blow, and Jud was down once more, this time senseless. The weapon lay in the dust. The bullet had gone wide.

The crowd yelled their approval, and, even while they applauded, the people were asking each of his neighbor: "Who is he? Who is he?"

Several men rushed in, and Dan, seeing the bully safe in as many hands as could lay hold of him, turned to discover the young woman whom he had met at the depot kneeling in the street over the still unconscious Denny. With her handkerchief she was wiping the blood and dirt from the boy's forehead. Dan had only time to wonder at the calmness of her face and manner when the crowd closed in about them.

Then the Doctor pushed his way through the throng, and the people, at sight of the familiar figure, obeyed his energetic orders and drew aside. A carriage was brought and Dan lifted the unconscious lad in his arms. The Doctor spoke shortly to the young woman, "You come too." And with the Doctor the two strangers in Corinth took Denny to his home.

In the excitement no one thought of introductions, while the people seeing their hero driving in the carriage with a young woman, also a stranger, changed their question from, "Who is he?" to "Who are they?"

When Denny had regained consciousness, and everything possible for his comfort and for the assistance of his distracted mother, had been done; and the physician had assured them that the lad would be as good as ever in a day or two, the men crossed the street to the little white house.

"Well," ejaculated Martha when Dan had been

presented, and the incident on the street briefly
related, "I'm mighty glad I cooked them three
roosters."

Dan laughed his big, hearty laugh, "I'm glad, too,"
he said. "Doctor used to drive me wild out in the
woods with tales of your cooking."

The Doctor could see that Martha was pleased at
this by the way she fussed with her apron.

"We always hoped that he would bring you with
him on some of his trips," continued Dan, "we all
wanted so much to meet you."

To the Doctor's astonishment, Martha stammered,
"I—maybe I will go some day." Then her manner
underwent a change as if she had suddenly remembered something. "You'll excuse me now while I
put the dinner on," she said stiffly. "Just make
yourself to home; preachers always do in this
house, even if Doctor don't belong." She hurried
away, and Dan looked at his host with his mother's
questioning eyes. The Doctor knew what it was.
Dan had felt it even in the house of his dearest
friend. It was the preacher Martha had welcomed,
welcomed him professionally because he was a
preacher. And the Doctor felt again *that* something
that had come between him and the lad.

"Martha doesn't care for fishing," he said gently.

Then they went out on the porch, and the old man
pointed out to Dan his room across the way—the
room that looked out upon the garden and the monument.

"Several of your congregation wanted to have you
in their homes," he explained. "But I felt—I

thought you might like to be—it was near me you see —and handy to the church." He pointed to the building up the street.

"Yes," Dan answered, looking at his old friend curiously—such broken speech was not natural to the Doctor—"You are quite right. It was very kind of you; you know how I will like it to be near you." Then looking at the monument he asked whose it was.

The Doctor hesitated again. Dan faced him waiting for an answer.

"That—oh, that's our statesman. You will need time to fully appreciate that work of art, and what it means to Corinth. It will grow on you. It's been growing on me for several years."

The young man was about to ask another question regarding the monument, when he paused. The girl who had gone to Denny in the street was coming from the little cottage. As she walked away under the great trees that lined the sidewalk, the two men stood watching her. Dan's question about the monument was forgotten.

"I wonder who she is," he said in a low voice.

The Doctor recalled the meeting at the depot and chuckled, and just then Martha called to dinner.

And the people on the street corners, at the ladies' bazaar, in the stores, the church booths and in the homes, were talking; talking of the exhibition of the man from Windy Cove, and asking each of his neighbor: "Who are they?"

CHAPTER V.

HOPE FARWELL'S MINISTRY.

"Useful hands they were, made for real service."

AFTER dinner was over and they had visited awhile, the Doctor introduced Dan to his landlady across the way and, making some trivial excuse about business, left the boy in his room. The fact is that the Doctor wished to be alone. If he could have done it decently, he would have gone off somewhere with his fishing tackle. As he could not go fishing, he did the next best thing. He went to his office.

The streets were not so crowded now, for the people were at the ball game, and the Doctor made his way down town without interruption. As he went he tried to think out what it was that had come between him and the boy whom he had known so intimately for so many years. Stopping at the post office, he found a letter in his care addressed to "Rev. Daniel H. Matthews." In his abstraction he was about to hand the letter in at the window with the explanation that he knew no such person, when a voice at his elbow said: "Is Brother Matthews fully rested from his tiresome journey, Doctor?"

The Doctor's abstraction vanished instantly, he jammed that letter into his pocket and faced the speaker.

"Yes," he growled, "I think Brother Matthews is fully rested. As he is a grown man of unusual strength, and in perfect health of body at least, and the tiresome journey was a trip of only four hours, in a comfortable railway coach, I think I may say that he is fully recovered."

Then the Doctor slipped away. But he had discovered what it was that had come between the boy and himself. The *man*, Dan Matthews, was no longer the Doctor's boy. He was "Reverend," "Brother," the *preacher*. All the morning it had been making itself felt, that something that sets preachers apart. The Doctor wondered how his young hill-bred giant would stand being coddled and petted and loved by the wives and mothers of men who, for their daily bread, met the world barehanded, and whose hardships were accepted by them and by these same mothers and wives as a matter of course.

By this time the Doctor had reached his office, and the sight of the familiar old rooms that had been the scene of so many revelations of real tragedies and genuine hardships, known only to the sufferer and to him professionally, forced him to continue his thought.

"There was Dr. Harry, for instance. Who, beside his old negro housekeeper, ever petted and coddled *him?* Who ever thought of setting him apart? Whoever asked if he were rested from his tiresome journey—journeys made not in comfortable coaches on the railroad, but in his buggy over all kinds of roads, at all times of day or night, in all sorts of weather winter and summer, rain and sleet and snow? Whoever 'Reverended' or 'Brothered' him? Oh no, he was only a man, a physician. It was his business to kill himself trying to keep other people alive."

Dr. Harry Abbott had been first, the Doctor's assistant, then his partner, and now at last his successor. Of a fine old Southern family, his people had lost everything in the war when Harry was only a lad. The father was killed in battle and the mother died a year later, leaving the boy alone in the world. Thrown upon his own resources for the necessities of life, he had managed somehow to live and to educate himself, besides working his way through both preparatory and medical schools, choosing his profession for love of it. He came to Dr. Oldham from school, when the Doctor was beginning to feel the burden of his large practice too heavily, and it was while he was the old physician's assistant that the people learned to call him Dr. Harry. And Dr. Harry he is to this day. How that boy has worked! His profession and his church (for he is a member, a deacon now, in the Memorial Church) have occupied every working minute of his life, and many hours beside that he should have given to sleep.

As the months passed Dr. Oldham placed more and more responsibilities upon him, and at the end of the second year took him into full partnership. It was about this time that Dr. Harry bought the old Wilson Carter place, and brought from his boyhood home two former slaves of his father to keep house for him, Old Uncle George and his wife Mam Liz.

Every year the younger man took more and more of the load from his partner's shoulders, until the older physician retired from active practice; and never has there been a word but of confidence and friendship between them. Their only difference is, that Harry will go to prayer meeting, when the Doctor declares he should go to bed; and that he will not go fishing. Always he has been the same courteous, kindly gentleman, intent only upon his profession, keeping abreast of the new things pertaining to his work, but ever considerate of the old Doctor's whims and fancies. Even now that Dr. Oldham has stepped down and out Harry insists that he leave his old desk in its place, and still talks over his cases with him.

The Doctor was sitting in his dilapidated office chair thinking over all this, when he heard his brother physician's step on the stairs. Harry came in, dusty and worn, from a long ride in the country on an all-night case. His tired face lit up when he saw his friend.

"Hello, Doctor! Glad to see you. Has he come? How is he?" While he was speaking the physician dropped his case, slipped out of his coat, and was in the lavatory burying his face in cold water by the time the other was ready to answer. That was Harry, he was never in a hurry, never seemed to move fast, but people never ceased to wonder at his quickness.

"He's all right," the Doctor muttered, his mind slipping back into the channel that had started him off to thinking of his fellow physician. "Got in on the ten-forty. But you look fagged enough. Why the devil don't you rest, Harry?"

Standing in the doorway rubbing his face, neck, and chest with a coarse towel the young man laughed, "Rest, what would I do with a vacation? I'll be all right, when I get outside of one of Mam Liz's dinners. It was that baby of Jensen's that kept me. Poor little chap. I thought two or three times he was going to make a die of it sure, but I guess he'll pull through now."

Dr. Oldham knew the Jensens well, eighteen miles over the worst roads in the country. He growled hoarsely: "It'll be more years than there are miles between here and Jensen's before you get a cent out of that case. You're a fool for making the trip; why don't you let 'em get that old bushwhacker at Salem, he's only three miles away?"

Harry pulled on his coat and dropped into his chair with a grin. "What'll you give me to collect some of your old accounts, Doctor? The Jensens say that the reason they have me is because you have always been their physician."

Then the Doctor in characteristic language expressed his opinion of the whole Jensen tribe, while Harry calmly glanced through some letters on his desk.

"See here, Doctor," he exclaimed, wheeling around in his chair and interrupting the old man's eloquent discourse. "Here is a letter from Dr. Miles—says he is sending a nurse; just what we want." He tossed the letter to the other. "There'll be the deuce to pay at Judge Strong's when she arrives. Whew!

I guess I better trot over home and get a bite and forty winks. A Jensen breakfast, as you may remember, isn't just the most staying thing for a civilized stomach, and I need to be fit when I call at the Strong mansion. Wonder when the nurse will get here."

"She's here now," said the old Doctor, and he then told him about the meeting at the depot and the fight on the street. "But go on and get your nap," he finished. "I'll look after her."

Harry had just taken his hat when there came a knock on the door leading into the little waiting room. He hung his hat back in the closet, and dropped into his chair again with a comical expression of resignation on his face. But his voice was cheerful, when he said: "Come in."

The door opened. The young lady of the depot entered. The old physician took a good look at her this time. He saw a girl of fine, strong form and good height, with clear skin, showing perfect health, large, gray eyes—serious enough, but with a laugh back of all their seriousness, brown hair, firm, rounded chin and a generous sensitive mouth. Particularly he noticed her hands—beautifully modeled, useful hands they were, made for real service. Altogether she gave him the impression of being very much alive, and very much a woman.

"Is this Dr. Abbott?" she asked, looking at Harry, who had risen from his chair. When she spoke the old man again noted her voice, it was low and clear.

"I am Dr. Abbott," replied Harry.

"I am Hope Farwell," she answered. "Dr. Miles,

you know, asked me to come. You wanted a nurse for a special case, I believe."

"Oh, yes," exclaimed Harry, "we have the letter here. We were just speaking of you, Miss Farwell. This is Dr. Oldham; perhaps Dr. Miles told you of him."

She turned with a smile. "Yes indeed, Dr. Miles told me. I believe we have met before, Doctor."

The girl broke into a merry laugh when the old man answered, gruffly: "I should think we had. I was just telling Harry there when you came in."

Then the younger physician asked, "How soon can you be ready to go on this case, Nurse?"

She looked at him with a faint expression of surprise. "Why I'm ready now, Doctor."

And the old Doctor broke in so savagely that they both looked at him in astonishment as he said: "But this is a hard case. You'll be up most of the night. You're tired out from your trip."

"Why, Doctor," said the young woman, "it is my business to be ready at any time. Being up nights is part of my profession. Surely you know that. Besides, that trip was really a good rest, the first good rest I've had for a long time."

"I know, of course," he answered. "I was thinking of something else. You must pardon me, Miss. Harry there will explain that I am subject to these little attacks."

"Oh, I know already," she returned smiling. "Dr. Miles told me all about you." And there was something in her laughing gray eyes that made the rough old man wonder just what it was that his friend Miles had told her.

"All right, get back to business you two," he growled. "I'll not interrupt again. Tell her about the case, Harry."

The young woman's face was serious in a moment, and she gave the physician the most careful attention as he explained the case for which he had written Dr. Miles to send a trained nurse of certain qualifications.

The Judge Strong of this story is an only son of the old Judge who moved Corinth. He is a large man—physically, as large as the Doctor, but where the Doctor is fat the Judge is lean. He inherited, not only his father's title (a purely honorary one) but his father's property, his position as an Elder in the church, and his general disposition; together with his taste and skill in collecting mortgages and acquiring real estate. The old Judge had but the one child. The Judge of this story, though just passing middle age, has no children at all. Seemingly there is no room in his heart for more than his church and his properties—his mind being thus wholly occupied with titles to heaven and to earth. With Sapphira, his wife, he lives in a big house on Strong Avenue, beyond the Strong Memorial Church, with never so much as a pet dog or cat to roughen the well-kept lawn or romp, perchance, in the garden. The patient whom Miss Farwell had come to nurse, was Sapphira's sister, a widow with neither child nor home. The Judge had been forced by his fear of public sentiment to give her shelter, and he had been compelled by Dr. Oldham and Dr. Harry to employ a nurse. The case would not be a pleasant one; Miss Farwell would need all that abundant stock of tact and patience which Dr. Miles had declared she possessed.

All this Dr. Harry explained to her, and when he had finished she asked in the most matter-of-fact tone: "And what are your instructions, Doctor?"

That caught Harry. It caught the old Doctor, too. Not even a comment on the disagreeable position she knew she would have in the Strong household, for Harry had not slighted the hard facts! She understood clearly what she was going into.

A light came into the young physician's eyes that his old friend liked to see. "I guess Miles knew what he was talking about in his letter," said the old Doctor. And the young woman's face flushed warmly at his words and look.

Then in his professional tones Dr. Harry instructed her more fully as to the patient's condition —a nervous trouble greatly aggravated by the Judge's disposition.

"Nice job, isn't it, Miss Farwell?" Harry finished. She smiled. "When do I go on, Doctor?"

Harry stepped to the telephone and called up the Strong mansion. "This you, Judge?" he said into the instrument. "The nurse from Chicago is here; came today. We want her to go on the case at once. Can you send your man to the depot for her trunk?"

By the look on his face the old Doctor knew what Harry was getting. The younger physician's jaw was set and his eyes were blazing, but his voice was calm and easy. "But Judge, you remember the agreement. Dr. Oldham is here now if you wish to speak to him. We shall hold you to the exact letter of your bargain, Judge. I am very sorry but——. Very well sir. I will be at your home with the nurse in a few moments. Please have a room ready. And by the way, Judge, I must tell you again that my patient is in a serious condition. I warn you that we will hold you responsible if anything happens to interfere with our arrangements for her treatment. Good-bye."

He turned to the nurse with a wry face. "It's pretty bad, Miss Farwell."

Then, ringing up the village drayman, he arranged to have the young woman's trunk taken to the house. When the man had called for the checks Harry said: "Now, Nurse, my buggy is here, and if you are ready I guess we had better follow your trunk pretty closely."

From the window the old Doctor watched them get into the buggy, and drive off down the street. Mechanically he opened the letter from Dr. Miles, which he still held in his hand. "An ideal nurse, who has taken up the work for love of it,—have known the family for years—thoroughbreds—just the kind to send a Kentuckian like you——I warn you look out,—I want her back again."

The Doctor chuckled when he remembered Harry's look as he talked to the young woman. "If ever a man needed a wife Harry does," he thought. "Who knows what might happen?"

Who knows, indeed?

Then the Doctor went home to Dan. He found him in Denny's garden, with Denny enthroned on the big rock—listening to his fun, while Deborah, from the house, looked on, unable to believe that it was "the parson sure enough out there wid Denny," —Denny who was to have been a priest himself one day, but who would never now be good for much of anything.

CHAPTER VI.

THE CALLING OF DAN MATTHEWS.

" 'In the battle of life we cannot hire a substitute; whatever work one volunteers to make his own he must look upon as his ministry to the race.' "

AN, with the Doctor and Mrs. Oldham were to take supper and spend the evening at Elder Jordan's. Martha went over early in the afternoon, leaving the two men to follow.

As they were passing the monument, Dan stopped. "Did you know him?" he asked curiously, when he had read the inscription. It was not like Dan to be curious.

The Doctor answered briefly: "I was there when he was born and was his family physician all his life, and I was with him when he died."

Something in the doctor's voice made Dan look at him intently for a moment, then in a low tone: "He was a good man?"

"One of the best I ever knew, too good for this town. Look at that thing. They say that expressed their appreciation of him—and it does," he finished grimly.

"But," said Dan, in a puzzled way, turning once more to the monument, "this inscription—" he read again the sentence from the statesman's speech on the forgotten issue of his passing day.

The Doctor said nothing.

Then gazing up at the cast-iron figure posed stiffly with outstretched arm in the attitude of a public speaker, Dan asked: "Is that like him?"

"Like him! It's like nothing but the people who conceived it," growled the Doctor indignantly. "If that man were living he would not be always talking about issues that have no meaning at this day. He would be giving himself to the problems that trouble us now. This thing," he rapped the monument with his stick until it gave forth a dull, hollow sound, "this thing is not a memorial to the life and character of my friend. It memorializes the dead issue to which he gave himself at one passing moment of his life, and which, had he lived, he would have forgotten, as the changing times brought new issues to be met as he met this old one. He was too great, too brave, to ever stand still and let the world go by. He was always on the firing line. This thing—" he rapped the hollow iron shaft again contemptuously, and the hollow sound seemed to add emphasis to his words— "this is a dead monument to a dead issue. Instead of speaking of his life, it cries aloud in hideous emphasis that he is dead."

They stood silently for a moment then Dan said, quietly: "After all, Doctor, they meant well."

"And that," retorted the old man grimly, "is what we doctors say when we see our mistakes go by in the hearse."

They went on up the street until they reached the church. Here Dan stopped again. He read the inscription cut large in the stone over the door, "The

Strong Memorial Church." Again Dan turned to his friend inquiringly.

"Judge Strong, the old Judge," explained the Doctor. "That's his picture in the big stained-glass window there."

In all his intentions Nathaniel Jordan was one of the best of men. Surely, if in the hereafter, any man receives credit for always doing what his conscience dictates, Nathan will. He was one of those characters who give up living ten years before they die. Nathan stayed on for the church's good.

Miss Charity, the Elder's only child is—well, she was born, raised and educated for a parson's wife. The Doctor says that she didn't even cry like other babies. At three she had taken a prize in Sunday school for committing Golden texts, at seven she was baptized, and knew the reason why, at twelve she played the organ in Christian Endeavor. At fourteen she was teaching a class, leading prayer meeting, attending conventions, was president of the Local Union, and pointed with pride to the fact that she was on more committees than any other single individual in the Memorial Church. The walls of her room were literally covered with badges, medals, tokens, prizes and emblems, with the picture of every conspicuous church worker and leader of her denomination. Between times the girl studied the early history of her church, read the religious papers and in other ways fitted herself for her life work. Poor Charity! She was so cursed with a holy ambition, that to her men were not men, they simply *were* or were *not* preachers.

When Dan and the Doctor reached the Jordan home they found this daughter of the church at the front gate watching for them, a look of eager hope and expectancy on her face. The Elder himself with his wife and Mrs. Oldham were on the front porch. Martha could scarcely wait for the usual greeting and the introduction of Dan to Mrs. Jordan, before she opened on the Doctor with, "It's a great pity Doctor, that you couldn't bring Brother Matthews here before the last possible minute; supper is ready right now. A body would think you had an important case, if they didn't know that you were too old to do anything any more."

"We did have an important case, my dear," the Doctor replied, "and it was Dan who caused our delay."

"That's it; lay it on to somebody else like you always do. What in the world could poor Brother Matthews be doing to keep him from a good meal?"

"He was studying—let me see, what was it, Dan? Art, Political Economy—or Theology?"

Dan smiled. "I think it might have been the theory and practice of medicine," he returned. At which they both laughed and the others joined in, though for his life the Doctor couldn't see why.

"Well," said the Elder, when he had finished his shrill cackle, "we better go in and discuss supper awhile; that's always a satisfactory subject at least." Which was a pretty good one for Nathaniel.

When the meal was finished, they all went out on the front porch again, where it soon became evident that Nathaniel did not propose to waste more time in light and frivolous conversation. By his familiar and ponderous "Ahem—ahem!" even Dan understood that he was anxious to get down to the real business of the evening, and that he was determined to do his full duty, or—as he would have said—"to keep that which was committed unto him."

"Ahem—ahem!" A hush fell upon the little company, the women turned their chairs expectantly, and the Doctor slipped over to the end of the porch to enjoy his evening cigar. The Elder had the field.

With another and still louder "Ahem!" he began. "I am sorry that Brother Strong is not here this evening. Judge Strong that is, Brother Matthews; he is our other Elder, you understand. I expected him but he has evidently been detained."

The Doctor, thinking of Dr. Harry and the nurse, chuckled, and Nathan turned a look of solemn inquiry in his direction.

"Ahem—ahem,—you did not come to Corinth directly from your home, I understand, Brother Matthews?"

The Doctor could see Dan's face by the light from the open window. He fancied it wore a look of amused understanding.

"No," answered the minister, "I spent yesterday in the city."

"Ahem—ahem," coughed the Elder. "Found an acquaintance on the train coming up, didn't you? We noticed you talking to a young woman at the car window."

Dan paused a moment before answering, and the Doctor could feel the interest of the company. Then the boy said, dryly, "Yes, I may say though, that she is something more than an acquaintance."

Smothered exclamations from the women. "Ah hah," from the Elder. The Doctor grinned to himself in the dark. "The young scamp!"

"Ahem! She had a pretty face, we noticed; are you—that is, have you known her long?"

"Several years, sir; the lady you saw is my mother. I went with her to the city day before yesterday, where she wished to do some shopping, and accompanied her on her way home as far as Corinth."

More exclamations from the women.

"Why, Doctor, you never told us it was his mother," cried Martha, and Nathaniel turned toward the end of the porch with a look of righteous indignation.

"You never asked me," chuckled the Doctor.

After this the two older women drifted into the house. Charity settled herself in an attitude of rapt attention, and the program was continued.

"Ahem. You may not be aware of it Brother Matthews, but I know a great deal about your family, sir."

"Indeed," exclaimed Dan.

"Yes sir. You see I have some mining interests in that district, quite profitable interests I may say. Judge Strong and I together have quite extensive interests. Two or three years ago we made a good many trips into your part of the country, where we heard a great deal of your people. Your mother seems to be a remarkable woman of considerable influence. Too bad she is not a regular member of the church. Our preachers often tell us, and I believe it is true, that people who do so much good out of the church really injure the cause more than anything else."

Dan made no answer to this, but as the Doctor saw his face in the light it wore a mingled expression of astonishment and doubt.

The Elder proceeded, "They used to tell us some great stories about your father, too. Big man, isn't he?"

"Yes sir, fairly good size."

"Yes, I remember some of his fights we used to hear about; and there was another member of the family, they mentioned a good deal. Dad—Dad—"

"Howitt," said Dan softly.

"That's it, Howitt. A kind of a shepherd, wasn't he? Discovered the big mine on your father's place. One of your father's fights was about the old man. Ahem—ahem—I judge you take after your father. I don't know just what to think about your whipping that fellow this morning. Someone had to do something of course, but—ahem, for a minister it was rather unusual. I don't know how the people will take it."

"I'm afraid that I forgot that I was a minister," said Dan uneasily. "I hope, sir, you do not think that I did wrong."

"Ahem—ahem, I can't say that it was wrong exactly, but as I said, we don't know how the people will take it. But there's one thing sure," and the Elder's shrill cackle rang out, "it will bring a big crowd to hear you preach. Well, well, that's off the subject. Ahem—Brother Matthews, why haven't your people opened that big mine in Dewey Bald?"

"I expect it would be better for me to let father or mother explain that to you, sir," answered Dan, as cool and calm as the evening.

"Yes, yes of course, but it's rather strange, rather unusual you know, to find a young man of your make-up and opportunities for wealth, entering the ministry. You could educate a great many preachers, sir, if you would develop that mine."

"Father and mother have always taught us children that in the battle of life one cannot hire a substitute; that whatever work one volunteers to make his own he must look upon as his ministry to the race. I believe that the church is an institution divinely given to serve the world, and that, more than any other, it helps men to the highest possible life. I volunteered for the work I have undertaken, because naturally I wish my life to count for the greatest possible good; and because I feel that I can serve men better in the church than in any other way."

"Whew!" thought the Doctor, "that was something for Nathan to chew on." The lad's face when he spoke made his old friend's nerves tingle. His was a new conception of the ministry, new to the Doctor at least. Forgetting his cigar he awaited the Elder's reply with breathless interest.

"Ahem—ahem, you feel then that you have no special Divine call to the work?"

"I have always been taught at home, sir, that every man is divinely called to his work, if that work is for the good of all men. His faithfulness or unfaithfulness to the call is revealed in the *motives* that prompt him to choose his field." The boy paused a moment and then added slowly—and no one who heard him could doubt his deep conviction—"Yes sir, I feel that I am divinely called to preach the gospel."

"Ahem—ahem, I trust, Brother Matthews, that you are not taken up with these new fads and fancies that are turning the minds of the people from the true worship of God."

"It is my desire, sir, to lead people to the true worship of God. I believe that nothing will accomplish that end but the simple old Jerusalem gospel."

The Doctor lit his cigar again. They seemed to be getting upon safer ground.

"I am glad to hear that—" said the Elder heartily —"very glad. I feared from the way you spoke, you might be going astray. There is a great work for you here in Corinth—a great work. Our old brother who preceded you was a good man, sound in the faith in every way, but he didn't seem to take somehow. The fact is the other churches—ahem— are getting about all our congregation."

Then for an hour or more, Elder Jordan, for the new minister's benefit, discussed in detail the religious history of Corinth, with the past, present and future of Memorial Church; while Charity, drinking in every word of the oft-heard discussion, grew ever more entranced with the possibilities of the new pastor's ministry, and the Doctor sat alone at the farther end of the porch. The Elder finished with: "Well, well, Brother Matthews, you are young, strong, unmarried, and with your reputation as a college man and an athlete you ought to do great things for Memorial Church. We are counting on you to build us up wonderfully. And let me say too, that we are one of the oldest and best known congregations in our brotherhood here in the state. We have had some great preachers here. You can make a reputation that will put you to the top of your—ah, calling."

Dan was just saying, "I hope I will please you, sir," when the women appeared in the doorway. Martha had her bonnet on.

"Come, come Nathan," said Mrs. Jordan, "you mustn't keep poor Brother Matthews up another minute. He must be nearly worn out with his long journey and all the excitement."

The Doctor thought again of the girl who had made the same journey in the car behind Dan, and who had also shared the excitement. He wondered how the nurse was enjoying her evening and when she would get to bed. "That's so," exclaimed the Doctor, rising to his feet. "We're all a lot of brutes to treat the poor boy so."

Dan whirled on him with a look that set the old man to laughing, "That's all right, sonny," he chuckled. "Come on, I've been asleep for an hour."

CHAPTER VII.

FROM DEBORAH'S PORCH.

"'With nothin' to think of all the time but the Blessed Jesus an' the Holy Mother; an' all the people so respectful, an' lookin' up to you. Sure 'tis a grand thing, Doctor, to be a priest.'"

NATHANIEL JORDAN'S prediction proved true

In the two days between Dan's arrival and his first Sunday in Corinth, the Ally was actively engaged in making known the identity of the big stranger, who had so skillfully punished the man from Windy Cove. Also the name and profession of the young woman who had gone to Denny's assistance were fully revealed.

The new minister of the Memorial Church was the sensation of the hour. The building could scarcely hold the crowd, while the rival churches were deserted, save only by the few faithful "pillars" who were held in their places by the deep conviction that heaven itself would fall should they fail to support their own particular faith. With the people who had attended the fair, the Ally journeyed far into the country, and the roads being good with promise of a moon to drive home by, the country folk for miles around came to worship God, and, incidentally, to see the preacher who had fought and vanquished the celebrated Jud. Many were there that day who had not been inside a church before for years. The Ally went also, but then the Ally, they say, is a regular attendant at all the services of every church.

Judge Strong, with an expression of pious satisfaction on his hard face, occupied his own particular corner. From another corner Elder Jordan watched for signs of false doctrine. Charity, except when busy at the organ, never took her adoring eyes from the preacher's face. At the last moment before the sermon, Dr. Harry slipped into the seat beside the Doctor. And many other earnest souls there were who depended upon the church as the only source of their life's inspiration and strength.

Facing this crowd that even in the small town of Corinth represented every class and kind, Dan felt it all; the vulgar curiosity, the craving for sensation, the admiration, the suspicion, the true welcome, the antagonism, the spiritual dependence. And the young man from the mountains and the schools, who had entered the ministry from the truest motives, with the highest ideals, shrank back and was afraid.

Dan was, literally, to this church and people a messenger from another world. It was not strange that many of the people thought, "How out of place this big fellow looks in the pulpit." Many of them felt dimly, too, that which the Doctor had always felt, that this man was somehow a revelation of something that might have been, that ought to be. But no one tried to search out the reason why.

The theme of the new minister's sermon was, "The

Faith of the Fathers," and it must have been a good
one, because Martha said the next day, that it was
the finest thing she had ever heard; and she had it
figured out somehow that the members of neighboring churches, who were there, got some straight gospel for once in their lives. Elder Jordan assured the
Doctor in a confidential whisper, that it was a splendid effort. The Doctor knew that Dan was splendid,
and he could see that the boy had fairly hypnotized
the crowd, but he could not understand why it should
have been much of an effort. He confided to Martha
that "so far as he could see, the sermon might have
been taken from the barrel of any one of the preachers that had served the Memorial Church since its
establishment." But the sermon was new and fresh
to Dan, and so gained something of interest and
strength from the earnestness and personality of the
speaker. "The boy had only to hold that gait,"
reflected the Doctor, "and he would, as Nathan had
said, land at the very top of his profession."

In the evening, the Doctor slipped away from
church as soon as the services were over, leaving Dan
with those who always stay until the janitor begins
turning out the lights. Martha would walk home
with fellow workers in the Ladies' Aid, who lived a
few doors beyond, and the Doctor wished to be alone.

Crossing the street to avoid the crowd, he walked
slowly along under the big trees, trying to accustom
himself to the thought of his boy dressed in the
conventional minister's garb, delivering time worn
conventionalities in a manner as conventional. It
was to this strange thinking old man, almost as if he

had seen Dan behind the grated doors of a prison cell.

Very slowly he went along, unmindful of aught but the thoughts that troubled him, until, coming to the Widow Mulhall's little cottage, where Deborah and Denny were sitting on the porch, he paused. Across the street in front of his own home, Martha and her friends were holding an animated conversation.

"Come in, come in, Doctor," called Deborah's cheery voice, "it's a fine evenin' it is and only beginnin'. I was just tellin' Denny that 'tis a shame folks have to waste such nights in sleep. Come right in, I'll fetch another chair—take the big rocker there, Doctor, that's right. And how are you? Denny? Oh the bye is all right again just as you said; sure the minister had him out in the garden that same afternoon. 'Twas the blessin' of God, though, that his Reverence was there to keep that devil from batin' the poor lad to death. I hope you'll not be forgettin' the way to our gate entirely now, Doctor, that you'll be crossin' the street so often to the house beyond the garden there."

In the Widow's voice there was a hint of her Irish ancestry, as, in her kind blue eyes, buxom figure and cordial manner, there was more than a hint of her warm-hearted, whole-souled nature.

"How do you like your new neighbor, Deborah?" asked the Doctor.

"Ah, Doctor, it's a fine big man he is, a danged fine man inside an' out. Denny and me are almighty proud, havin' him so close. He's that sociable, too, not at all like a priest. It's every blessed day since he's been here he's comin' over to Denny in the garden, and helpin' him with the things, a-talkin' away all the time. ' 'Tis the very exercise I need,' says he. 'And it's a real kindness for ye to let me work a bit now and then,' says he. But sure we kin see, 'tis the big heart of him, wishful to help the bye. But it's queer notioned he is fer a preacher."

"Didn't I see you and Denny at church this evening?" asked the Doctor.

"You did that, sir. You see not havin' no church of our own within reach of our legs, an' bein' real wishful to hear a bit of a prayer and a sermon like, Denny an' me slips into the protestant meetings now and then. After all there's no real harm in it now, do you think, Doctor?"

"Harm to you and Denny, or the church?" the Doctor asked.

"Aw, go on now, Doctor you do be always havin' your joke," she laughed. "Harm to neither or both or all, I mane, for, of course—well, let it go. I guess that while Denny and me do be sayin' our prayers in our little cabin on this side of the street, and you are a-sayin' yours in your fine house across the way, 'tis the same blessed Father of us all gets them both. I misdoubt if God had much to do wid layin' out the streets of Corinth anyhow. I've heard how 'twas the old Judge Strong did that."

"And what do you think of Mr. Matthews' sermon?"

"It's ashamed I am to say it, Doctor, but I niver heard him."

"Never heard him? But I thought you were there."

"And we was, sir, so we was. And Denny here can tell you the whole thing, but for myself I niver heard a blessed word, after the singin' and the preacher stood up."

"Why, what was the matter?"

"The preacher himself."

"The preacher?"

"Yes sir. 'Twas this way, Doctor, upon my soul I couldn't hear what he was a-sayin' for lookin' at the man himself. With him a-standin' up there so big an' strong an'—an' clean like through an' through an' the look on his face! It set me to thinkin' of all that I used to dream fer—fer my Denny here. Ye mind what a fine lookin' man poor Jack was, sir, tho' I do say it, and how Denny here, from a baby, was the very image of him. I always knowed he was a-goin' to grow up another Jack for strength an' looks. And you know yourself how our hearts was set on havin' him a priest, him havin' such a turn that way, bein' crazy on books and studyin' an' the likes—an' now—now here we are, sir. My man gone, an' my boy just able to drag his poor broken body around, an' good fer nothin' but to dig in the dirt. No sir, I couldn't hear the sermon fer lookin' at the preacher an' thinkin'."

Denny moved his twisted, misshapen body uneasily, "Oh, come now, mother," he said, "let's don't be spoilin' the fine night fer the Doctor with our troubles."

"Indade, that we will not," said Deborah cheerfully. "Don't you think Denny's garden's been doin' fine this summer, Doctor?"

"Fine," said the Doctor heartily. "But then it's always fine. There's lots of us would like to know how he makes it do so well."

Denny gave a pleased laugh.

"Aw now Doctor you're flatterin' me. They have been doin' pretty well though—pretty well fer me."

"I tell you what it is, Doctor," said Deborah, "the bye naturally loves them things into growin'. If people would be takin' as good care of their children as Denny does for his cabbage and truck it would be a blessin' to the world."

"It is funny, Doctor," put in Denny, "but do you know those things out there seem just like people to me. I tell mother it ain't so bad after all, not bein' a priest. The minister was a-sayin' yesterday, that the people needed more than their souls looked after. If I can't be tellin' people how to live, I can be growin' good things to keep them alive, and maybe that's not so bad as it might be."

"I don't know what we'd be doin' at all, if it wasn't fer that same garden," added Deborah, "with clothes, and wood and groceries to buy, to say nothin' of the interest that's always comin' due. We—"

"Whist," said Denny in a low tone as a light flashed up in the corner window of the house on the other side of the garden. "There's the minister come home."

Reverently they watched the light and the moving shadow in the room. The moon, through the branches of the trees along the street, threw waving patches of soft light over the dark green of the little lawn. Martha's friends had moved on, Martha herself had retired. The street was seemingly deserted and very still.

Leaning forward in her chair Deborah spoke in a whisper. "We can always tell when he's in of nights, and when he goes to bed. Ye see it's almost like we was livin' in the same house with him. An' a great comfort it is to us too, wid him such a good man, our havin' him so near. Poor bye I'll warrant he's tired tonight. But oh, it must be a grand thing, Doctor, to be a doin' such holy work, an' a livin' with God Almighty like, with nothin' to think of all the time but the Blessed Jesus and the Holy Mother; an' all the people so respectful, an' lookin' up to you. Sure 'tis a grand thing, Doctor, to be a priest, savin' your presence sir, for I know how you've little truck wid churches, tho' the lady your wife does enough fer two."

The Doctor rose to go for he saw that the hour was late. As he stood on the steps ready to depart the steady flow of Deborah's talk continued, when Denny interrupted again, pointing toward a woman who was crossing to the other side of the street. She walked slowly, and, reaching the sidewalk in front of the Doctor's house, hesitated, in a troubled, undecided way. Approaching the gate, she paused, then drew back and moved on slowly up the street. Her movements and manner gave the impression that she was in trouble, perhaps in pain.

"There's something wrong there," said the Doctor. "Who is it? Can you see who it is, Denny?"

"Yes, sir," he answered, and Deborah broke in, "it's that poor girl of—of Jim Conner's, sir."

The Doctor, at once nervous and agitated, was not a little worried and could make no reply, knowing that it was Jim Conner who had killed Deborah's husband.

"Poor thing," murmured Deborah. "For the love of God, look at that now, Doctor!"

The girl had reached the corner, and had fallen or thrown herself in a crouching heap against the monument.

The widow was starting for the street, but Denny caught her arm: "No—no mother, you mustn't do that, you know how she's scared to death of you; let the Doctor go."

The physician was already on his way as fast as his old legs would take him.

CHAPTER VIII.

THE WORK OF THE ALLY.

"In the little room that looked out upon the Monument and the garden, Dan—all unknowing—slept. And over all brooded the spirit that lives in Corinth—the Ally—that dread, mysterious thing that never sleeps."

RACE CONNER is a type common to every village, town and city in the land, the saddest of all sad creatures—a good girl with a bad reputation.

Her reputation Grace owed first to her father's misdeeds, for which the girl could in no way be to blame, and second, to the all-powerful Ally, without whom the making of any reputation, good or bad, is impossible.

The Doctor knew the girl well. When she was a little tot and a member of Martha's Sunday school class, she was at the house frequently. Later as a member of the church she herself was a teacher and an active worker. Then came the father's crime and conviction, followed soon by the mother's death, and the girl was left to shift for herself. She had kept herself alive by working here and there, in the canning factory and restaurants, and wherever she could. No one would give her a place in a home.

The young people in the church, imitating their elders, shunned her, and it was not considered good policy to permit her to continue teaching in the Sunday school. No mother wanted her child to associate with a criminal's daughter; naturally she drifted away from the regular services, and soon it was publicly announced that her name had been dropped from the roll of membership. After that she never came.

It was not long until the girl had such a name that no self respecting man or woman dared be caught recognizing her on the street.

The people always spoke of her as "that Grace Conner."

The girl, hurt so often, grew to fear everyone. She strove to avoid meeting people on the street, or meeting them, passed with downcast eyes, not daring to greet them. Barely able to earn bread to keep life within her poor body, her clothing grew shabby, her form thin and worn; and these very evidences of her goodness of character worked to accomplish her ruin. But she was a good girl through it all, a good girl with a bad reputation.

She was cowering at the foot of the monument, her face buried in her hands, when the Doctor touched her on the shoulder. She started and turned up to him the saddest face the old physician had ever seen.

"What's the matter, my girl?" he said as kindly as he could.

She shook her head and buried her face in her hands again.

"Please go away and let me alone."

"Come, come," said the Doctor laying his hand

on her shoulder again. "This won't do; you must tell me what's wrong. You can't stay out here on the street at this time of the night."

At his tone she raised her head again. "This time of the night! What difference does it make to anyone whether I am on the street or not?"

"It makes a big difference to you, my girl," the Doctor answered. "You should be home and in bed."

God! What a laugh she gave!

"Home! In bed!" She laughed again.

"Stop that!" said the physician sharply, for he saw that just a touch more, and she would be over the line. "Stand up here and tell me what's the matter; are you sick?"

She rose to her feet with his help.

"No sir."

"Well, what have you been doing?"

"Nothing, Doctor. I—I was just walking around."

"Why don't you go back to the Hotel? You are working there, are you not?"

At this she wrung her hands and looked about in a dazed way, but answered nothing.

"See here, Grace," said the physician, "you know me, surely—old Doctor Oldham, can't you tell me what it is that's wrong?"

She made no answer.

"Come, let me take you to the Hotel," he urged; "it's only a step."

"No—no," she moaned, "I can't go there. I don't live there any more."

"Well where do you live now?" he asked.

"Over in Old Town."

"But why did you leave your place at the Hotel?"

"A—a man there said something that I didn't like, and then the proprietor told me that I must go, because some of the people were talking about me, and I was giving the Hotel a bad name. Oh, Doctor, I ain't a bad girl, I ain't never been, but folks are driving me to it. That or—or—" she hesitated.

What could he say?

"It's the same everywhere I try to work," she continued in a hopeless tone. "At the canning factory the other girls said their folks wouldn't let them work there if I didn't go. I haven't been able to earn a cent since I left the Hotel. I don't know what to do, —oh, I don't know what to do!" She broke down crying.

"Look here, why didn't you come to me?" the Doctor asked roughly. "You knew you could come to me. Didn't I tell you to?"

"I—I was afraid. I'm afraid of everybody." She shivered and looked over her shoulder.

The Doctor saw that this thing had gone far enough. "Come with me," he said. "You must have something to eat."

He started to lead her across the street toward Mrs. Mulhall whom he could see at the gate watching them. But the girl hung back.

"No, no," she panted in her excitement. "Not there, I dare not go there." The Doctor hesitated.

"Well, come to my house then," he said. She went as far as the gate then she stopped again.

"I can't, Doctor. Mrs. Oldham, I can't—" The girl was right. The Doctor was never so ashamed in all his life. After a little, he said with decision, "Look here, Grace, you sit down on the porch for a few minutes. Martha is in bed and fast asleep long ago." He stole away as quietly as possible, and in a little while returned with a basket full of such provisions as he could find in the pantry. He was chuckling to himself as he thought of Martha when she discovered the theft in the morning, and cursing half aloud the thing that made it necessary for him to steal from his own pantry for the girl whom he would have taken into his home so gladly, if——

He made her eat some of the cold chicken and bread and drink a glass of milk. And when she was feeling better, walked with her down the street a little way, to be sure that she was all right.

"I can't thank you enough, Doctor," she said, "you have saved me from—"

"Don't try," he broke in. He did not want her to get on that line again. "Go on home like a good girl now, and mind you look carefully in the bottom of that basket." He had put a little bill there, the only money he had in the house. "This will help until times are better for you, and mind now, if you run against it again, come to me or go to Dr. Harry at the office, and tell him that you want me."

He watched her down the street and then went home, stopping for a word of explanation to Deborah and Denny, who were waiting at the gate.

The light was still burning in Dan's window when the Doctor again entered his own yard. He thought once that he would run in on the minister for a minute, and then remembered that "the boy would be tired after his great effort defending the faith of Memorial Church." It was long past the old man's bed time. He told himself that he was an old fool to be prowling about so late at night, and that he would hear from Martha all right tomorrow. Then, as he climbed into bed, he chuckled again, thinking of the empty kitchen pantry and that missing basket.

The light in Dan's room went out. Some belated person passed, going home for the night; a little later, another. Then a man and woman, walking closely, talking in low tones, strolled slowly by in the shadow of the big trees. The quick step of a horse and the sound of buggy-wheels came swiftly nearer and nearer, passed and died away in the stillness. It was Dr. Harry answering a call. In Judge Strong's big, brown house, a nurse in her uniform of blue and white, by the dim light of a night-lamp, leaned over her patient with a glass of water. In Old Town a young woman in shabby dress, with a basket on her arm, hurried—trembling and frightened—across the lonely, grass-grown square. Under the quiet stars in the soft moonlight, the cast-iron monument stood—grim and cold and sinister. In the peace and quiet of the night, Denny's garden wrought its mystery. In the little room that looked out upon the monument and the garden, Dan—all unknowing—slept.

And over all brooded the spirit that lives in Corinth—the Ally—that dread, mysterious thing that never sleeps.

CHAPTER IX.

THE EDGE OF THE BATTLEFIELD.

"But it was as if his superior officers had ordered him to mark time, while his whole soul was eager for the command to charge."

DAN was trying to prepare his evening sermon for the third Sunday of what the old Doctor called his Corinthian ministry. The afternoon was half gone, when he arose from his study table. All day he had been at it, and all day the devils of dissatisfaction had rioted in his soul—or wherever it is that such devils are supposed to riot.

The three weeks had not been idle weeks for Dan. He had made many pastoral calls at the homes of his congregation; he had attended numberless committee meetings. Already he was beginning to feel the tug of his people's need—the world old need of sympathy and inspiration, of courage and cheer; the need of the soldier for the battle-cry of his comrades, the need of the striving runner for the lusty shout of his friends, the need of the toiling servant for the "well-done" of his master.

Keenly sensitive to this great unvoiced cry of life, the young man answered in his heart, "Here am I, use me." Standing before his people he felt as one who, on the edge of a battlefield longs, with all his heart, to throw himself into the fight. But it was as if his superior officers had ordered him to mark time, while his whole soul was eager for the command to charge.

Why do people go to church? What do men ask of their religion? What have they the right to expect from those who assume to lead them in their worship? Already these questions were being shouted at him from the innermost depths of his consciousness. He felt the answer that his Master would give. But always between him and those to whom he would speak there came the thought of his employers. And he found himself, while speaking to the people, nervously watching the faces of the men by whose permission he spoke. So it came that he was not satisfied with his work that afternoon, and he tossed aside his sermon to leave his study for the fresh air and sunshine of the open fields. From his roses the Doctor hailed him as he went down the street, but the boy only answered with a greeting and a wave of his hand. Dan did not need the Doctor that day. Straight out into the country he went walking fast, down one hill—up another, across a creek, over fences, through a pasture into the woods. An hour of this at a good hard pace, and he felt better. The old familiar voices of hill and field and forest and stream soothed and calmed him. The physical exercise satisfied to some extent his instinct and passion for action.

Coming back through Old Town, and leisurely climbing the hill on the road that leads past the old Academy, he paused frequently to look back over the ever widening view, and to drink deep of the pure, sun-filled air. At the top of the hill, reluctant to go back to the town that lay beyond, he stood contemplating the ancient school building that held so bravely its commanding position, and looked so pitiful in its shabby old age. Then passing through a gap in the tumble-down fence, and crossing the weed-filled yard, he entered the building.

For a while he wandered curiously about the time-worn rooms, reading the names scratched on the plaster walls, cut in the desks and seats, on the window casing, and on the big square posts that, in the lower rooms, supported the ceiling. He laughed to himself, as he noticed how the sides of these posts facing away from the raised platform at the end of the room were most elaborately carved. It suggested so vividly the life that had once stirred within the old walls.

Several of the names were already familiar to him. He tried to imagine the venerable heads of families he knew, as they were in the days when they sat upon these worn benches. Did Judge Strong or Elder Jordan, perhaps, throw one of those spit-balls that stuck so hard and fast to the ceiling? And did some of the grandmothers he had met giggle and hide their faces at Nathaniel's cunning evasion of the teacher's quick effort to locate the successful marksman? Had those staid pillars of the church ever been swayed and bent by passions of young manhood and womanhood? Had their minds ever been stirred by the questions and doubts of youth? Had their hearts ever throbbed with eager longing to know—to feel life in its fullness?

Seating himself at one of the battered desks he tried to bring back the days that were gone, and to see about him the faces of those who once had filled the room with the strength and gladness of their youth. He felt strangely old in thus trying to feel a boy among those boys and girls of the days long gone.

Who among the boys would be his own particular chum? Elder Jordan? He smiled. And who, (the blood mounted to his cheek at the thought) who among the girls would be— Out of the mists of his revery came a face—a face that was strangely often in his mind since that day when he arrived in Corinth. Several times he had caught passing glimpses of her; once he had met her on the street and ventured to bow. And Dr. Harry, with whom he had already begun an enduring friendship, had told him much to add to his interest in her. But to dream about the stranger in this way—

"What nonsense!" he exclaimed aloud, and rising, strode to the window to clear his mind of those too strong fancies by a sight of the world in which he lived and to which he belonged.

The next moment he drew back with a start—a young woman in the uniform of a trained nurse was entering the yard.

CHAPTER X.

A MATTER OF OPINION.

" 'Who spoke of condemnation? Is that just the question? Are you not unfair?' "

MISS FARWELL had heard much of the new pastor of the Memorial Church. Dr. Harry frequently urged her to attend services; Deborah, when Hope had seen her was eloquent in his praise. Mrs. Strong and the ladies who called at the house spoke of him often. But for the first two weeks of her stay at Judge Strong's the nurse had been confined so closely to the care of her patient that she had heard nothing to identify the preacher with the big stranger whom she had met at the depot the day of her arrival.

By the time Miss Farwell began hearing of the new preacher the interest occasioned by his defense of Denny had already died down, and it chanced that no one mentioned it in her presence when speaking of him, while each time he had called at the Strong home the nurse had been absent or busy. Thus it happened that so far as she knew, Miss Farwell had never met the minister about whom she had heard so much. But she had several times seen the big fellow, who had apologized at such length for running into her at the depot, and who had gone so quickly to the assistance of Denny. It was natural, under such conditions, that she should remember him. It was natural, too, that she never dreamed of connecting the young hero of the street fight with the Reverend Matthews of the Memorial Church.

Her patient had so far improved that the nurse was now able to leave her for an hour or two in the afternoon, and the young woman had gone for a walk just beyond the outskirts of the village. Coming to the top of the hill she had turned aside from the dusty highway, thinking to enjoy the view from the shade of a great oak that grew on a grassy knoll in the center of the school grounds.

Dan watched her as she made her way slowly across the yard, his eyes bright with admiration for her womanly grace as she stopped, here and there, to pick a wild flower from the tangle of grass and weeds. Reaching the tree she seated herself and, laying her parasol on the grass by her side, began arranging the blossoms she had gathered—pausing, now and then, to look over the rolling country of field and woods that, dotted by farm houses with their buildings and stacks, stretched away into the blue distance.

The young fellow at the window gazed at her with almost superstitious awe. That her face had come before him so vividly, as he sat dreaming in the old school-room, at the very moment when she was turning into the yard, moved him greatly. His blood tingled at the odd premonition that this woman was somehow to play a great part in his life. Nothing seemed more natural than that he should have come to this spot this afternoon. Neither was it at all strange that, in her walk, she too, should be attracted by the beauty of the place. But the feeling forced itself upon him nevertheless that this perfectly natural incident was a great event in his life. He knew that he would go to her presently. He was painfully aware that he ought not to be thus secretly watching her, but he hesitated as one about to take a step that could never be retraced.

She started when he appeared in the doorway of the building and half-arose from her place. Then recognizing him she dropped back on the grass; and there was a half-amused frown on her face, though her cheeks were red. She was indignant with herself that she should be blushing like a schoolgirl at the presence of this stranger whose name even she did not know.

"I beg your pardon, Miss Farwell, I fear that I startled you," he said, hat in hand. Already Dan had grown so accustomed to being greeted by strangers, that it never occurred to him that this lady did not know who he was.

She saw the sunlight on his shaggy red-brown hair, and the fine poise of the well-shaped head, as she answered shortly, "You did."

Woman-like she was making him feel her anger at herself; and also woman-like, when she saw his embarrassment at her blunt words and manner, she smiled.

"I am sorry," he said, but he did not offer to go on his way.

When she made no reply but began rearranging her handful of blossoms, he spoke again, remarking on the beauty of the view before them; and ventured to ask if the knoll was to her a favorite spot, adding that it was his first visit to the place.

"I have never been here before either," she answered. The brief silence that followed was broken by Dan.

"We seem to have made a discovery," he said, wondering why she should seem confused at his simple remark. "I know I ought to go," he continued. "I will if you say the word, but—" he paused.

"You were here first," she returned with a smile. Really, she thought, there was no reason why she should drive him away. He was so evidently a gentleman, and the place was on the public thoroughfare.

"Then I may stay?" He dropped on the grass at her feet with an exclamation of satisfaction and pleasure.

Looking away over the landscape where the clouds and shadows were racing, and the warm autumn light lay on the varying shades of green and brown, he remarked: "Do you know when I see a bit of out-doors like that, on such a day as this, or when I am out in the woods or up in the hills, I wonder what men build churches for, anyway. I fear I must be something of a pagan, for I often feel that I can worship God best in his own temple. Quite heathenish isn't it?" He laughed, but under the laugh there was a note of troubled seriousness.

She looked at him curiously. "And is it heathenish to worship God outside of a church? If it is I fear that I, too, am a heathen."

He noted the words "I, too," and saw instantly that she did not know him but had understood from his words that he was not a church man. He felt that he ought to correct her false impression, that he ought to tell her who and what he was, but he was possessed of a curious feeling of reluctance to declare his calling.

The truth is, Dan Matthews did not want to meet this woman as a priest, but as a man. He had already learned how the moment the preacher was announced the man was pushed into the background.

While he hesitated she watched him with increasing interest. His words had pleased her; she waited for him to speak again.

"I suppose your profession does keep you from anything like regular church attendance," he said.

"Yes," she answered, "I have found that sick people do not as a rule observe a one-day-in-seven religion. But it is not my professional duties that keep me from church."

"You are not then—"

"Decidedly I am not," she answered.

"Really, you surprise me. I thought of course you were a member of some church."

There was a touch of impatience in her quick reply. "You thought 'of course'? And why of course, please?"

He started to answer, but she went on quickly, "I know why; because I am a woman, *the weaker sex!*"

It is not possible to describe the fine touch in her voice when she said "the weaker sex." It was so delicately done, that it had none of the coarseness that commonly marks like expressions, when used by some women. Dan was surprised to feel that it emphasized the fineness of her character, as well as its strength.

"Because I am not a man must I be *useless?*" she continued. "Is a woman's life of so little influence in the world that she can spend it in *make-believe living* as little girls play at being grown up? Have I not as great a right to my paganism as you call it, as you have to yours?"

Again he saw his opportunity and realized that he ought to correct her mistake in assuming from his words that he was not a man of church affiliation, but again he passed it by saying slowly, instead: "I think your kind of paganism must be a very splendid thing; no one could think of one in that dress as useless."

"I did not mean—"

"I understand I think," he said earnestly, "but won't you tell me why you feel so about the church?"

She laughed as she returned, "One might think from your awful seriousness that you were a preacher. Father Confessor, if you please—" she began mockingly, then stopped—arrested by the expression of his face. "Oh I beg your pardon, have I been rude?"

With a forced laugh he answered, "Oh no, indeed, not at all. It is only that your views of the Christian religion surprise me."

"My views of the Christian religion," she repeated, very serious now. "I did not know that my views of Christianity were mentioned."

He was bewildered. "But the church! You were speaking of the church."

"And the church and Christianity are one and the same of course." Again with a touch of sarcasm, more pronounced, "You will tell me next, I suppose, that a minister really ministers."

Dan was astonished and hurt. He had learned much of the spirit of Christianity in his backwoods home, but he knew nothing of churches except that which the school had taught him. He had accepted the church to which he belonged at its own valuation, highly colored by biased historians. Such words as these were to his ears little less than sacrilege. He was shocked that they should come from one whose personality and evident character had impressed him so strongly. His voice was doubtful and perplexed as he said: "But is not that true church of Christ, which is composed of his true disciples, Christian? Surely, they can no more be separated than the sun can be separated from the sunshine; and is not the ministry a vital part of that church?"

Miss Farwell, seeing him so troubled, wondered whether she understood him. She felt that she was talking too freely to this stranger, but his questions drew her on, and she was curiously anxious that he should understand her.

"I was not thinking of that true church composed of the true disciples of Christ," she returned. "And that is just it, don't you see? *This true church that is so inseparable from the religion of Christ is so far forgotten that it never enters into any thought of the church at all.* The sun always shines, it is true, but we do not always have the sunshine. There are the dark and stormy days, you know, and sometimes there is an eclipse. To me these are the dark days, so dark that I wonder sometimes if it is not an eclipse." She paused then added deliberately, "This selfish, wasteful, cruel, heartless thing that men have built up around their opinions, and whims, and ambitions, has so come between the people and the Christianity of the Christ, that they are beginning to question if, indeed, there is anywhere such a thing as the true church."

Again Dan was startled at her words and by her passionate earnestness; the more so that, in the manner of her speaking as in her words, there was an impersonal touch very unusual to those who speak on religious topics. And there was a note of sadness in her voice as well. It was as if she spoke to him professionally of the sickness of some one dear to her and sought to keep her love for her patient from influencing her calm consideration of the case.

His next words were forced from him almost against his will. And his eyes had that wide questioning look so like that of his mother. "And the ministry," he said.

She answered, "You ask if the ministry is not a vital part of the church, and your very question expresses conditions clearly. What conception of Christianity is it that makes it possible for us to even think of the ministry as a *part* of the church? Why, the true church *is* a ministry! There can be no other reason for its existence. But don't you see how we have come to think of the ministry as we have come to think of the church? It is to us, as you say, a part of this great organization that men have created and control, and in this we are right, for this church has made the minister, and this minister has in turn made the church. They are indeed inseparable."

Dan caught up a flower that she had dropped and began picking it to pieces with trembling fingers.

"To me," he said slowly, "the minister is a servant of God. I believe, of course, that whatever work a man does in life he must do as his service to the race and in that sense he serves God. But the ministry—" he reached for another flower, choosing his words carefully, "the ministry is, to me, the highest service to which a man may be called."

She did not reply but looked away over the valley.

"Tell me," he said, "is it not so?"

"If you believe it, then to you it is so," she answered.

"But you—" he urged, "how do you look upon the minister?"

"Why should I tell you? What difference does it make what I think? You forget that we are strangers." She smiled. "Let us talk about the weather; that's a safe topic."

"I *had* forgotten that we are strangers," he said, with an answering smile. "But I am interested in what you have said because you—you have evidently thought much upon the matter, and your profession must certainly give you opportunities for observation. Tell me, how do you look upon the minister and his work?"

She studied him intently before she answered. Then—as if satisfied with what she found in his face, she said calmly: "To me he is the most useless creature in all the world. He is a man set apart from all those who live lives of service, who do the work of the world. And then that he should be distinguished from these world-workers, these servers, by this noblest of all titles—*a minister,* is the bitterest irony that the mind of the race ever conceived."

Her companion's face was white now as he answered quickly, "But surely a minister of the gospel is doing God's will and is therefore serving God."

She answered as quickly, "Man serves God only by serving men. There can be no ministry but the ministry of man to man."

"But the minister is a man."

"The world cannot accept him as such, because his individuality is lost in the church to which he belongs. Other institutions employ a man's time, the church employs his life; he has no existence outside his profession. There is no outside the church for him. The world cannot know him as a man, for he is all preacher."

"But the church employs him to minister to the world?"

"I cannot see that it does so at all. On the contrary a church employs a pastor to serve itself. To the churches Christianity has become a question of fidelity to a church and creed and not to the spirit of Christ. The minister's standing and success in his calling, the amount of his salary, even, depends upon his devotion to the particular views of the church that calls him and his ability to please those who pay him for pleasing them. His service to the world does not enter into the transaction any more than when you buy the latest novel of your favorite author, or purchase a picture that pleases you, or buy a ticket to hear your favorite musician. We do not pretend, when we do these things that we are ministering to the world, or that we are moved to spend our money thus to serve God, even though there may be in the book, the picture, or the music, many things that will make the world better."

The big fellow moved uneasily.

"But" he urged, eagerly, "the church is a sacred institution. It is not to be compared to the institutions of men. Its very purpose is so holy, so different from other organizations."

"Which of the hundreds of different sects with their different creeds do you mean by the church?" she asked quickly. "Or do you mean all? And if all are equally sacred, with the same holy purpose, why are they at such variance with each other and why is there such useless competition between them? How are these institutions—organized and controlled, as they are, by men, different from other institutions, organized and controlled by the same men? Surely you are aware that there are thousands of institutions and organizations in the world with aims as distinctly Christian as the professed object of the church. Why are these not as holy and sacred?"

"But the church is of divine origin."

"So is this tree; so is the material in that old building; so are those farms yonder. To me it is only the spirit of God in a thing that can make it holy or sacred. Surely there is as much of God manifest in a field of grain as in any of these churches; why, then, is not a corn field a holy institution and why not the farmer who tends the field, a minister of God?"

"You would condemn then everyone in the church?" he asked bitterly. "I cannot think that— I know—" he paused.

"Condemn?" she answered questioningly, "I condemn?" Those deep gray eyes were turned full upon him, and he saw her face grow tender and sad, while the sweet voice trembled with emotion. "Who spoke of condemnation? Is that just the question? Are you not unfair? In my—" she spoke the words solemnly, "my ministry, I have stood at the bedside of too many heroes and heroines not to know that the church is filled with the truest and bravest. And that—Oh! don't you see—that is the awful pity of it all. That those true, brave, noble lives should be the—the cloud that hides the sun? As for the ministry, one in my profession could scarcely help knowing the grand lives that are hidden in this useless class set apart by the church to push its interests. The ministers are useless only because they are not free. They cannot help themselves. They are slaves, not servants. Their first duty is, not service to the soul-sick world that so much needs their ministry, but obedience to the whims of this hideous monster that they have created and now must obey or—" she paused.

"Or what?" he said.

She continued as if she had not heard: "They are valued for their fidelity to other men's standards, never for the worth of their own lives. They are hired to give always the opinions of others, and they are denied the only thing that can make any life of worth—freedom of self-expression. The surest road to failure for them is to hold or express opinions of their own. They are held, not as necessities, but as a luxury, like heaven itself, for which if men have the means to spare, they pay. They can have no real fellowship with the servants of the race, for they are set apart by the church not to a ministry but from it. Their very personal influence is less than the influence of other good men because the world accepts it as professional. It is the way they earn their living."

"But do you think that the ministers themselves wish to be so set apart?" asked Dan. "I—I am sure they must all crave that fellowship with the workers."

"I think that is true," she answered. "I am sure it is of the many grand, good men in the ministry whom I have known."

"Oh," he said quickly, "then there are good men in the ministry?"

"Yes," she retorted, "just as there are gold and precious stones ornamenting heathen gods and pagan temples, and their goodness is as useless. For whether they wish it or not the facts remain that their masters set them apart and that they are separated, and I notice that most of them accept gracefully the special privileges, and wear the title and all the marks of their calling that emphasize the distinction between them and their fellow men."

"Yet you wear a distinguishing dress," he said. "I knew your calling the first time I saw you."

She laughed merrily.

"Well what amuses you?" he demanded, smiling himself at her merriment.

"Oh, it's so funny to see such a big man so helpless. Really couldn't you find an argument of more weight? Besides you didn't know my profession the first time you saw me. I only wear these clothes when I am at work, just as a mechanic wears his overalls—and they are just as necessary, as you know. The first time you—you bumped into me, I dressed like other people and I had paid full fare, too. Nurses don't get clergy credentials from the railroad."

With this she sprang to her feet. "Look how long the shadows are! I must go right back to my patient this minute."

As she spoke she was all at once painfully conscious again that this man was a stranger. What must he think of her? How could she explain that it was not her habit to talk thus freely to men whom she did not know? She wished that he would tell her his name at least.

Slowly—silently they walked together across the

weed-grown yard. As they passed through the gap in the tumble-down fence, Dan turned to look back. It seemed to him ages since he had entered the yard.

"What's the matter, have you lost something?" she asked.

"No—that is—I—perhaps I have. But never mind, it is of no great importance, and anyway I could not find it. I think I will say good-bye now," he added. "I'm not going to town just yet."

Again she wondered at his face, it was so troubled.

He watched her down the street until her blue dress, with its white trimming became a blur in the shadows. Then he struck out once more for the open country.

CHAPTER XI.

REFLECTIONS.

"And gradually, out of the material of his school experience, he built again the old bulwark, behind which he could laugh at his confusion of the hour before."

SINCE that first chance meeting at the depot when he had looked into the nurse's eyes and heard her voice only for a moment, Dan had not been able to put the young woman wholly out of his mind. The incident on the street when she had gone to Denny, and the scene that followed in Denny's home had strengthened the first impression, while the meeting at the old Academy yard had stirred depths in his nature never touched before. The very things she had said to him were so evidently born out of a nature great in its passion for truth and in its capacity for feeling that, even though her words were biting and stung, he could not but rejoice in the beauty and strength of the spirit they revealed.

The usual trite criticisms of the church Dan had heard, and had already learned to think somewhat lightly of the kind of people who commonly make them. But this young woman—so wholesome, so good to look at in her sweet seriousness, so strong in her womanliness and withal so useful in what she called her ministry—this woman was—well, she was different.

Her words were all the more potent, coming as they did after the disquieting thoughts and the feeling of dissatisfaction that had driven him from his study that afternoon. The young minister could not at first rid himself of the hateful suggestion that there might be much truth in the things she had said. After all under the fine words, the platitudes and the professions, the fact remained he *was* earning his daily bread by being obedient to those who hired him. He had already begun to feel that his work was not so much to give what he could to meet the people's need as to do what he could to supply the wants of Memorial Church, and that his very chance to serve depended upon his satisfying these self-constituted judges. He saw too, that these same judges, his masters, felt the dignity of their position heavily upon them, and would not be in the least backward about rendering their decision. They would let him know what things pleased them and what things were not to their liking. Their opinions and commandments would not always be in definite words, perhaps, but they would be none the less clearly and forcibly given for all that.

He had spoken truly when he had told Miss Farwell, as they parted, that he had lost something. And now, as he walked the country road, he sought earnestly to regain it; to find again his certainty of mind; to steady his shaken confidence in the work to which he had given his life.

Dan's character was too strong, his conviction too powerful, his purpose too genuine, for him to be easily turned from any determined line of thought or action. Certainly it would require more than the words of a stranger to swing him far from his course, even though he felt that there might be a degree of truth in them. And so, as he walked, his mind began shaping answers to the nurse's criticism and gradually, out of the material of his school experience, he built again the old bulwark, behind which he could laugh at his confusion of the hour before.

But withal Dan's admiration of the young woman's mind and character was not lessened. More, he felt that she had in some way given him a deeper view into her life and thoughts than was due a mere stranger. He was conscious, too, of a sense of shame that he had, in a way, accepted her confidence under false pretense. He had let her believe he was not what he was. But, he argued with himself, he had not intentionally deceived her and he smiled at last to think how she would enjoy the situation with him when she learned the truth.

How different she was from any of the women he had known in the church! They mostly accepted their religious views as they would take the doctor's prescription—without question.

And how like she was to his mother!

Then came the inevitable thought—what a triumph it would be if he could win such a character to the church. What an opportunity! Could he do it? He must.

With that the minister began putting his thoughts in shape for a sermon on the ministry. Determined to make it the effort of his life, he planned how he would announce it next Sunday for the following week, and how, with Dr. Harry's assistance, he would perhaps secure her attendance at the service.

Meanwhile Hope Farwell passing quickly along the village street on her way home from the old Academy yard, was beset by many varied and conflicting emotions. Recalling her conversation with the man who was to her so nearly a total stranger, she felt that she had been too earnest, too frank. It troubled her to think how she had laid bare her deepest feelings. She could not understand how she had so far forgotten her habitual reserve. There was a something in that young man, so tall and strong, and withal so clean looking, that had called from her, in spite of herself, this exposition of her innermost life and thoughts. She ought not to have yielded so easily to the subtle demand that he— unconsciously no doubt—had made.

It was as though she had flung wide open the door to that sacred, inner chamber at which only the most intimate of her friends were privileged to knock. He had come into the field of her life in the most commonplace manner—through the natural incident of their meeting. He should have stopped there, or should have been halted by her. The hour should have been spent in conversation on such trivial and commonplace topics as usually occupy strangers upon such occasions, and they should have parted strangers still. She felt that after this exhibition of herself, as she termed it in her mind, she at least was no stranger to him. And she was angry with herself, and ashamed, when she reflected how deeply into her life he had entered; angry with him too, in a way, that he had gained this admittance with apparently no effort.

She reflected too, that while she had so freely opened the door to him, and had admitted him with a confidence wholly inexcusable, he had in no way returned that confidence. She searched her memory for some word—some expression of his, that would even hint at what he thought, or believed, or was, within himself; something that would justify her in feeling that she knew him even a little. But there was nothing. It was as though this stranger, whom she had admitted into the privacy of the inner chamber, had worn mask and gown. No self-betraying expression had escaped him. He had not even told her his name. While she had laid out for his inspection the strongest passions of her life; had felt herself urged to show him all, and had kept nothing hidden. He had looked and had gone away making no comment.

"Of course," she thought, "he is a gentleman, and he is cultured and refined, and a good man too." Of this she was sure, but that was nothing. One does not talk as she had talked to a man just because he is not a ruffian or a boor. She wanted to know him as she had made herself known to him. She could not say why.

The nurse's work in Corinth was nearly finished; she would probably never meet this man again. She started at the thought. Would she ever meet him again? What did it matter? And yet—she would not confess it even to herself, but it did, somehow, seem to matter. Of one thing she was sure—he was well worth knowing. She had felt that there was a depth, a richness, a genuineness to him, and it was this feeling, this certainty of him, that had led her to such openness. Yes—she was sure there were treasures there—deep within, for those whom he chose to admit. She wished—(why should she not confess it after all)—she wished that she might be admitted.

Hope Farwell was alone in the world with no near living relatives. She had only her friends; and friends to her meant more than to those who have others dearer to them by ties of blood.

That evening when Dr. Harry was leaving the house after his visit to his patient, the nurse went with him to the door, as usual, for any word of instruction he might wish to give her privately.

"Well, Miss Hope," he said, "you've done it."

"What have I done?" she asked, startled.

"Saved my patient in there. She would have gone without a doubt, if you had not come when you did. It's your case all right."

"Then I'm glad I came," she said quietly. "And I may go back soon now, may I not, Doctor?"

He hesitated, slowly drawing on his gloves.

"Must you go back Miss Farwell? I—we need you so much here in Corinth. There are so many cases you know where all depends upon the nurse. There is not a trained nurse this side of St. Louis. I am sure I could keep you busy." There was something more than professional interest in the keen eyes that looked so intently into her own.

"Thank you Doctor, you are very kind, but you know Dr. Miles expects me. He warned me the last thing before I left, that he was only lending me to you for this particular case. You know how he says those things."

"Yes," said the man grimly, "I know Miles. It is one of the secrets of his success, that he will be satisfied with nothing but the best. He warned me, too."

He watched her keenly. "It would be just like Miles," he thought, "to tell the young woman of the particular nature of the warning." But Miss Farwell betrayed no embarrassing knowledge, and the doctor said, "You did not promise to return to Chicago did you?"

She answered slowly, "No, but he expects me, and I had no thought of staying, only for this case."

"Well won't you think of it seriously? There are many nurses in Chicago. I don't mean many like you—" interrupting himself hastily—"but here there is no one at all," and in his low-spoken words there was a note of interest more than professional.

She lifted her face frankly and let him look deep into her eyes as she answered—"I appreciate your argument, Dr. Abbott, and—I will think about it."

He turned his eyes away, and his tone was quite professional as he said heartily, "Thank you, Miss Farwell. I shall not give up hoping that we may keep you. Good night!"

"Isn't he a dear, good man?" exclaimed the invalid, as the nurse re-entered the sick room.

"Yes," she answered, "he is a good man, one of the best I think, that I have ever known."

The patient continued eagerly, "He told me the ladies could come here for their Aid Society meeting next week, if you would stay to take care of me. You will, won't you dear?"

The nurse busy with the medicine the doctor had left did not answer at once.

"I would like it so much," came the voice from the bed.

Hope turned and went quickly to her patient saying with a smile, "Of course I will stay if you wish it. I believe the meeting will do you good."

"Oh thank you, and you'll get to meet our new minister then, sure. Just to think you have never seen him, and he has called several times, but you have always happened to be out or in your room."

"Yes," said the young woman, "I have managed to miss him every time."

Something in the voice, always so kind and gentle, caused the sick woman to turn her head on the pillow and look at her nurse intently.

"And you haven't been to church, since you have been here, either."

"Oh, but you know I am like your good doctor in that, I can plead professional duties."

"Dr. Harry is always there when he can possibly go. I never thought of it before. Will you mind, dearie, if I ask you whether you are a Christian or not? I told Sapphira this afternoon that I knew you were."

"Yes," said Hope, "you are right. I cannot often go to church, but—" and there was a ring of seriousness in her voice now, "I am a Christian if trying to follow faithfully the teachings of the Christ is Christianity."

"I was sure you were," murmured the other, "Brother Matthews will be so glad to meet you. I know you will like him."

To which the nurse answered, "But you will be in no condition for the visit of the ladies, if I don't take better care of you now. Did you know that you were going to sleep? Well you are. You have had a busy day, and you are not to speak another word except 'good night.' I am going to turn the light real low—so—And now I am going to sit here and tell you about my walk. You're just to shut your eyes and listen and rest—rest—rest."

And the low, sweet voice told of the flowers and the grass and the trees, the fields lying warm in the sunlight, with the flitting cloud-shadows, and the hills stretching away into the blue, until no troubled thought was left in the mind of the sick woman. Like a child she slept.

But as the nurse talked to make her patient forget, the incident of the afternoon came back, and while the sick woman slept, Hope Farwell sat going over again in her mind the conversation on the grassy knoll in the old Academy yard, recalling every word, every look, every expression. What was his work in life? He was no idler, she was sure. He had the air of a true worker, of one who was spending his life to some purpose. She wondered again at the expression on his face as she had seen it when they parted. Should she go back to the great city and lose herself in her work, or—she smiled to herself—should she yield to Dr. Abbott's argument and stay in Corinth a little longer?

CHAPTER XII.

THE NURSE FORGETS.

"He seemed so made for fine and strong things."

THE affairs of Memorial Church were booming.

Or, in the more orthodox language of Elder Jordan, in an article to the official paper of the denomination, "the congregation had taken on new life, and the Lord's work was being pushed with a zeal and determination never before equalled. The audiences were steadily increasing. The interest was reviving in every department, and the world would soon see grand old Memorial Church taking first place in Corinth, if not in the state. Already Reverend Matthews had been asked to deliver a special sermon to the L. M. of J. B.'s, who would attend the service in a body, wearing the full regalia of the order. Surely God had abundantly blessed the brethren in sending them such an able preacher."

The week following Dan's talk with Miss Farwell in the old Academy yard, the ladies of the Aid Society assembled early, and in unusual numbers, for their meeting at the home of Judge Strong. As the announcement from the pulpit had it—there was business of great importance to transact; also there was work on hand that must be finished.

The business of importance was the planning of a

great entertainment to be given in the opera house, by local talent, both in and out of the church, for the purpose of raising money that the church still owed their former pastor. The unfinished work was a quilt of a complicated wheel pattern. Every spoke of each wheel contained the name of some individual who had paid ten cents for the honor. The hubs cost twenty-five cents. When finished this "beautiful work of the Lord" (they said their work was the Lord's work) was to be sold to the highest bidder; thereby netting a sum of money for the pulpit furniture fund, nearly equal to the cost to anyone of the leading workers, for the society's entertainment, in a single afternoon or evening, for what would appear in the Sunday issue of the Daily Corinthian as a "social event."

It must not be understood that all the women enrolled as members of Dan's congregation belonged to the Ladies' Aid. Only the workers were active in that important part of the "Body of Christ." Many there were in the congregation, quiet, deeply—truly —religious souls, who had not the time for this service, but in the scheme of things as they are, those were not classed as active members. They were not of the inner circle on the inside. They were reckoned as counting only on the roll of membership. But it was the strength, the soul, the ruling power, the spirit of this Temple of God that assembled that afternoon at Judge Strong's big, brown house, on Strong Avenue, just beyond Strong Memorial Church.

The Ally came also. The Ally, it is said, never misses a Ladies' Aid meeting in Corinth.

Miss Farwell was there with her patient as she had promised, and Mrs. Strong took particular care that as fast as they arrived each one of her guests met the young woman. To some—women of the middle class—the trained nurse, in her blue dress with white cap and apron, was an object of unusual interest. They did not know whether to rank her with servants, stenographers, sales-ladies or teachers. But the leading ladies (see the Daily Corinthian) were very sure of themselves. This young woman worked for wages in the homes of people, waited on people; therefore she was a working girl—a servant.

No one wasted much time with the stranger. The introduction was acknowledged with a word or a cool nod and an unintelligible murmur of something that meant nothing, or—worse—with a patronizing air, a sham cordiality elaborately assumed, which said plainly "I acknowledge the introduction here, because this is the Lord's business. You will be sure please, that you make no mistake should we chance to meet again." And immediately the new arrival would produce the modern weapon of the Christian warfare, needle, thread and thimble; and—hurrying to the side of some valiant comrade of her own set—join bravely in the fray.

That quilt was attacked with a spirit that was worth at least a half column in the denominational weekly, while the sound of the conflict might almost have been heard as far as Widow Mulhall's garden where Denny was cheerily digging away, with his one good side, while the useless, crippled arm swung from the twisted shoulder.

To Miss Farwell sitting quietly—unobserved, but observing—there came a confused sound of many voices speaking at once, with now and then a sentence in a tone stronger than the common din.

"She said the Memorial Church didn't believe in the Spirit anyhow, and that all we wanted was to get 'em in. . . . I told them that Brother Matthews would surely be getting some of their folks before the year was out, if they kept on coming to our services. . . . I says, says I—'Brother Matthews never said that; you'd better read your Bible. If you can show me in the Book where you get your authority for it, I'll quit the Memorial Church right then and join yours'. . . . Yes, all their people were out. . . . Sure, he's their church clerk. I heard him say with my own ears that Brother Matthews was the biggest preacher that had ever been in Corinth. . . . I'll venture that sermon next Sunday on 'The Christian Ministry' will give them something to think about. . . . The old Doctor never misses a service now. Wouldn't it be great if we was to get him? . . . Wasn't that solo the sweetest thing? . . . Wish he would join; we'd be sure of him then. . . . They would like mighty well to get him away from us if they could. He'll stay fast enough as long as Charity plays the organ!"

There was a laugh at this last from a group near the window and Miss Charity blushed as she answered, "I've worked hard enough to get him, and I certainly intend to keep him if I can! I've been urging all the girls to be particularly nice to him."

Someone nearer to Miss Farwell said, in low tone — Of course there's nothing in it. Charity's just keeping him in the choir. She wouldn't think of anyone but the preacher. I tell you if Brother Matthews knows what's best for him, he won't miss that chance. I guess if the truth was known old Nathan's about the best fixed of anyone in Corinth."

Sometimes a group would put their heads closer together and by the quick glances in her direction the nurse felt that she was contributing her full share to the success of the meeting. On one of these occasions she turned her back on the company to speak a few words to her patient who was sitting in an easy chair a little apart from the circle.

The invalid's face was all aglow. "Isn't it fine!" she said. "I feel as if I had been out of the world. It's so kind of these dear sisters to have the meeting here today so that I could look on. It's so good of you too, dear, to stay so they could come." She laughed. "Do you know, I think they're all a little bit afraid of you."

The nurse smiled and was about to reply when there was a sudden hush in the room and her patient whispered excitedly, "He's come! Now you'll get to meet our minister!"

Mrs. Strong's voice in the hall could be heard greeting the new arrival, and answering her the deeper tones of a man's voice.

Miss Farwell started. Where had she heard that

voice before? Then she felt him enter the room and heard the ladies greeting him. Something held her from turning and she remained with her back to the company, watching her patient's face, as the eyes of the invalid followed the minister about the room.

Charity alone was noting the young woman's too obvious lack of interest.

The hum had already commenced again when Mrs. Strong's hand was placed lightly on the nurse's arm.

"Miss Farwell, I want you to meet our minister, Reverend Matthews."

There was an amused smile on Dan's face as he held out his hand. "I believe Miss Farwell and I have met before."

But the young woman ignored the out-stretched hand, and her voice had an edge, as she answered, "It is possible sir. I am forced to meet so many strangers in my profession, you know, but I—I have forgotten you."

Charity was still watching suspiciously. At the minister's words she started and a touch of color came into her pale cheeks, while at Miss Farwell's answer the look of suspicion in her eyes deepened. What could it mean?

Dan's embarrassment was unmistakable. Before he could find words to reply, the sick woman exclaimed, "Why, how strange! Do tell us about it, Brother Matthews. Was it here in Corinth?"

In a flash the minister saw his predicament. If he said he had met the young lady in Corinth they would know that it was impossible that she should have literally forgotten him. He understood the meaning of her words. These women would give them a hundred meanings. If he admitted that he was wrong and that he had not met her, there was always the chance of the people learning of that hour spent on the Academy grounds.

Meanwhile the young woman made him understand that she realized the difficulties of his position, and all awaited his next words with interest. Looking straight into her eyes he said, "I seem to have made a mistake. I beg your pardon, Miss Farwell."

She smiled. It was almost as good as if he had deliberately lied, but it was the best he could do.

"Please do not mention it," she returned, with a meaning for him alone. "I am sorry that I will not be here next Sunday to hear your sermon on 'The Christian Ministry!' So many have urged me to attend. There is no doubt it will be interesting."

"You are leaving Corinth, then?" he asked.

At the same moment her patient and Mrs. Strong exclaimed, "Oh Miss Hope, we thought you had decided to stay. We can't let you go so soon."

She turned from the man to answer the invalid.

"Yes I must go. I did not know the last time we talked it over, but something has happened since that makes it necessary. I shall leave tomorrow. And now, if you will excuse me please, I will run away for a few moments to get my things together. You are doing so nicely, you really don't need me at all, and there is no reason why I should stay longer— now that I have met the minister." She bowed slightly to Dan and slipped from the room.

The women looked significantly at one another,

and the minister too came in for his full share of the curious glances. There was something in the incident that they could not understand and because Dan was a man they naturally felt that he was somehow to blame. It was not long until Charity, under the pretext of showing him a sacred song which she had found in one of Mrs. Strong's books, led him to another room, away from the curious crowd.

All the week Dan had looked forward to this meeting of the Ladies' Aid Society for he knew that he would see the nurse again. Charmed by the young woman's personality and mind, and filled with his purpose to win her to the church, he was determined, if chance did not bring it about, to seek another opportunity to talk with her. He had smiled often to himself, at what he thought would be a good joke between them, when she came to know of his calling. Like many such jokes it was not so funny after all. Instead of laughing with him she had given him to understand that the incident was closed, that there must be no attempt on his part to continue the acquaintance—that, indeed, she would not acknowledge that she had ever met him, and that she was so much in earnest that she was leaving Corinth the next day because of him.

"Really, Brother Matthews, if I have offended you in any way, I am very sorry." Dan awoke with a start. He and Charity were alone in the room. From the open door, came the busy hum of the workers in the Master's vineyard.

"I beg your pardon, what were you saying?" he murmured.

"I have asked you three times if you liked the music last Sunday."

Apologizingly he answered, "Really I am not fit company for anyone today."

"I noticed that you seemed troubled. Can I help you in any way? Is it the church?" she asked gently.

He laughed, "Oh no, it's nothing that anyone can help. It's myself. Please don't bother about it. I believe if you will excuse me, and make my excuses to the ladies in there, I will go. I really have some work to do."

She was watching his face so closely that she had not noticed the nurse who passed the window and entered the garden. Dan rose to his feet as he spoke.

"Why, Brother Matthews, the ladies expect you to stay for their business meeting, you know. This is very strange."

"Strange! There is nothing strange about it. I have more important matters that demand my attention—that is all. It is not necessary to interrupt them now, you can explain when the business meeting opens. They would excuse me I am sure, if they knew how important it was." And before poor Charity had time to fairly grasp the situation he was gone, slipping into the hall for his hat, and out by a side door.

Miss Farwell from meeting the minister, had gone directly to her room, but she could not go about her packing. Dropping into a chair by the window she sat staring into the tops of the big maples. She did not see the trees. She saw a vast stretch of rolling country, dotted with farm-buildings and stacks, across which the flying cloud-shadows raced, a weed-grown yard with a gap in the tumble-down fence, an old deserted school building, and a big clean-looking man standing, with the sun-light on his red-brown hair.

"And he—he was that." She had thought him something so fine and strong. He seemed so made for fine and strong things. And he had let her go on—leading her to talk as she would have talked only to intimate friends who would understand. She had so wanted him to understand. And then he had thought it all a joke! The gray eyes filled with angry tears, and the fine chin quivered. She sprang to her feet. "I won't!" she said aloud, "I won't!"

Why should she indeed think a second time of this stranger—this preacher? The room seemed close. She felt that she could not stay another minute in the house, with those people down stairs. Catching up a book, she crept down the back way and on out to a vine covered arbor that stood in a secluded corner of the garden.

Miss Farwell had been in her retreat but a few minutes when the sound of a step on the gravel walk startled her. Then the doorway was darkened by a tall, broad-shouldered figure, and a voice said, "May I come in?"

The gray eyes flashed once in his direction. Then she calmly opened her book, without a further glance, or a sign to betray her knowledge of his presence.

"May I come in?" he asked again.

She turned a page seeming not to hear.

Once more the man repeated the same words slowly —sadly.

The young woman turned another page of her book.

Then suddenly the doorway was empty. She rose quickly from her place and started forward. Then she stopped.

Charity met him on his way to the gate.

"Have you finished that important business so soon?" she asked sharply. Then with concern at the expression of his face she exclaimed, "Tell me, won't you, what is the matter!"

He tried to laugh and when he spoke, his voice was not his voice at all.

The daughter of the church turned to watch her minister as he passed through the gate, out of the yard and down the street. Then she went slowly down the path to the arbor, where she found a young woman crouched on the wooden bench weeping bitter tears—a book on the floor at her feet.

Quickly Charity drew back. Very quietly she went down the walk again. And as she went, she seemed all at once to have grown whiter and thin and old.

CHAPTER XIII.

DR. HARRY'S CASE.

"'Whatever or whoever is responsible for the existence of such people and such conditions is a problem for the age to solve. The fact is, they are here.'"

THE meeting of the Ladies' Aid adjourned and its members, with sighs and exclamations of satisfaction over work well done, separated to go to their homes—where there were suppers to prepare for hungry husbands, and children of the flesh.

Thus always in the scheme of things as they are, the duties of life conflict with the duties of religion. The faithful members of Memorial Church were always being interrupted in their work for the Lord by the demands of the world. And as they saw it, there was nothing for them to do but to bear their crosses bravely. What a blessed thought it is that God understands many things that are beyond our ken!

The whistles blew for quitting time. The six o'clock train from the West pulled into the yards, stopped—puffing a few moments at the water tank—and thundered on its way again. On the street, business men and those who labored with their hands hurried from the scenes of their daily toil, while the country folk untied their teams and saddle-horses from the hitch-racks to return to their waiting families and stock on the distant farms.

A few miles out on the main road leading northward the home-going farmers passed a tired horse hitched to a dusty, mud-stained top-buggy, plodding steadily toward the village. Without exception they hailed the driver of the single rig heartily. It was Dr. Harry returning from a case in the backwoods country beyond Hebron.

The deep-chested, long-limbed bay, known to every child for miles around, was picking her own way over the country roads, for the lines hung slack. Without a hint from her driver the good horse slowed to a walk on the rough places and quickened her pace again when the road was good, and of her own accord, turned out for the passing teams. The man in the buggy returned the greetings of his friends mechanically, scarcely noticing who they were.

It was Jo Mason's wife this time. Jo was a good fellow but wholly incapable of grasping, single-handed, the problem of daily life for himself and brood. There were ten children in almost as many years. Understanding so little of life's responsibilities the man's dependence upon his wife was pitiful, if not criminal. With tears streaming down his lean, hungry face he had begged, "Do somethin', Doc! My God Almighty, you jest got to do somethin'!"

For hours Dr. Harry had been trying to do something. Out there in the woods, in that wretched, poverty-stricken home, with only a neighbor woman of the same class to help he had been fighting a losing fight.

And now while the bay mare was making her tired way home he was still fighting—still trying to do something. His professional knowledge and experience told him that he could not win; that, at best, he could do no more than delay his defeat a few days, and his common sense urged him to dismiss the case from his mind. But there was something in Dr. Harry stronger than his common sense; something greater than his professional skill. And so he must go on fighting until the very end.

It was nearly twilight when he reached the edge of the hill on the farther side of the valley. He could see the lights of the town twinkling against the dark mass of tree and hill and building, while on the faintly-glowing sky the steeple of Memorial Church, the cupola of the old Academy building, and the court-house tower were cut in black. Down into the dusk of the valley the bay picked her way, and when they had gained the hill on the edge of town it was dark. Now the tired horse quickened her pace, for the home barn and Uncle George were not far away. But as they drew near the big brown house of Judge Strong, she felt the first touch of the reins and came to a walk, turning in to the familiar hitching post with reluctance.

At that moment a tall figure left the Judge's gate to pass swiftly down the street in the dusk.

Before the bay quite came to a stop at the post her master's hand turned her head into the street again, and his familiar voice bade her, somewhat sharply, to "go on!" In mild surprise she broke into a quick trot. How was the good horse to know that her driver's impatience was all with himself, and was caused by seeing his friend, the minister coming—as he thought—from the Strong mansion? Or how was Dr. Harry to know that Dan had only paused at the gate as if to enter, and had passed on when he saw the physician turning in?

Farther down the street at the little white cottage near the monument, the bay mare was pulled again to a walk, and this time she was permitted to turn in to the curb and stop.

The old Doctor was sitting on the porch. "Hello!" he called cheerily, "Come in."

"Not tonight, thank you Doctor, I can't stop," answered the younger man. At his words the old physician left his chair and came stiffly down the walk to the buggy. When he was quite close, with one hand grasping the seat, Dr. Harry said in a low tone, "I'm just in from Mason's."

"Ah huh," grunted the other. Then inquiringly —"Well?"

"It's—it's pretty bad Doctor."

The old man's voice rumbled up from the depth of his chest, "Nothing to do, eh? You know I told you it was there. Been in her family way back. Seen it ever since she was a girl."

"Yes I knew it was of no use, of course. But you know how it is, Doctor."

The white head nodded understandingly as Dr. Harry's hand was slowly raised to his eyes.

"Yes I know Harry. Jo take it pretty bad?"

"Couldn't do anything with him, poor fellow, and those children, too—"

Both men were silent. Slowly the younger man took up the reins. "I just stopped to tell you, Doctor."

"Ah huh. Well, you go home and rest. Get a good night whatever you do. You'll have to go out again, I suppose. Call me if anything turns up; I'm good for a little yet. You've got to get some rest, Harry, do you hear!" he spoke roughly.

"Thank you, Doctor. I don't think I will need to disturb you, though; everybody else is doing nicely. I can't think of anything that is likely to call me out."

"Well, go to bed anyway."

"I will, good night, Doctor."

"Good night, Harry."

The mare trotted on down the dark street, past the twinkling lights. The Doctor stood by the curb until he heard the buggy wheels rattle over the railroad tracks, then turned to walk stiffly back to his seat on the porch.

Soon the tired horse was in the hands of old Uncle George, while Mam Liz ministered to the weary doctor. The old black woman lingered in the dining room after serving his dinner, hovering about the table, calling his attention to various dishes, watching his face the while with an expression of anxiety upon her own wrinkled countenance. At last Harry looked up at her with a smile.

"Well Mam Liz, what is it? Haven't I been good today?"

"No sah, Mars Harry yo ain't. Yo been plumb bad, an' I feel jest like I uster when yo was er little trick an' I tuk yo 'cross my knee an' walloped yo good."

"Why, Mammy, what have I done now? Wasn't that new dress what you wanted? You can change it, you know, for anything you like."

"Law, chile, 'tain't *me*. Yo ole Mammy mighty proud o' them dress goods—they's too fine fo ole nigger like me. 'Tain't nothin' yo done to other folks, Mars Harry. Hit's what yo all's doin' to yoself." A tear stole down the dusky cheek. "Think I can't see how yo—yo plumb tuckered out? Yo ain't slep in yo bed fo three nights 'ceptin' jest fo a hour one mo'nin' when other folks was er gettin' up, an' only the Good Lawd knows when yo eats."

The doctor laughed. "There, there Mammy, you can see me eating now all right can't you?" But the old woman shook her head mournfully.

Harry continued, "One of your dinners, you know, is worth at least six of other folks' cooking. Fact—" he added grimly, "I believe I might safely say a dozen." Then he gave her a laughing description of his attempt to cook breakfast for himself and the ten children at the Masons that morning.

The old woman was proudly indignant, "Dem po'r triflin' white trash! To think o' yo' doin' that to sech as them! Ain't no sense 'tall in sech doin's, no how, Mars Harry. What right dey got to ax yo', any how? Dey shore ain't got no claim on yo'—an' yo' ain't got no call to jump every time sech as them crooks they fingers."

Dr. Harry shook his head solemnly.

"Now Mam Liz, I'm afraid you're an aristocrat."

"Cos I's a 'ristocrat. Ain't I a Abbott? Ain't I bo'n in de fambly in yo' grandaddy's time—ain't I nuss yo' Pa an' yo? 'Ristocrat! Huh! Deed I is. No sah, Mars Harry, yo' ought to know, yo ain't got no call to sarve sech as them!"

"I don't know," he returned slowly, "I'm afraid I have."

"Have what?"

"A call to serve such as them." He repeated her words slowly. "I don't know why they are, or how they came to be. Whatever or whoever is responsible for the existence of such people and such conditions is a problem for the age to solve. The fact is, they are here. And while the age is solving the problem, I am sure that we as individuals have a call to personally minister to their immediate needs." The doctor had spoken half to himself, following a thought that was often in his mind.

It was a little too much for the old servant. She watched him with a puzzled expression on her face.

"Talkin' 'bout ministers, de Pa'son was here to see yo' yest'day evenin'."

"Brother Matthews? I am sorry I was not at home."

"Yes sah, I was sorry too; he's a right pious-lookin' man, he sho is. I don tole him de Lawd only knowed whar yo' was or when yo'd git back. He laughed an' says he sho de Lawd wasn't far away wherever yo' was, an' that I mus' tell yo' hit was only a little call, nothin' of impo'tance—so's yo wouldn't bother 'bout it, I reckon."

Dr. Harry rose from the table. "Perhaps he will run in this evening. No, this is prayer meeting night. Heigh-ho!" He stretched his tired body— "I ought—"

The old woman interrupted him. "Now look a here Mars Harry, yo' ain't goin' to leave this yer house tonight. Yo' goin' jest put on yo' slippa's an' jacket an' set down in thar an' smoke yo' pipe a lille an' then yo' goin' to bed. Yo' ain't et 'nough to keep er chicken 'live, an' yo' eyes like two holes burned in er blanket. Won't yo' stop home an' res', honey?" she coaxed, following him into the hall. "Yo' plumb tuckered."

The weary physician looked through the door into the library where the lamp threw a soft light over the big table. The magazines and papers lay unopened, just as they had been brought from the office by Uncle George. A book that for a month, Harry had been trying to read, was lying where he had dropped it to answer a call. While he hesitated, the old negro came shuffling in with the doctor's smoking jacket and slippers.

"Yes sah, here dey is—an' de mare's all right— ain't hurted a bit—takin' her feed like er good one. Oh, I tell yo' der ain't no betta on de road dan her."

Dr. Harry laughed. "Uncle George, I give you my honest professional opinion—Mother Eve was sure a brunette." As he spoke he slipped out of his coat and Mam Liz took it from his hand, while

Uncle George helped him into the comfortable jacket.

"He—he—he—" chuckled the old servant. "A brunette, he—he. That air's yo Liz, ol' 'oman, yo' sho brunette. Yes sah, 'pon my word, Mars Harry, I believe yo'. He—he—"

And the black woman's deep voice rolled out— "Yo' go on now—yo' two, 'tain't so—'cause Adam he sho po'r white trash. Ain't no decent colored body goin' to have no truck wid sech as him."

With the doctor's shoes in his hand the old servant stood up, "Anythin' else, sah? No? Good night, sah! Good night, Mars Harry!" They slipped noiselessly from the room.

Is there, after all, anything more beautiful in life than the ministry of such humble ones, whose service is the only expression of their love?

Many of the Master's truths have been shamefully neglected by those into whose hands they were committed. Many of His grandest lessons are ignored by His disciples, who ambitious for place and power —quarrel among themselves. Many of His noblest laws have been twisted out of all resemblance to His spirit by those who interpret them to meet the demands of their own particular sects and systems. But of all the truths the Master has given to men, none, perhaps, has been more neglected, or abused than the simple truth He illustrated so vividly when He washed His disciples' feet.

Left alone Dr. Harry picked up one magazine after another, only to turn the leaves impatiently and

—after a moment—toss them aside. He glanced at his medical journal and found it dull. He took up his book only to lay it down again. Decidedly he could not read. The house with its empty rooms was so big and still. He seated himself at his piano but had scarcely touched the keys, when he rose again to go to the window.

"After all," he thought, "it would have been better to have gone to prayer meeting. I am not fit to be alone tonight. If I could only go to bed and sleep, but I feel as if I had forgotten how. Those Masons certainly got on my nerves." Indeed, the strain was plainly visible, for his face was worn and haggard. In his ears poor Jo's prayer was ringing, "Do somethin' Doc! My God Almighty, you jest got to do somethin'!"

Turning from the window the doctor's eyes fell on his medicine case, which Uncle George had brought in from the buggy and placed near the hall door.

"Why not?" he thought.

Picking up the case he went to the table, where he opened it hesitatingly.

"After all, why not?" he repeated half-aloud. "I would give it to a patient in my condition."

"But the patient wouldn't know what it was," a voice within himself answered.

"I need something. I—" his hand went out toward the case—"I have never done it before."

"You have seen others who have," said the voice again.

"This is an exceptionally trying time," he argued.

"There will be many more such times in your practice."

"But I must get some rest!" he cried, "I must!" He reached again for the open case but paused—startled by the ringing of the door-bell.

Obeying the impulse of the moment he dropped into his chair and caught up a paper.

Mam Liz's voice, in guarded tones came from the hall, "Yes marm, he's to home, but he's plumb tuckered out. Is yo' got to see him? Yo' ain't wantin' him to go out agin is yo'?"

Another voice answered, but the listening doctor could not distinguish the reply.

"Oh sho mam. Come in, come in. He's in the library."

A moment the nurse stood, hesitating, in the doorway.

Dr. Harry sprang to his feet. "Miss Farwell! I'm glad to see you. I—" Then he stopped looking at her in astonishment.

Very softly she closed the door behind her, and—going to the table—closed the medicine case. Then lifting her eyes to him with a meaning look she said simply, "I am glad, too."

He turned his face away. "You—you saw?"

"The window shades were up. I could not help it."

He dropped into the chair. "I'm a weak fool, Miss Farwell. No man in my profession has a right to be so weak."

"Yes, that's it," she said gently. "Your profession—those who depend upon you for their own lives and the lives of their dear ones—you must remember that always. Your ministry."

He raised his face and looked at her squarely. "I never did this before. You believe me, Miss Farwell, that this is the first time?"

She returned his look frankly. "Yes," she said. "I believe you, and I believe it will be the last."

And it was.

For there was something in that voice, something in the calm still depth of those gray eyes that remained with Dr. Harry Abbott and whenever afterwards he reached the limit of his strength, whenever he gave so much of himself in the service of others that there was nothing left for himself—this incident came back to him, that something held him—kept him strong.

Very quickly the nurse changed the subject and led the physician's mind away from the sadness and horror of his work that had so nearly wrought such havoc. The big empty house no longer seemed so big and empty. She made him light his pipe again and soon the man felt his tired nerves relax while the weary brain ceased to hammer away at the problems it could not solve.

Then at last she told him why she had come—to bid him good-bye.

"But I thought you were going to stay!" he cried.

"I had thought of doing so," she admitted. "But something—something makes it necessary for me to go."

His arguments and pleadings were in vain. Her

only answer was, "I cannot, Dr. Abbott, truly I cannot." Nor would she tell him more than that it was necessary for her to go.

"But we need you so. I need you; there is no one can take your place—Hope—" Then he stopped.

She was frankly permitting him to look deep into her eyes. "I am sorry, Doctor, but I must go." And the strength of her held him and made him strong.

"Just one thing, Miss Farwell. You are not going because of—because of me?"

She held out her hand. "No indeed, Doctor. Whatever you think, please don't think that."

He would have accompanied her home but she would not permit it and insisted so strongly that he retire at once, that he was forced to yield. But he would not say good-bye, declaring that he would be at the depot in the morning to see her off.

Mrs. Oldham, coming home from prayer meeting, found her husband still sitting on the porch. When she could not force him to listen to reason and go to bed, she left him to his thoughts. A little later the old Doctor saw the tall form of the minister turn in at the gate opposite. Then the light in the corner window flashed brightly. A few moments more, and he saw a woman coming down the street, going toward Judge Strong's. Nearing the house across the way, she slackened her pace, walking very slowly. Under the corner window she almost stopped. As she went on she turned once to look back, then disappeared under the trees in the dusk.

It was almost morning when Miss Farwell was

awakened by a loud knocking at the front door. Then Mrs. Strong came quickly up stairs to the nurse's room. The young woman was on her feet instantly.

"That old negro of Dr. Abbott is here asking for you," explained Mrs. Strong. "He says Dr. Harry sent him and that he must see you. What in the world can it mean?"

CHAPTER XIV.

THAT GIRL OF CONNER'S.

"'You will tell the people that this poor child wanted to kill herself, and the people will call it suicide. But, by God—it's murder! Murder—I tell you!'"

LIPPING into her clothing the nurse went down to the front door where Uncle George was waiting. A horse and buggy stood at the front gate.

"Evenin' mam, is yo' de nurse?" said the old negro, lifting his cap.

"Yes, I am the nurse, Miss Farwell. Dr. Abbott sent you for me?"

"'Deed he did, mam, 'deed he did—said I was to fetch yo' wid big Jim out dar. Tol' me to say hit was er 'mergency case. I dunno what dat is, but dey sho needs yo' powerful bad over in Old Town—'deed dey does."

The latter part of this speech was delivered to the empty doorway. The nurse was already back in her room.

The old negro rubbed his chin with a trembling hand, as he turned with a puzzled look on his black face from the open door to the horse and buggy and back to the door again.

"Dat young 'oman run lak a scared rabbit," he muttered. "What de ole scratch I do now?"

Before he could decide upon any course of action, Miss Farwell, fully dressed was by his side again, and half way to the gate before he could get under way.

"Come," she said, "you should have been in the buggy ready to start."

"Yas'm, yas'm, comin' comin'," he answered, breaking into a trot for the rig, and climbing in by her side. "Come Jim, git! Yo' black villen, don' yo' know, dis here's er 'mergency case? Yo' sho got to lay yo' laigs to de groun' dis night er yo' goin' to git left sartin! 'Mergency case!" he chuckled. "Dat mak him go, Miss. Funny I nebber knowed dat 'fore."

Sure enough, the black horse was covering the ground at a pace that fairly took Miss Farwell's breath. The quick steady beat of the iron-shod feet and the rattle of the buggy wheels echoed loudly in the gray stillness. Above the tops of the giant maples that lined the road, the nurse saw the stars paling in the first faint glow of the coming day, while here and there in the homes of some early-rising workers the lights flashed out, and the people—with the name of Dr. Harry on their lips—paused to listen to the hurried passing of big Jim.

"Can you tell me something of the case?" asked the nurse.

"Case? Oh you mean de po'r gal what tried to kill herse'f. Yes, Miss, I sho can. Yo' see hit's dis away. Hit's dat po'r Conner gal, her whose Daddy done killed Jack Mulhall, de town marshal yo' know. De Conners used to be nice folks, all

147

'ceptin' Jim. He drink a little sometimes, an' den he was plumb bad. Seems lak he got worse dat way. An' since dey took him off an' Mrs. Conner died de gal, she don't git 'long somehow. Since she left de hotel she's been livin' over in Old Town along some colored folks, upstairs in de old town-hall building. I knows 'bout hit 'y see, coz Liz an' me we all got friends, Jake Smith an' his folks, livin' in de same buildin', yo see. Wal, lately de gal don't 'pear to be doin' even as well as usual, an' de folks dey got plumb scared she ac' so queer like. Sometime in de night, Jake an' Mandy dey waked up hearin' a moanin' an' a cryin' in de po'r gal's room. Dey call at de door but dey ain't no answer an' so dey stan 'round for 'while 'thout knowin' what to do, till de cryin' an' screechin' gits worse, an' things 'pears to be smashin' round lak. Den Mandy say to de folks what's been waked up an' is standin' 'round de door she ain't goin' to stan dare doin' nothin' no mo', an' she fo'ce open de door an' goes in.

"Yes sah, Miss Nurse, Mandy say dat gal jest throwin' herself 'round de room an' screechin', an' Mandy grab her jest as she 'bout to jump out de winder. She won't say nothin' but how she's burnin' up an' Mandy she send Jake to me quick. I sho don' want to wake Dr. Harry, Miss coz he's done tuckered out, but I'se scared not to, coz once 'fore I didn't wake him when somebody want him an' I ain't nebber done hit no mo'. Go on dar, Jim. Yes sah, Mars Harry Abbott he's a debbil, Miss, when he's mad, 'deed he is, jest lak de old Mars—he's daddy. So I calls him easy-like but Lawd—he's up an' dress 'fore I can hook up big Jim here, an' we come fer Old Town on de run. Quick as he get in de room he calls out de winder fo' me to drive quick's I can to de Judge's an' fotch yo'. An' dat's all I know—'ceptin' Dr. Harry say hit's a 'mergency case. We most dare now. Go on Jim—go on sah!" '

While the old negro was speaking the big horse was whirling them through the quiet streets of the village. As Uncle George finished they reached the top of Academy Hill, where Miss Farwell saw the old school building—ghostly and still in the mists that hung about it like a shroud, the tumble-down fence with the gap leading into the weed-grown yard, the grassy knoll and the oak—all wet and sodden now, and—below, the valley—with its homes and fields hidden in the thick fog, suggestive of hidden and mysterious depths.

"Is yo' cold, Miss? We's mos dar, now." The nurse had shivered as with a sudden chill.

Turning sharply to the north a minute later they entered the square of Old Town where a herd of lean cows were just getting up from their beds to pick a scanty breakfast from the grass that grew where once the farmer folk had tied their teams, and in front of the ruined structure that had once been the principal store of the village, a mother sow grunted to her squealing brood.

Long without touch of painter's brush, the few wretched buildings that remained were the color of the mist. To the nurse—like the fog that hid the valley—they suggested cold mysterious depths of life, untouched by any ray of promised sun. And out of that dull gray abyss a woman's voice broke sharply, on the stillness, in a scream of pain.

"Dat's her, dat's de po'r gal, now, nurse. Up dare where yo' sees dat light."

Uncle George brought the big black to a stand in front of the ancient town-hall and court-house, a two-story, frame building with the stairway on the outside. A group of negroes huddled—with awed faces—at the foot of the stairs drew back as the nurse sprang from the buggy and ran lightly up the shaky old steps. The narrow, dirty hallway was crowded with more negroes. The odor of the place was sickening.

Miss Farwell pushed her way through and entered the room where Dr. Harry, assisted by a big black woman, was holding his struggling patient on the bed. The walls and ceiling of the room—stained by the accumulated smoke of years, the rough bare floor, the window—without shade or curtain, the only furniture—a rude table and a chair or two, a little stove set on broken bricks, a handful of battered dishes and cooking utensils, a trunk, and the bed with its ragged quilts and comforts, all cried aloud the old, old familiar cry of bitter poverty.

Dr. Harry glanced up as the nurse entered.

"Carbolic acid," he said quietly, "but she didn't get quite enough. I managed to give her the antidote and a hypodermic. We better repeat the hypodermic I think."

Without a word the nurse took her place at the bedside. When the patient, under the influence of the drug, had grown more quiet, Dr. Harry dismissed the negro woman with a few kind words, and the promise that he would send for her if she could help them in any way. Then when he had sent the others away from the room and the hallway he turned to the nurse.

"Miss Farwell, I am sorry that I was forced to send for you, but you can see that there was nothing else to do. I knew you would come without loss of time, and I dared not leave her without a white woman in the room." He paused and went to the bedside. "Poor, poor little girl. She tried so hard to die, nurse; she will try again the moment she regains consciousness. These good colored people would do anything for her, but she must see one of her own race when she opens her eyes." He paused seemingly at a loss for words.

Miss Farwell spoke for the first time, "She is a good girl, Doctor? Not that it matters you know, but—"

Dr. Harry spoke positively, "Yes, she is a good girl; it is not that, nurse."

"Then how—" Miss Farwell glanced around the room. "Then why is she here?"

No one ever heard Dr. Harry Abbott speak a bitter word, but there was a strange note in his voice as he answered slowly, "She is here because there seems to be no other place for her to go. She did this because there seemed to be nothing else for her to do."

Then briefly he related the sad history of this good girl with a bad reputation. "Dr. Oldham and I tried to help her," he said, "but some ugly stories got started and somehow Grace heard them. After that she avoided us."

For a little while there was silence in the room. When Dr. Harry again turned from his patient to the nurse, Miss Farwell was busily writing upon his tablet of prescription blanks with a stub of a pencil which she had taken from her pocket. The doctor watched her curiously for a moment, then arose, and taking his hat, said briskly: "I will not keep you longer than an hour Miss Farwell. I think I know of a woman whom I can get for today at least, and perhaps by tonight we can find someone else, or arrange it somehow. I'll be back in plenty of time, so don't worry. Your train does not go until ten-thirty, you know. If the woman can't come at once, I'll ask Dr. Oldham to relieve you."

The nurse looked at him with smiling eyes, "I am very sorry, Dr. Abbott, if I am not giving satisfaction," she said.

The physician returned her look with amazement, "Not giving satisfaction! What in the world do you mean?"

"Why you seem to be dismissing me," she answered demurely. "I understood that you sent for me to take this case."

At the light that broke over his face she dropped her eyes and wrote another line on the paper before her.

"Do you mean—" he began, then he stopped.

"I mean," she answered, "that unless you send me away I shall stay on duty."

"But Dr. Miles—that case in Chicago. I understood from you that it was very important."

She smiled at him again. "There is nothing so important as the thing that needs doing now," she answered. "And," she finished slowly, turning her eyes toward the unconscious girl on the bed—"I do seem to be needed here."

"And you understand there will be no—no fees in this case?" he asked.

The color mounted to her face. "Is our work always a question of fees, Doctor? I am surprised, cannot I collect my bill when you receive yours?"

He held out his hand impulsively.

"Forgive me, Miss Farwell, but it is too good to be true. I can't say any more now. You *are* needed here—you cannot know how badly. I—we all need you." She gently released her hand, and he continued in a more matter-of-fact tone, "I will go now to make a call or two so that I can be with you later. Your patient will be all right for at least three hours. I'll send Uncle George with your breakfast."

"Never mind the breakfast," she said. "If you will have your man bring these things, I will get along nicely." She handed him a prescription blank. "Here is a list that Mrs. Strong will give him from my room. And here—" she gave him another blank, "is a list he may get at the grocery. And here—" she handed him the third blank, "is a list he may get at some dry goods store. I have not my purse with me so he will need to bring the bills. The merchants will know him of course—"

Dr. Harry looked from the slips in his hand to the young woman.

"You must not do that, Miss Farwell. Really—"

She interrupted, "Doctor, this is my case, you know."

"It was mine first," he answered grimly.

"But Doctor—"

"Shall I send you my bill, too?" he asked.

A few moments later she heard the quick step of big Jim and the rattle of the wheels.

Two hours had passed when in response to a low knock, the nurse opened the door to find Dr. Oldham standing in the narrow hall. The old physician was breathing heavily from his effort in climbing the rickety stairs. His arms were full of roses.

Miss Farwell exclaimed with delight, "Oh Doctor, just what I was wishing for!"

"Uh huh," he grunted. "I thought so. They'll do her good. Harry told me what you were up to. Thought I better come along in case you should need any help."

He drew a chair to the bedside, while the nurse with her sleeves rolled up returned to the work which his knock at the door had interrupted.

Clean, white sheets, pillows and coverings had replaced the tattered quilt on the bed. The floor was swept. The litter about the stove was gone, and in its place was a big armful of wood neatly piled, the personal offering of Uncle George, who had returned quickly with the things for which the nurse had sent. The dirt and dust had vanished from the windows. The glaring light was softened by some sort of curtain material, that the young woman had managed to fix in place. The bare old cupboard shelves covered with fresh paper were filled with provisions, and the nurse, washing the last of the dishes and utensils, was placing them carefully in order. She finished as Dr. Oldham turned from the patient, and—throwing over the rough table a cloth of bright colors—began deftly arranging in such dishes as the place afforded, the flowers he had brought. Already the perfume of the roses was driving from the chamber that peculiar, sickening odor of poverty.

The old physician, trained by long years of service to habits of close observation, noted every detail in the changed room. Silently he watched the strong, beautifully formed young woman in the nurse's uniform, bending over his flowers, handling them with the touch of love while on her face, and in the clear gray eyes, shone the light that a few truly great painters have succeeded in giving to their pictures of the Mother Mary.

The keen old eyes under their white brows filled and the Doctor turned hastily back to the figure on the bed. A worn figure it was—thin and looking old —with lines of care and anxiety, of constant pain and ceaseless fear, of dread and hopelessness. Only a faint suggestion of youth was there, only a hint of the beauty of young womanhood that might have been; nay that would have been—that should have been.

Miss Farwell started as the old man with a sudden exclamation—stood erect. He faced the young woman with blazing eyes and quivering face—his voice shaken with passion, as he said: "Nurse, you and Harry tell me this is suicide." He made a gesture toward the still form on the bed. "You will tell the people that this poor child wanted to kill herself, and the people will call it suicide. But, by God—it's murder! Murder—I tell you! She did not want to kill herself. She wanted to live, to be strong and beautiful like you. But this community with its churches and Sunday schools and prayer meetings wouldn't let her. They denied her the poor privilege of working for the food she needed. They refused even a word of real sympathy. They hounded her into this stinking hole to live with the negroes. She may die, nurse, and if she does—as truly as there is a Creator, who loves his creatures—her death will be upon the unspeakably cruel, pious, self-worshiping, churchified, spiritually-rotten people in this town! It's *murder!* I tell you, by God—it's *murder!*" The old man dropped into his chair exhausted by his passionate outburst.

For a few moments there was no sound in the room save the heavy breathing of the physician. The nurse stood gazing at him—a look of mingled sadness and horror on her face.

Then the figure on the bed stirred. The sick girl's eyes opened to stare wildly—wonderingly, about the room. With a low word to the Doctor, Miss Farwell went quickly to her patient.

CHAPTER XV.

THE MINISTER'S OPPORTUNITY.

"He saw only the opportunity so mysteriously opened to him."

HEN Dan left Miss Farwell in the summer house at Judge Strong's he went straight to his room.

Two or three people whom he met on the way turned when he had passed to look back at him. Mrs. James talking over the fence with her next door neighbor, wondered when he failed to return her greeting. And Denny from his garden hailed him joyfully. But Dan did not check his pace. Reaching his own gate he broke fairly into a run, and leaping up the stairway, rushed into his room, closing and locking his door. Then he stood, breathing hard, and smiling grimly at the foolish impulse that had made him act for all the world like a thief escaping with his booty.

He puzzled over this strange feeling that possessed him, the feeling that he had taken something that did not belong to him, until the thought struck him that there might, after all, be good reason for the fancy; that it might indeed be more than a fancy.

Pacing to and fro the length of his little study he recalled every detail of that meeting in the Academy yard. And as he remembered how he had consciously refrained from making known his position to the young woman—not once, but several times when he knew that he should have spoken, and how his questions, combined with the evident false impression that his words had given her had led her to speak thoughts she would never have dreamed of expressing had she known him, the conviction grew that he had indeed—like a thief, taken something that did not belong to him. And as he realized more and more how his silence must appear to her as premeditated, and reflected how her fine nature would shrink from what she could not but view as a coarse ungentlemanly trick he grew hot with shame. No wonder, he told himself, that he had instinctively shrunk from looking into the faces of the people whom he had met and had fled to the privacy of his rooms.

Dan did not spare himself that afternoon, and yet beneath all the self scorn he felt, there was a deeper sub-conscious conviction, that he was not—at heart—guilty of the thing with which he charged himself. This very conviction, though felt but dimly, made him rage the more. He had the hopeless feeling of one caught in a trap—of one convicted of a crime of which in the eyes of the law he was guilty, but which he knew he had unwittingly committed.

The big fellow in so closely analyzing the woman's thoughts and feelings, and in taking so completely her point of view, neglected himself. He could not realize how true to *himself* he had been that afternoon, or how truly the impulse that had prompted him to deny his calling was an instinct of his own strong manhood—the instinct to be accepted or rejected for what he was within himself, rather than for the mere accident of his calling and position in life.

One thing was clear, he must see Miss Farwell again. She must listen to his explanation and apology. She must somehow understand. For apart from his interest in the young woman herself, there was that purpose of the minister to win her to the church. It was a monstrous thought that he himself should be the means of strengthening her feeling against the cause to which he had given his life. So he had gone to Judge Strong's home early that evening determined to see her. But at the gate, when he saw Dr. Harry turning in as if to stop, he had passed on in the dusk. Later at prayer meeting his thoughts were far from the subject under discussion. His own public petition was so faltering and uncertain that Elder Jordan watched him suspiciously.

It would be interesting to know just how much the interest of the man in the woman colored and strengthened the purpose of the preacher to win this soul so antagonistic to his church.

The next day, Dan was putting the finishing touches to his sermon on "The Christian Ministry" when his landlady interrupted him with the news of the attempted suicide in Old Town. Upon hearing that the girl had at one time been a member of his congregation, he went at once to learn more of the particulars from Dr. Oldham. He found his old friend who had returned from Old Town a half hour before, sitting in his big chair on the front porch gazing at the cast-iron monument across the way. To the young man's questions the Doctor returned only monosyllables or grunts and growls that might mean anything or nothing at all. Plainly the Doctor did not wish to talk. His face was dark and forbidding, and under his scowling brows, his eyes—when Dan caught a glimpse of them—were hard and fierce. The young man had never seen his friend in such a mood and he could not understand.

Dan did not know that the kind-hearted old physician had just learned from his wife that the girl with the bad reputation had called at the house to see him a few hours before she had made the attempt to end her life, and that she had been sent away by the careful Martha with the excuse that the doctor was too busy to see her. Neither could the boy know how the old man's love for him was keeping him silent lest, in his present frame of mind, he say things that would strengthen that something which they each felt had come between them.

Suddenly the Doctor turned his gaze from the monument and flashed a meaning look straight into the brown eyes of the young minister. "She was a member of your church. Why don't you go to see her? Ask the nurse if there is anything the church can do." As Dan went down the walk he added, "Tell Miss Farwell that I sent you." Then smiling grimly he growled to himself, "You'll get valuable material for that sermon on the ministry, or I miss my guess."

The nurse! The nurse! He was to see her again! The thought danced in Dan's brain. How strangely the opportunity had come. The young minister felt that the whole thing had, in some mysterious way, been planned to the end he desired. In the care that the church would give this poor girl the nurse would see how wrongly she had judged it. She would be forced to listen to him now. Surely God had given him this opportunity!

What—the poor suicide?

Oh, but Dan was not thinking of the suicide. That would come later. Just now his mind and heart were too full of his own desire to win this young woman to the church. He saw only the opportunity so mysteriously opened to him. Dan was thoroughly orthodox.

So in the brightness of the afternoon the pastor of Memorial Church went along the street that, in the gray chill of the early morning, had echoed the hurried steps of the doctor's horse. The homes— so silent when the nurse had passed on her mission— were now full of life. The big trees—dank and still then, now stirred softly in the breeze, and rang with the songs of their feathered denizens. The pale stars were lost in the infinite blue and the sunlight warmed and filled the air—flooding street and home and lawn and flower and tree with its golden beauty. At the top of Academy Hill Dan paused. For him no shroud of mist wrapped the picturesque old building; no fog of mysterious depths hid the charming landscape.

Recalling the things the nurse had said to him there under the oak on the grassy knoll, and thinking of his sermon in answer—he smiled. It was a good sermon, he thought, with honest pride—strong, logical, convincing.

And it was—*at that moment.*

With a confident stride he went on his way.

CHAPTER XVI.

DAN SEES THE OTHER SIDE.

" 'What right have you, Mr. Matthews, to say that you do not understand—that you do not know? It is your business to understand—to know.' "

MISS FARWELL was alone with her patient. Dr. Harry, who had returned soon after the girl regained consciousness, had gone out into the country, promising to look in again during the evening on his way home, and the old Doctor finding that there was no need for him to remain had left a few moments later.

Except to answer their direct questions the sick girl had spoken no word, but lay motionless—her face turned toward the wall. Several times the nurse tried gently to arouse her, but save for a puzzled, half-frightened, half-defiant look in the wide-open eyes, there was no response, though she took her medicine obediently. But when Miss Farwell after bathing the girl's face, and brushing and braiding her hair, dressed her in a clean, white gown, the frightened defiant look gave place to one of wondering gratitude, and a little later she seemed to sleep.

She was still sleeping when Miss Farwell, who was standing by the window watching a group of negro children playing ball in the square, saw a man approaching the group from the direction of the village.

The young woman's face flushed as she recognized the unmistakable figure of the minister.

Then an angry light shone in the gray eyes, and she drew back with a low exclamation. As in evident answer to his question, a half dozen hands were pointed toward the window where she stood. Watching, she saw him coming toward the building.

His purpose was clear. What should she do? Her first angry impulse was to refuse to admit him. What right had he to attempt to see her after her so positive dismissal? Then she thought—perhaps he was coming to see the sick girl. What right had she to refuse to admit him, when it could in no way harm her patient? The room, after all, was the home of the young woman on the bed—the nurse was only there in her professional capacity.

Miss Farwell began to feel that she was playing a part in a mighty drama; that the cue had been given for the entrance of another actor. She had nothing to do with the play save to act well her part. It was not for her to arrange the lines or manage the parts of the other players. The feeling possessed her that, indeed, she had somewhere rehearsed the scene many times before. Stepping quickly to the bed she saw that her patient was still apparently sleeping. Then she stood trembling, listening to the step in the hall as Dan approached.

He knocked the second time before she could summon strength to cross the room and open the door.

"May I come in?" he asked hat in hand.

At his words—the same that he had spoken a few

hours before in the garden—the nurse's face grew crimson. She made no answer, but in the eyes that looked straight into his, Dan read a question and his own face grew red as he said, "I called to see your patient. Dr. Oldham asked me to come."

"Certainly; come in." She stepped aside and the minister entered the sick-room. Mechanically, without a word she placed a chair for him near the bed, then crossed the room to stand by the window. But he did not sit down.

Presently Dan turned to the nurse. "She is asleep?" he asked in a low tone.

Miss Farwell's answer was calmly—unmistakably professional. Looking at her watch she answered, "She has been sleeping nearly two hours."

"Is there—will she recover?"

"Dr. Abbott says there is no reason why she should not if we can turn her from her determination to die."

Always Dan had been intensely in love with life. He had a strong, full-blooded young man's horror of death. He could think of it only as a fitting close to a long, useful life, or as a possible release from months of sickness and pain. That anyone young, and in good health, with the world of beauty and years of usefulness before them, with the opportunities and duties of life calling, should willfully seek to die, was a monstrous thought. After all the boy knew so little. He was only beginning to sense vaguely the great forces that make and mar humankind.

At the calm words of the nurse he turned quickly

toward the bed with a shudder. "Her determination to die!" he repeated in an awed whisper.

Miss Farwell was watching him curiously.

He whispered half to himself, wonderingly, "Why should she wish to die?"

"Why should she wish to live?" The nurse's cold tones startled him.

He turned to her perplexed, wondering, speechless.

"I—I—do not understand," he said at last.

"I don't suppose you do," she answered grimly. "How could you? Your ministry is a matter of schools and theories, of doctrines and beliefs. This is a matter of life."

"My church—" he began, remembering his sermon.

But she interrupted him, "Your church does not understand, either; it is so busy earning money to pay its ministers that it has no time for such things as this."

"But they do not know," he faltered. "I did not dream that such a thing as this could be." He looked about the room and then at the still form on the bed, with a shudder.

"You a minister of Christ's gospel and ignorant of these things? And yet this is not an uncommon case, sir. I could tell you of many similar cases that have come under my own observation, though not all of them have chosen to die. This girl could have made a living; I suppose you understand. But she is a good girl; so there was nothing for her but this. All she asked was a chance—only a chance."

The minister was silent. He could not answer.

The nurse continued, "What right have you, Mr. Matthews, to say that you do not understand—that you do not know? It is your business to understand —to know. And your church—what right has it to plead ignorance of the life about its very doors? If such things are not its business what business has this institution that professes to exist for the salvation of men; that hires men like you—as you yourself told me—to minister to the world? What right I say, have you or your church to be ignorant of these everyday conditions of life? Dr. Abbott must know his work. I must know mine. Our teachers, our legal and professional men, our public officers, our mechanics and laborers, must all know and understand their work. The world demands it of us, and the world is beginning to demand that you and your church know your business." As the nurse spoke in low tones her voice was filled with sorrowful, passionate earnestness.

And Dan, Big Dan, sat like a child before her— his face white, his brown eyes wide with that questioning look. His own voice trembled as he answered, "But the people are not beasts. They do not realize. At heart they—we are kind; we do not mean to be carelessly cruel. Do you believe this, Miss Farwell?"

She turned from him wearily, as if in despair at trying to make him understand.

"Of course I believe it," she answered. "But how does that affect the situation? The same thing could be said, I suppose, of those who crucified the Christ, and burned the martyrs at the stake. It is this system, that has enslaved the people, that feeds itself upon the strength that should be given to their fellow men. They give so much time and thought and love to their churches and creeds, that they have nothing left—nothing for girls like these." Her voice broke and she went to the window.

In the silence Dan gazed at the form on the bed—gazed as if fascinated. From without came the shouts of the negro boys at their game of ball, and the sound of the people moving about in other parts of the building.

"Is there—is there no one who cares?" Dan said, at last in a hoarse whisper.

"No one has made her feel that they care," the nurse answered, turning back to him, and her manner and tone were cold again.

"But you," he persisted, "surely you care."

At this the gray eyes filled and the full voice trembled as she answered, "Yes, yes I care. How could I help it? Oh, if we can only make her feel that we—that someone wants her, that there is a place for her, that there are those who need her!" She went to the bedside and stood looking down at the still form. "I can't—I won't—I won't let her go."

"Let us help you, Miss Farwell," said Dan. "Dr. Oldham suggested that I ask you if the church could not do something. I am sure they would gladly help if I were to present the case."

The nurse wheeled on him with indignant, scornful eyes.

He faltered, "This is the churches' work, you know."

"Yes," she returned, and her words stung. "You are quite right, this *is* the churches' work."

He gazed at her in amazement as she continued hotly, "You have made it very evident Mr. Matthews, that you know nothing of this matter. I have no doubt that your church members would respond with a liberal collection if you were to picture what you have seen here this afternoon in an eloquent public appeal. Some in the fullness of their emotions would offer their personal service. Others I am sure would send flowers. But I suggest that for your sake, before you present this matter to your church you ask Dr. Oldham to give you a full history of the case. Ask him to tell you why Grace Conner is trying to die. And now you will pardon me, but in consideration of my patient, who may waken at any moment, I dare not take the responsibility of permitting you to prolong this call."

Too bewildered and hurt to attempt any reply, he left the room and she stood listening to his steps as he went slowly down the hall and out of the building.

From the window she watched as he crossed the old square, watched as he passed from sight up the weed-grown street. The cruel words had leaped from her lips unbidden. Already she regretted them deeply. She knew instinctively that the minister had come from a genuine desire to be helpful. She should have been more kind, but his unfortunate words had brought to her mind in a flash, the whole hideous picture of the poor girl's broken life. And the suggestion of such help as the church would give now, came with such biting irony, that she was almost beside herself.

The situation was not at all new to Miss Farwell. Her profession placed her constantly in touch with such ministries. She remembered a saloonkeeper who had contributed liberally to the funeral expenses of a child who had been killed by its drunken father. The young woman had never before spoken in such cruel anger. Was she growing bitter? She wondered. All at once her cheeks were wet with scalding tears.

Dan found the Doctor sitting on the porch just as he had left him. Was it only an hour before?

CHAPTER XVII.

THE TRAGEDY.

"Now, for the first time, he was face to face with existing conditions. Not the theory but the practice confronted him now. Not the traditional, but the actual. It was, indeed, a tragedy."

AN went heavily up the path between the roses, while the Doctor observed him closely. The young minister did not sit down.

"Well?" said the Doctor.

Dan's voice was strained and unnatural. "Will you come over to my room?"

Without a word the old man followed him.

In the privacy of his little study the boy said, "Doctor, you had a reason for telling me to ask Miss Farwell if the church could do anything for—for that poor girl. And the nurse told me to ask you about the case. I want you to tell me about her—*all* about her. Why is she living in that wretched place with those negroes? Why did she attempt to kill herself? I want to know about this girl as you know her—as Miss Farwell knows."

The old physician made no reply but sat silent—studying the young man who paced up and down the room. When his friend did not speak Dan said again, "Doctor you must tell me! I'm not a child. What is this thing that you should so hesitate to talk

171

to me freely? I must know and you must tell me now."

"I guess you are right, boy," returned the other slowly.

To Big Dan, born with the passion for service in his very blood and reared amid the simple surroundings of his mountain home, where the religion and teaching of the old Shepherd had been felt for a generation, where every soul was held a neighbor—with a neighbor's right to the assistance of the community, and where no one—not even the nameless "wood's colt"—was made to suffer for the accident of birth or family, but stood and was judged upon his own life and living, the story of Grace Conner was a revelation almost too hideous in its injustice to be believed.

When the Doctor finished there was a tense silence in the minister's little study. It was as though the two men were witnessing a grim tragedy.

Trained under the influence of his parents and from them receiving the highest ideals of life and his duty to the race, Dan had been drawn irresistibly by the theoretical self-sacrificing heroism and traditionally glorious ministry of the church. Now, for the first time, he was face to face with existing conditions. Not the theory but the practice confronted him now. Not the traditional, but the actual.

It was, indeed, a tragedy.

The boy's face was drawn and white. His eyes—wide with that questioning look—burned with a light that his old friend had not seen in them before—the light of suffering—of agonizing doubt.

In his professional duties the Doctor had been forced to school himself to watch the keenest suffering unmoved, lest his emotions bias his judgment—upon the accuracy of which depended the life of his patient. He had been taught to cause the cruelest pain with unshaken nerve by the fact that a human life under his knife depended upon the steadiness of his hand. But his sympathy had never been dulled—only controlled and hidden. So, long years of contact with what might be called a disease of society, had accustomed him to the sight of conditions —the revelation of which came with such a shock to the younger man. But the Doctor could still appreciate what the revelation meant to the boy. Knowing Dan from his childhood, familiar with his home-training, and watching his growth and development with personal, loving interest, the old physician had realized how singularly susceptible his character was to the beautiful beliefs of the church. He had foreseen, too, something of the boy's suffering when he should be brought face to face with the raw, naked truths of life. And Dan, as he sat now searching the rugged, but kindly face of his friend, realized faintly why the Doctor had shrunk from talking to him of the sick girl.

Slowly the minister rose from his chair. Aimlessly—as one in perplexing, troubled thought—he went to the window and, standing there, looked out with unseeing eyes upon the cast-iron monument on the opposite corner of the street. Then he moved restlessly to the other window, and, with eyes still unseeing, looked down into the little garden of the crippled boy—the garden with the big moss and vine-grown rock in its center. Then he went to his study table and stood idly moving the books and papers about. His eye mechanically followed the closely written lines on the sheets of paper that were lying as he had left them that morning. He started. The next moment, with quick impatient movement, he crushed the pages of the manuscript in his powerful hands and threw them into the waste basket. He faced the Doctor with a grim smile.

"My sermon on 'The Christian Ministry.' "

CHAPTER XVIII.

TO SAVE A LIFE.

"It was not Hope Farwell's way to theorize about the causes of the wreck, or to speculate as to the value of inventions for making more efficient the life-saving service, when there was a definite, immediate, personal something to be done for the bit of life that so closely touched her own."

NURSE!"

Miss Farwell turned quickly. The girl on the bed was watching her with wide wondering eyes. She forced a smile. "Yes, dear, what is it? Did you have a good sleep?"

"I was not asleep. I—oh nurse, is it true?"

Hope laid a firm, cool hand on the hot forehead, and looked kindly down into the wondering eyes.

"You were awake while the minister was here?"

"Yes I—I—heard it all. Is it—is it true?"

"Is what true, child?"

"That you care, that anyone cares?"

Miss Farwell's face shone now with that mother-look as she lowered her head until the sick girl could see straight into the deep gray eyes. The poor creature gazed hungrily—breathlessly.

"Now don't you know that I care?" whispered the nurse, and the other burst into tears, grasping the nurse's hand in both her own and with a reviving hope clinging to it convulsively.

"I'm not bad, nurse," she sobbed. "I have always

been a good girl even when—when I was so hungry. But they—they talked so about me, and made people think I was bad until I was ashamed to meet anyone. Then they put me out of the church, and nobody would give me work in their homes, and they drove me away from every place I got, until there was no place but this, and I was so frightened here alone with all these negroes in the house. Oh nurse, I didn't want to do it—I didn't want to do it. But I thought no one cared—no one."

"They did not mean to be cruel, dear," said the nurse softly. "They did not understand. You heard the minister say they would help you now."

The girl gripped Miss Farwell's hand with a shudder.

"They put me out of the church. Don't let them come, don't! Promise me you won't let them in."

The other calmed her. "There, there dear, I will take care of you. And no one can put you away from God; you must remember that."

"Is there a God, do you think?" whispered the girl.

"Yes, yes dear. All the cruelty in the world can't take God away from us if we hold on. We all make mistakes, you know, dear—terrible mistakes sometimes. People with the kindest, truest hearts sometimes do cruel things without thinking. Why, I suppose those who crucified Jesus were kind and good in their way. Only they didn't understand what they were doing, you see. You will learn by-and-by to feel sorry for these people, just as Jesus wept over those who he knew were going to torture and kill him. But first you must get well and strong again. You will now, won't you dear?"

And the whispered answer came, "Yes, nurse. I'll try now that I know you care."

So the strong young woman with the face of the Mother Mary talked to the poor outcast girl, helping her to forget, turning her thoughts from the sadness and bitterness of her experience to the gladness and beauty of a possible future, until—when the sun lighted up the windows on the other side of the square with flaming fire, and all the sky was filled with the glory of his going—the sick girl slept, clinging still to her nurse's hand.

In the twilight Miss Farwell sat in earnest thought. Deeply religious—as all true workers must be—she sought to know her part in the coming scenes of the drama in which she found herself cast.

The young woman felt that she must leave Corinth. Her experience with Dan had made the place unbearable to her. And, since the scene that afternoon, she felt, more than ever, that she should go. She had no friends in Corinth save her patient at Judge Strong's, Mrs. Strong, the two doctors, Deborah and Denny. At home she had many friends. Then from the standpoint of her profession—and Hope Farwell loved her profession—her opportunities in the city with Dr. Miles were too great to be lightly thrown aside.

But what of the girl? This girl so helpless, so alone—who buffeted and bruised, had been tossed senseless at her very feet by the wild storms of life. Miss Farwell knew the fury of the storm; she had witnessed before the awful strength of those forces that overwhelmed Grace Conner. She knew, too, that there were many others struggling hopelessly in the pitiless grasp of circumstances beyond their strength—single handed—to overcome.

As one watching a distant wreck from a place of safety on shore, the nurse grieved deeply at the relentless cruelty of these ungoverned forces, and mourned at her own powerlessness to check them. But she felt especially responsible for this poor creature who had been cast within her reach. Here was work to her hand. This she could do and it must be done now, without hesitation or delay. She could not prevent the shipwrecks; she could, perhaps, save the life of this one who had felt the fury of the storm. It was not Hope Farwell's way to theorize about the causes of the wreck, or to speculate as to the value of inventions for making more efficient the life-saving service, when there was a definite, immediate, personal something to be done for the bit of life that so closely touched her own.

There was no doubt in the nurse's mind now but that the girl would live and regain her health. But what then? The people would see that she was cared for as long as she was sick. Who among them would give her a place when she was no longer an object of ostentatious charity? Her very attempted suicide would mark her in the community more strongly than ever, and she would be met on every hand by suspicion, distrust and cruel curiosity. Then, indeed, she would need a friend—someone to believe in her and to love her. Of what use to save the life tossed up by the storm, only to set it adrift again? As Miss Farwell meditated in the twilight the conviction grew that her responsibility could end only when the life was safe.

It is, after all, a little thing to save a life; it is a great thing to make it safe. Indeed, in a larger sense a life is never saved until it is safe.

When Dr. Harry called, later in the evening as he had promised, he handed the nurse an envelope. "Mr. Matthews asked me to give you this," he said. "I met him just as he was crossing the square. He would not come in but turned back toward town."

He watched her curiously as she broke the seal and read the brief note.

> "I have seen Dr. Oldham and he has told about your patient. You are right—I cannot present the matter to my people. I thank you. But this cannot prevent my own personal ministry. Please use the enclosed for Miss Conner, without mentioning my name. You must not deny me this."

The "enclosed" was a bill, large and generous.

Miss Farwell handed the letter to Dr. Harry with the briefest explanation possible. For a long time the doctor sat in brown study. Then making no comment further than asking her to use the money as the minister had directed, he questioned her as to the patient's condition. When she had finished her report he drew a long breath.

"We are all right now, nurse. She will get over this nicely and in a week or two will be as good as ever. But—what then?"

CHAPTER XIX.

ON FISHING.

"'It is not for you to waste your time in useless speculation as to the unknowable source of your life-stream, or in seeking to trace it in the ocean. It is enough for you that it is, and that, while it runs its brief course, it is yours to make it yield its blessings. For this you must train your hand and eye and brain—you must be in life a fisherman.'"

COME boy," said the Doctor at last, laying his hand upon the young minister's shoulder. "Come, boy—let's go fishing. I know a dandy place about twelve miles from here. We'll coax Martha to fix us up a bite and start at daylight. What do you say?"

"But I can't!" cried Dan. "Tomorrow is Saturday and I have nothing now for Sunday morning." He looked toward the waste basket where lay his sermon on "The Christian Ministry."

"Humph," grunted the Doctor. "You'll find a better one when you get away from this. Older men than you, Dan, have fought this thing all their lives. Don't think that you can settle it in a couple of days thinking. Take time to fish a little; it'll help a lot. There's nothing like a running stream to clear one's mind and set one's thoughts going in fresh channels. I want you to see Gordon's Mills. Come boy, let's go fishing."

The evening was spent in preparation, eager anticipation and discussion of the craft, prompted by the Doctor. And as they overhauled flies and rods and lines and reels, and recalled the many delightful days spent as they proposed to spend the morrow, the young man's thoughts were led away from the first real tragedy of his soul. At daylight, after a breakfast of their own cooking—partly prepared the night before by Martha, who unquestionably viewed the minister's going away on a Saturday with doubtful eyes—they were off.

When they left the town far behind and—following the ridge road in the clear wine-like air of the early day—entered the woods, the Doctor laughed aloud as Dan burst forth with a wild boyish yell.

"I couldn't help it Doctor, it did itself," he said in half apology. "It's so good to be out in the woods with you again. I feel as if I were being re-created already."

"Yell again," said the physician with another laugh, and added dryly, "I won't tell."

Gordon's Mills, on Gordon's creek, lay in a deep, narrow valley, shut in and hidden from the world, by many miles of rolling, forest-covered hills. The mill, the general store and post office, and the blacksmith shop were connected with Corinth, twelve miles away, by daily stage—a rickety old spring wagon that carried the mail and any chance passenger. Pure and clear and cold the creek came welling to the surface of the earth full-grown, from vast, mysterious, subterranean caverns in the heart of the hills—and, from the brim of its basin, rushed, boiling and roaring, along to the river two miles distant, checked only by the dam at the mill. For a little way above the dam the waters lay still and deep, with patches of long mosses, vines and rushes, waving in its quiet clearness—forming shadowy dens for lusty trout, while the open places—shining fields and lanes —reflected, as a mirror, the steep green-clad bluff, and the trees that bent far over until their drooping branches touched the gleaming surface.

As the two friends tramped the little path at the foot of the bluff, or waded, with legs well-braced, the tumbling torrent, and sent their flies hither and yon across the boiling flood to be snatched by the strong-hearted denizens of the stream, Dan felt the life and freshness and strength of God's good world entering into his being. At dinner time they built a little fire to make their coffee and broil a generous portion of their catch. Then lying at ease on the bank of the great spring, they talked as only those can talk who get close enough to the great heart of Mother Nature to feel strongly their common kinship with her and with their fellows.

After one of those long silences that come so easily at such a time, Dan tossed a pebble far out into the big pool and watched it sink down, down, down, until he lost it in the unknown depths.

"Doctor, where does it come from?"

"Where does what come from?"

"This stream. You say its volume is always the same—that it is unaffected by heavy rains or long droughts. How do you account for it?"

"I don't account for it," grunted the Doctor, with a twinkle in his eye, "I fish in it."

Dan laughed. "And that," he said slowly, "is your philosophy of life."

The other made no answer.

Choosing another pebble carefully, Dan said, "Speaking as a preacher—please elaborate."

"Speaking as a practitioner—you try it," returned the Doctor.

The big fellow stretched himself out on his back, with his hands clasped beneath his head. He spoke deliberately.

"Well, you do not know from whence your life comes, and it goes after a short course, to lose itself with many others in the great stream that reaches—at last, and is lost in—the Infinite." The Doctor seemed interested. Dan continued, half talking to himself: "It is not for you to waste your time in useless speculation as to the unknowable source of your life-stream, or in seeking to trace it in the ocean. It is enough for you that it is, and that, while it runs its brief course, it is yours to make it yield its blessings. For this you must train your hand and eye and brain—you must be in life a fisherman."

"Very well done," murmured the Doctor, "for a preacher. Stick to the knowable things, and don't stick at the unknowable; that is my law and my gospel."

Dan retorted, "Now let's watch the practitioner make a cast."

"Humph! Why don't you stop it, boy?"

"Stop what?" Dan sat up.

The other pointed to the great basin of water that —though the stream rushed away in such volume and speed—was never diminished, being constantly renewed from its invisible, unknown source.

The young man shook his head, awed by the contemplation of the mighty, hidden power.

And the Doctor—poet now—said: "No more can the great stream of love, that is in the race for the race and that finds expression in sympathy and service, be finally stopped. Fed by hidden, eternal sources it will somehow find its way to the surface. Checked and hampered, for the moment, by obstacles of circumstances or conditions, it is not stopped, for no circumstance can touch the source. And love will keep coming—breaking down or rising over the barrier, it may be—cutting for itself new channels, if need be. For every Judge Strong and his kind there is a Hope Farwell and her kind. For every cast-iron, ecclesiastical dogma there is a living, growing truth."

Dan's sermon the next day, given in place of the one announced, did not please the whole of his people.

"It was all very fine and sounded very pretty," said Martha, "but I would like to know, Brother Matthews, where does the church come in?"

CHAPTER XX.

COMMON GROUND.

"'But we will find common ground,' he exclaimed. 'Look here, we have already found it! This garden—Denny's garden!'"

THE following Tuesday morning Dan was at work bright and early in Denny's garden. Many of the good members of Memorial Church would have said that Dan might better have been at work in his study.

The ruling classes in this congregation, that theoretically had no ruling classes, were beginning to hint among themselves of a humiliation beyond expression at the spectacle, now becoming so common, of their minister working with his coat off like an ordinary laboring man. He should have more respect for the dignity of the cloth. At least, if he had no pride of his own, he should have more regard for the feelings of his membership. Besides this they did not pay him to work in anybody's garden.

The grave and watchful keepers of the faith, who held themselves responsible to the God they thought they worshiped, for the belief of the man they had employed to prove to the world wherein it was all wrong and they were all right, watched their minister's growing interest in this Catholic family with increasing uneasiness.

The rest of the church, who were neither of the class nor of the keepers, but merely passengers, as it were, in the Ark of Salvation, looked on with puzzled interest. It was a new move in the game that added a spice of ginger to the play not wholly distasteful. From a safe distance the "passengers" kept one eye on the "class" and the other on the "keepers," with occasionally a stolen glance at Dan, and waited nervously for their cue.

The world outside the fold awaited developments with amused and breathless interest. Everybody secretly admired the stalwart young worker in the garden, and the entire community was grateful that he had given them something new to talk about. Memorial Church was filled at every service.

Meanwhile wholly unconscious of all this, Big Dan continued digging his way among the potatoes, helping the crippled boy to harvest and prepare for market the cabbages and other vegetables, that grew in the plot of ground under his study window, never dreaming that there was aught of interest either to church or town in the simple neighborly kindness. It is a fact—though Dan at this time, would not have admitted it, even to himself—that the hours spent in the garden, with Denny enthroned upon the big rock, and Deborah calling an occasional cheery word from the cottage, were by far the most pleasant hours of the day.

Every nerve and muscle in the splendid warm-blooded body of this young giant of the hills called for action. The one mastering passion of his soul was the passion for deeds—to do; to serve; to be used. He had felt himself called to the ministry by his desire to accomplish a work that would be of real worth to the world. He was already conscious of being somewhat out of place with the regular work of the church: the pastoral calls, which mean visiting, day after day, in the homes of the members to talk with the women about nothing at all, at hours when the men of the household are away laboring, with brain or hand, for the necessities of life; the meetings of the various women's societies, where the minister himself is the only man present, and the talk is all women's talk; the committee meetings, where hours are spent in discussing the most trivial matters with the most ponderous gravity—as though the salvation of the world depends upon the color of the pulpit carpet, or who should bake a cake for the next social.

For nearly a week now, Dan had found no time to touch the garden; he was resolved this day to make good his neglect. An hour before Denny was up the minister was ready for his work. As he went to get the garden-tools from the little lean-to woodshed, Deborah called from the kitchen, " 'Tis airly ye are this mornin' sir. It's not many that do be layin' awake all the night waitin' for the first crack o' day, so they can get up to somebody else's work fer thim."

The minister laughingly dodged the warm-hearted expressions of gratitude he saw coming. "I've been shirking lately," he said. "If I don't do better than this the boss will be firing me sure. How is he?"

"Fine sir, fine! He's not up yet. You'll hear

him yelling at you as soon as he sees what you're at."

"Good," ejaculated the other. "I'll get ahead of him this time. Perhaps I can get such a start before he turns out that he'll let me stay a while longer, as it would not be pleasant to get my discharge."

Passing laborers and business men on the way to their daily tasks, smiled at the coatless figure in the garden. Several called a pleasant greeting. The boy with the morning papers from the great city checked his whistle as he looked curiously over the fence, and the Doctor who came out on the porch looked across the street to the busy gardener and grunted with satisfaction as he turned to his roses.

But Dan's mind was not occupied altogether that morning by the work upon which his hands were engaged. Neither was he thinking only of his church duties, or planning sermons for the future. As he bent to his homely tasks his thoughts strayed continually to the young woman whom he had last seen beside the bed of the sick girl in the poverty-stricken room in Old Town. The beautiful freshness and sweetness of the morning and the perfume of the dewy things seemed subtly to suggest her. Thoughts of her seemed, somehow, to fit in with gardening.

He recalled every time he had met her. The times had not been many, and they were still strangers, but every occasion had been marked by something that seemed to fix it as unusual, making their meeting seem far from commonplace. He still had that feeling that she was to play a large part in his life and he was confident that they would meet again. He was wondering where and how when he looked up from his work to see her coming toward him, dressed in a fresh uniform of blue and white.

The young fellow stood speechless with wonder as she came on, picking her way daintily among the beds and rows, her skirts held carefully, her beautiful figure expressing health and strength and joyous, tingling life in every womanly curve and line.

There was something wonderfully intimate and sweetly suggestive in the picture they made that morning, these two—the strong young woman in her uniform of service going in the glow of the early day to the stalwart coatless man in the garden, to interrupt him in his homely labor.

"Good morning," she said with a smile. "I have been watching you from the house and decided that you were working altogether too industriously, and needed a breathing spell. Do you do everything so energetically?"

It is sadly true of most men today that the more you cover them up the better they look. Our civilization demands a coat, and the rule seems to be—the more civilization, the more coat. Dan Matthews is one of those rare men who look well in his shirt sleeves. His shoulders and body needed no shaped and padded garments to set them off. The young woman's eyes, in spite of her calm self-possession, betrayed her admiration as he stood before her so tall and straight—his powerful shoulders, deep chest and great muscled arms, so clearly revealed.

But Dan did not see the admiration in her eyes.

He was so bewildered by the mere fact of her presence that he failed to note this interesting detail.

He looked toward the house, then back to the young woman's face.

"You were watching me from the house," he repeated. "Really, I did not know that you—"

"Were your neighbors?" she finished. "Yes we are. Grace and I moved yesterday. You see," she continued eager to explain, "it was not good for her to remain in that place. It was all so suggestive of her suffering. I knew that Mrs. Mulhall had a room for rent, because I had planned to take it before I decided to go back to Chicago." She blushed as she recalled the thoughts that had led her to the decision, but went on resolutely. "The poor child has such a fear of everybody, that I thought it would help her to know that Mrs. Mulhall and Denny could be good to her, even though it was Denny's father, that her father—you know—"

Dan's eyes were shining. "Yes I know," he said.

"I explained to Mrs. Mulhall and, like the dear good soul she is, she understood at once and made the poor child feel better right away. I thought, too, that if Grace were living here with Mrs. Mulhall it might help the people to be kinder to her. Then someone will give her a chance to earn her living and she will be all right. The people will soon act differently when they see how Mrs. Mulhall feels, don't you think they will?"

Dan could scarcely find words. She was so entirely unconscious of the part she was playing—of this beautiful thing she was doing.

"And you?" he asked, "You are not going away?"

"Not until she gets a place. She will need me until she finds a home, you know. And Dr. Harry assures me there is plenty of work for me in Corinth. So Grace and I will keep house at Mrs. Mulhall's. Grace will do the work while I am busy. It will make her feel less dependent and," she added frankly, "it will not cost so much that way. And that brings me to what I came out here to say." She paused. "I wish to thank you, Mr. Matthews, for your help— for the money you sent. The poor child needed so many things, and—I want to beg your pardon for— for the shameful way I treated you when you called. I—I knew better, and Mrs. Mulhall has been telling me how much you have done for them. I—"

Dan interrupted, "Please don't, Miss Farwell; I understand. You were exactly right. I know, now." Then he added, slowly, "I want you to know, though, Miss Farwell, that I had no thought of being rude when we talked in the old Academy yard." She was silent and he went on, "I must make you understand that I am not the ill-mannered cad that I seemed. I—You know, this ministry"—he emphasized the word with a smile—"is so new to me—I am really so inexperienced!"

She glanced at him quickly.

He continued, "I had never before heard such thoughts as you expressed, and I was too puzzled to realize how my silence would appear to you when you knew."

"Then this is your first church?" she asked.

"Yes," he said, "and I am beginning to realize

how woefully ignorant I am of life. You know I was born and brought up in the backwoods. Until I went to college I knew only our simple country life; at college I knew only books and students. Then I came here."

As he talked the young woman's face cleared. It was something very refreshing to hear such a man declare his ignorance of life with the frankness of a boy. She held out her hand impulsively.

"Let's forget it all," she said. "It was a horrid mistake."

"And we are to be good friends?" he asked, grasping her outstretched hand.

Without replying the young woman quietly released her hand and drew back a few paces—she was trembling. She fought for self-control. There was something—what was it about this man? The touch of his hand—Hope Farwell was frightened by emotions new and strange to her.

She found a seat on the big rock and ignoring his question said, "So that's why you are so big and strong, and know so well how to work in a garden. I thought it was strange for one of your calling. I see now how natural it is for you."

"Yes," he smiled, "it is very natural—more so than preaching. But tell me—don't you think we should be good friends? We are going to be now, are we not?"

The young woman answered with quiet dignity, "Friendship Mr. Matthews means a great deal to me, and to you also, I am sure. Friends must have much in common. We have nothing, because—because everything that I said to you at the Academy, to me, is true. We do not live in the same world."

"But it's for myself—the man and not the minister—that I ask it," he urged eagerly.

She watched his face closely as she answered, "But you and your ministry are one and the same. Yourself—your life is your ministry. You are your ministry and your ministry is you."

"But we will find common ground," he exclaimed. "Look here, we have already found it! This garden —Denny's garden! We'll put a sign over the gate, 'No professional ministry shall enter here!'—The preacher lives up there." He pointed to his window. "The man, Dan Matthews, works in the garden here. To the man in the garden you may say what you like about the parson up there. We will differ, of course, but we may each gain something, as is right for friends, for we will each grant to the other the privilege of being true to self."

She hesitated; then slipping from the rock and looking him full in the face said, "I warn you it will not work. But for friendship's sake we will try."

Neither of them realized the deep significance of the terms, but in the days that followed, the people of Corinth had much—much more, to talk about. The Ally was well pleased and saw to it that the ladies of the Aid Society were not long in deciding that something must be done.

CHAPTER XXI.

THE WARNING.

"From God's sunny hillside pastures to the gloom and stench of the slaughter pens."

IT happened two weeks to the day after Dan and Miss Farwell met in Denny's garden.

The Ally had been busy to some purpose. The Ladies' Aid, having reached the point of declaring that something must be done, did something. The Elders of Memorial Church, in their official capacity, called on their pastor.

Dan was in the garden when the Elders came. The Doctor's wife declared that Dan spent most of his time in the garden now, and that, when there, he did nothing because that nurse was always helping him. Good Martha has the fatal gift of telling a bit of news so vividly that it gains much in the telling.

Miss Farwell was in the garden that afternoon with the minister and so was Denny, while Grace Conner and Deborah were sitting on the front porch of the little cottage when the two church fathers passed. Though neither of the men turned their heads, neither of them failed to see the two women on the porch and the three friends in the garden.

"For the love of Heaven, look there!" exclaimed Deborah in an excited whisper. "They're turnin' in at the minister's gate, an' him out there in the 'taters in his shirt, a-diggin' in the ground an' a-gassin' wid Denny an' Miss Hope. I misdoubt there's somethin' stirrin' to take thim to his door the day. I must run an' give him the word."

But Dan had seen and was already on his way to the front gate, drawing on his coat as he went. From the other side of the street the Doctor waved his hand to Dan encouragingly as the young man walked hastily down the sidewalk to overtake the church officials at the front door.

Truly in this denominational hippodrome, odd yoke-fellows are sometimes set to run together; the efforts of the children of light to equal in wisdom the children of darkness leading the church to clap its ecclesiastical harness upon anything that—by flattery, bribes or intimidation, can be led, coaxed or driven to pull at the particular congregational chariot to which the tugs are fast! When the people of Corinth speak of Judge Strong's religion, or his relation to the Memorial Church they wink—if the Judge is not looking. When Elder Jordan is mentioned their voices always have a note of respect and true regard. Elder Strong is always called "The Judge"; Nathaniel Jordan was known far and wide as "Elder Jordan." Thus does the community, as communities have a way of doing, touch the heart of the whole matter.

Dan recognized instinctively the difference in the characters of these two men, yet he had found them always of one mind in all matters of the church. He felt the subtle antagonism of Judge Strong, though he did not realize that the reason for it lay in the cunning instinct of a creature that recognized a natural enemy in all such spirits as his. He felt, too, the regard and growing appreciation of Elder Jordan. Yet the two churchmen were in perfect accord in their "brotherly administration."

When the officials met in Dan's study that day, their characters were unmistakable. That they were both in harness was also clear. The minister's favorite chair creaked in dismay as the Judge settled his heavy body, and twisted this way and that in an open effort to inspect every corner of the apartment with his narrow, suspicious eyes; while the older churchman sat by the window, studiously observing something outside. Dan experienced that strange feeling of uneasiness familiar to every schoolboy when called upon unexpectedly for the private interview with the teacher. The Elders had never visited him before. It was too evident that they had come now upon matters of painful importance.

At last Judge Strong's wandering eye came to rest upon Dan's favorite fishing-rod, that stood in a corner behind a book-case. The young man's face grew red in spite of him. It was impossible not to feel guilty of something in the presence of Judge Strong. Even Elder Jordan started as his brother official's metallic voice rang out, "I see that you follow in the footsteps of the early disciples in one thing, at least, Brother Matthews. You go fishing." He gave forth a shrill, cold laugh that—more than anything else—betrayed the real spirit he laughed to hide.

This remark was characteristic of Judge Strong.

On the surface it was the mild jest of a churchman, whose mind dwelt so habitually on the sacred Book, that even in his lightest vein he could not but express himself in terms and allusions of religious significance. Beneath the surface, his words carried an accusation, a condemnation, a sneer. His manner was the eager, expectant, self-congratulatory manner of a dog that has treed something. The Judge's method was skillfully chosen to give him this advantage: it made his meaning clear while it gave no possible opening for a reply to the real idea his words conveyed, and forced his listener to an embarrassed silence of self-condemnation, that secured the Judge in his assumed position of pious superiority.

Dan forced a smile. He felt that the Judge's laugh demanded it. "Yes," he said, "I am scriptural when it comes to fishing. Dr. Oldham and I had a fine day at Gordon's Mills."

"So I understand," said the other meaningly. "I suppose you and the old Doctor have some interesting talks on religion?"

It was impossible not to feel the sneering accusation under the words. It was as impossible to answer. Again Dan's face flushed as he said, "No, we do not discuss the church very often."

"No?" said the Judge. "I should think you would find him a good subject to practice on. Perhaps, though, he practices on you, heh?" Again he laughed.

"Ahem, ahem!" Elder Jordan gave his usual warning. Dan turned to the good old man with a feeling of relief. At least Nathaniel Jordan's words would bear their face value. "Perhaps, Brother Strong, we had better tell Brother Matthews the object of our call."

The Judge leaned back in his chair with the air of one about to be pleasantly entertained. He waved his hand with a gesture that said as plainly as words, "All right, Nathaniel, go ahead. I'm here if you need me, so don't be uneasy! If you find yourself unequal to the task, depend upon me to help you out."

The minister waited with an expectant air.

"Ahem, ahem! You must not think, Brother Matthews, that there is anything really wrong because we called. But we, ahem—we thought best to give you a brotherly warning. I'm sure you will take it in the spirit in which it is meant."

The Judge stirred uneasily in his chair, bending upon Dan such a look as—had he been a real judge—he might have cast upon a convicted criminal. Dan already felt guilty. He signified his assent to the Elder's statement and Nathaniel proceeded:

"You are a young man, Brother Matthews; I may say a very talented young man, and we are jealous for your success in this community and, ahem—for the standing of Memorial Church. Some of our ladies feel—I may say that we feel that you have been a little, ah—careless about some things of late. Elder Strong and I know from past experience that a preacher—a young unmarried preacher cannot be too careful. Not that we have the least idea that you mean any harm, you know—not the least in the world. But people will talk and—ahem, ahem!"

Dan's face was a study. He was so clearly mystified by the Elder's remarks that the good man found his duty even more embarrassing than he had anticipated.

Then Judge Strong threw a flood of light upon the situation in a characteristic manner. "That young woman, Grace Conner, has a mighty bad name in this town; and the other one, her friend the nurse, is a stranger. She was in my house for a month and—well, some things about her look mighty queer to me. She hasn't been inside a church since she came to Corinth. I would be the last man in the world to cast a suspicion on anyone but—" he finished with a shake of his head, and an expression of pious doubt on his crafty face that said he could, if he wished, tell many dark secrets of Miss Farwell's life.

Dan was on his feet instantly, his face flaming and his eyes gleaming with indignation. "I—" then he checked himself, confused, as—in a flash—he remembered who these men were and his relation to them in the church. "I beg your pardon," he finished slowly, and dropped back into his chair, biting his lips and clenching his big hands in an effort at self-control.

Elder Jordan broke in nervously. "Ahem, ahem! You understand, Brother Matthews, that the sisters —that we do not think that you mean any harm, but your standing in the community, you know, is such that we must shun every appearance of evil. We, ahem—we felt it our duty to call."

Big Dan, who had never met that spirit, the Ally, knew not how to answer his masters in the church. He tried to feel that their mission to him was of grave importance. He was tempted to laugh; their ponderous dignity seemed so ridiculous.

"Thank you, sir," he at last managed to say, gravely, "I think it is hardly necessary for me to attempt any explanation." He was still fighting for self-control and chose his words carefully. "I will consider this matter." Then he turned the conversation skillfully into other channels.

When the overseers of the church were gone the young pastor walked the floor of the room trying to grasp the true significance of the situation. Gradually the real meaning of the Elders' visit grew upon him. Because his own life was so big, so broad, because his ideals and ambitions were so high, so true to the spirit of the Christ whose service he thought he had entered, he could not believe his senses.

He might have found some shadow of reason, perhaps, for their fears regarding his friendship for the girl with the bad reputation, had the circumstances been other than they were, and had he not known who it was gave Grace Conner her bad name. But that his friendship for Miss Farwell, whose beautiful ministry was such an example of the spirit of the Christian religion; and that her care for the poor girl should be so quickly construed into something evil—his mind positively refused to entertain the thought. He felt that the visit of his church fathers was unreal. He was as one dazed by an unpleasant dream.

To come from the pure, wholesome atmosphere of his home and the inspiring study of the history of the Christian religion, to such a twisted, distorted, hideous corruption of the church policy and spirit, was, to Dan, like coming from God's sunny hillside pastures to the gloom and stench of the slaughter pens. He was stunned by the littleness, the meanness that had prompted the "kindly warning" of these leaders of the church.

Slowly he began to see what that spirit might mean to him.

No man of ordinary intelligence could long be in Memorial Church, without learning that it was ruled by a ring, as truly as any body politic was ever so ruled. Dan Matthews understood too clearly that his position in Memorial Church depended upon the "bosses" then in control. And he saw farther—saw, indeed, that his final success or failure in his chosen calling depended upon the standing that should be given him by this, his first charge; depended at the last upon these two men who had shown themselves, each in his own way, so easily influenced by the low, vicious tales of a few idle-minded town gossips.

As one in the dark—stepping without warning into a boggy hole—Dan groped for firmer ground.

As one standing alone in a wide plain sees on the distant horizon the threat of a gathering storm, and —watching, shudders at the shadow of a passing cloud, Dan stood—a feeling of loneliness and dread heavy upon him.

He longed for companionship, for someone to whom he could speak his heart. But to whom in Corinth could he go? These men who had just "advised him" were, theoretically, his intimate counselors; to them he was supposed, and had expected, to look—in his inexperience, for advice and help. These men, old in the service of the church—how would they answer his troubled thoughts? He shrugged his shoulders and smiled grimly. The Doctor? He smiled again.

Dan little dreamed how much that keen old fisherman already knew, from a skillful baiting of Martha, about the visit of the Elders that afternoon; while his knowledge of Dan's character from childhood, enabled the physician to guess more than a little of the thoughts that occupied the young man pacing the floor of his room. But the Doctor would not do for the young man that day.

Dan went to the window overlooking the garden. The nurse was still there, helping crippled Denny with his work. The minister's hoe was leaning against the big rock, as he had left it when he had caught up his coat. Should he go down? What would she say if he were to tell her of the Elders' mission?

Something caused Miss Farwell to look up just then and she saw him. She beckoned to him playfully, guardedly, like a schoolgirl. Smiling, he shook his head. He could not go.

More than ever, then, he felt very much alone.

CHAPTER XXII.

AS DR. HARRY SEES IT.

"Thus Dr. Harry presented another side of the problem to his bewildered friend—a phase of the question commonly ignored by every fiery reformer, whose particular reformation is the one—the only way."

THE friendship between Dan and Dr. Abbott had grown rapidly, as was natural, for the two men had much in common. In a town as small as Corinth, there are many opportunities for even the busiest men to meet, and scarcely a day passed that the doctor and the preacher did not exchange greetings, at least. As often as their duties permitted they were together; sometimes at the office or in Dan's rooms; again, of an evening, at Harry's home; or driving miles across country behind the bay mare or big Jim—the physician to see a patient, and the minister to be the "hitchin' post."

Harry was just turning from the telephone that evening when Dan entered the house.

"Hello, parson!" he cried heartily. "I was just this minute trying to get you. I couldn't think of anything to do to anybody else, so I thought I'd have a try at you. That wasn't such a bad guess either," he added, when he had a good look at his friend's face. "You evidently need to have something fixed. What is it, liver?" He led the way into the library.

"Not mine," said Dan shortly. "I don't believe I have one."

He pushed an arm chair to face the doctor's favorite seat by the table.

Harry chuckled as he reached for his pipe and tobacco. "You don't need to have one yourself in order to suffer from liver troubles. Speaking professionally, my opinion is that you preachers, as a class, are more likely to suffer from other people's livers than from your own, though it is also true that the average parson has more of his own than he knows what to do with."

"And what do you doctors prescribe when it is the other fellow's?" asked Dan.

The other struck a match. "Oh, there's a difference of opinion in the profession. The old Doctor, for instance, pins his faith to a split bamboo with a book of flies or a can of bait."

"And you?" Dan was smiling now.

The answer came through a cloud of smoke. "Just a pipe and a book."

Dan's smile vanished. "I fear your treatment would not agree with my constitution," he said grimly. "My system does not permit me to use the remedy you prescribe."

"Oh, I see. You mean the pipe." A paff of smoke punctuated the remark. The physician was watching his friend's face now, and the fun was gone from his voice as he said gravely, "Pardon me, Brother Matthews; I meant no slur upon your personal conviction touching—"

"Brother Matthews!" interrupted Dan, sharply,

"I thought we had agreed to drop all that. It's bad enough to be dodged and shunned by every man in town without your rubbing it in. As for my personal convictions, they have nothing to do with the case. In fact, my system does not permit me to have personal convictions."

Dr. Harry's eyes twinkled. "This system of yours seems to be in a bad way, Dan. What's wrong with it?"

"Wrong with it! Wrong with my system? Man alive, don't you know this is heresy! How can there be anything wrong with my system? Doesn't it relieve me of any responsibility in the matter of right and wrong? Doesn't it take from me all such burdens as personal convictions. Doesn't it fix my standard of goodness, and then doesn't it make goodness my profession? You, poor drudge; you and the rest of the merely humans must be good as a matter of sentiment! Thanks to my system my goodness is a matter of business; I am paid for being good. My system says that your pipe and, perhaps your book, are bad—sinful. I have nothing to do with it. I only obey and draw my salary."

"Oh, well," said Harry, soothingly, "there is the old Doctor's remedy. It's probably better on the whole."

"I tried that the other day," Dan growled.

"Worked, didn't it?"

Dan grinned in spite of himself. "At first the effects seemed to be very beneficial, but later I found that it was, er— somewhat irritating, and that it slightly aggravated the complaint."

The doctor was smiling now. "Suppose you try a little physical exercise occasionally—working in the garden or—"

Dan threw up his hands with a tragic gesture. "Suicide!" he almost shouted.

Then they both lay back in their chairs and fairly howled with laughter.

"Whew! That does a fellow good!" gasped Dan.

"I guess we have arrived," said Harry, with a final chuckle. "Thought we were way off the track once or twice; but I have located your liver trouble, all right. When did they call?"

"This afternoon. Did you know?"

The doctor nodded. "I have been expecting it for several days. I guess you were about the only person in Corinth who wasn't."

"Why didn't you tell me?"

"If I can avoid it, I never tell a patient of a coming operation until it's time to operate; then it's all over before they can get nervous."

Dan shuddered—the laugh was all out of him now. "I have certainly been on the table this afternoon," he said. "I need to talk it out with someone. That's what I came to you for."

"Perhaps you had better tell me the particulars," said Harry, quietly.

So Dan told him, and when he had finished they had both grown very serious.

"I was afraid of this, Dan," said Harry. "You'll need to be very careful—very careful."

The other started to speak, but the doctor checked him.

"I know. I know how you feel. What you say about the system and all that is all too true, and you haven't seen the worst of it yet, by a good deal."

"Do you mean to tell me that Miss Farwell will be made to suffer for her interest in that poor girl?" demanded Dan warmly.

"If Miss Farwell continues to live with Grace Conner at Mrs. Mulhall's, there is not a respectable home in this town that will receive her," answered the doctor bluntly.

"My God! are the people blind? Can't the church see what a beautiful—what a Christ-like thing she is doing?"

"You know Grace Conner's history," replied Harry, coolly. "What reason is there to think it will be different in Miss Farwell's case, so far as the attitude of the community goes?"

Dan could not keep his seat. In his agitation he walked the floor. Suddenly turning on the other he demanded, "Then I am to understand that my friendship with Miss Farwell will mean for me—"

Dr. Harry was silent. Indeed, how could he suggest, ever so indirectly, that the friendship between Dan and Miss Farwell should be discontinued. If the young woman had been anyone else, or if Dr. Harry himself had not— But why attempt explanation?

The minister continued tramping up and down the room, stopping now and then to face the doctor, who sat still in his chair by the library table, quietly smoking.

"This is horrible, Harry! I—I can't believe it!

So far as my friendship for Miss Farwell goes, that
is only an incident. It does not matter in itself."

Dr. Harry puffed vigorously. He thought to himself that this might be true, but something in Dan's
face and voice when he spoke—something of which
he himself was unconscious—made Harry glad that
he had not answered.

"It is the spirit of it all that matters," the minister continued, pausing again. "I never dreamed
that such a thing could be. That Grace Conner's
life should be ruined by the wicked carelessness of
these people seems bad enough. But that they should
take the same attitude toward Miss Farwell, simply
because she is seeking to do that Christian thing that
the church itself will not do, is—is monstrous!" He
turned impatiently to resume his restless movement.
Then, when his friend did not speak he continued
slowly, as though the words were forced from him
against his will: "And to think that they could be
so unmoved by the suffering of that poor girl, their
own victim, and so untouched by the example of Miss
Farwell; and then that they should give such grave
consideration and be so influenced by absolutely
groundless and vicious idle gossip! And that the
church of Christ, that Christianity itself, should be
so wholly in the hands of people so unspeakably
blind, so—contemptibly mean and small in their con-
ceptions of the religion of Jesus Christ!"

He confronted the doctor again and his face
flushed. "Why, Doctor, my whole career as a Christian minister depends upon the mere whim of these

people, who are moved by such a spirit as this. No matter what motives may prompt my course they have the power to prevent me from doing my work. This is one of the strongest and most influential churches in the brotherhood. They can give me such a name that my life-work will be ruined. What can I do?"

"You must be very careful, Dan," said Dr. Harry, slowly.

"Careful! And that means, I suppose, that I must bow to the people of this church—ruled as they are by such a spirit—as to my lords and masters; that I shall have no other God but this congregation; that I shall deny my own conscience for theirs; that I shall go about the trivial, nonsensical things they call my pastoral duties, in fear and trembling; that my ministry is to cringe when they speak, and do their will regardless of what I feel to be the will of Christ! Faugh!" Big Dan drew himself erect. "If this is what the call to the ministry means, I am beginning to understand some things that have always puzzled me greatly."

He dropped wearily into his chair.

"Tell me, Doctor," he demanded, "do the people generally, see these things?"

"It seems to me that everyone who thinks must see them," replied the other.

"Then why did no one tell me? Why did not the old Doctor explain the real condition of the church?"

"As a rule it is not a safe thing to attempt to tell a minister these things. Would you have listened,

Dan, if he had tried to tell you? Or, because he is not a church man, would you not have misunderstood his motives? The Doctor loves you, Dan."

"But you are a church man, a member of the official board of my congregation. If men like you know these things why are you in the church at all?"

Silently Dr. Harry re-filled and lighted his pipe. It was as if he deliberated over his reply. The membership of every church may be divided into three distinct classes: those who are the church; those who belong to the church; and those who are members, but who neither are, nor belong to. Dr. Harry was a member.

"Dan," said the physician, "I suppose it is very difficult for such men as you to understand the religious dependence of people like myself. We see the church's lack of appreciation of true worth of character, we know the vulgar, petty scheming and wire-pulling for place, the senseless craving for notoriety, and the prostitution of the spirit of Christ's teaching to denominational ends. We understand how the ministers are at the mercy of the lowest minds and the meanest spirits in their congregation; but, Dan, because we love the cause we do not talk of these things even to each other, for fear of being misunderstood. It is useless to talk of them to our ministers, for they dare not listen. Why man, I never in my life felt that I could talk to my pastor as I am talking to you!" He smiled. "I guess that I was afraid that they would tell Judge Strong, and that the church would put me out. And, with most of them, that—probably, is exactly what would have happened. I am not sure but you will consider me unsafe, and avoid me in the future," he added whimsically.

Dan smiled at his words, though they revealed so much to him.

Dr. Harry went on, "We remain in the church, and give it our support, I suppose, because we are dependent upon it for our religious life; because we know no religious life outside of it. It is the only institution that professes to be distinctively Christian, and we love its teaching in spite of its practice. We are always hoping that some one will show us a way out. And some one will!" He spoke passionately now, with deep conviction: "Some one must! This Godless mockery cannot continue. I have too much faith in the goodness of men to believe otherwise. I don't know how the change will come. But it will come and it will come from men in the church—men like you, Dan, who come to the ministry with the highest ideals. But you must be careful, mighty careful, not for your own sake, alone, but for the sake of the cause we both love. Some operations are exceedingly dangerous to the life of the patient; some medicines must be administered with care lest they kill instead of cure. Men like me, from long experience with professional reformers, look with distrust upon the preacher who talks about his church, even while we know that there is a great need."

Thus Dr. Harry presented another side of the problem to his bewildered friend—a phase of the question commonly ignored by every fiery reformer, whose particular reformation is *the* one—the only way.

Later Dan asked, "Do you think Miss Farwell understands what her course means, Doctor?"

Harry shook his head. "I wish I knew how much she understands. Already two or three people who expected to call her have told me they would find someone else. I have several cases now that need a trained nurse, but they won't have her because of what they have heard. And yet I promised her, you know, that she should have plenty of work."

"Have you told her this?" asked Dan.

Again Harry shook his head. "What's the good?"

"But she ought to be told," exclaimed the other.

"I know that, Dan. But I can't do it, after urging her, as I did, to stay in Corinth. You are the one to tell her, I am sure."

Then, as if to avoid any further discussion of the matter he rose. "You certainly have had enough of this for today, old man. I think I'll prescribe a little music, now, and, if you don't mind, I'll take some of my own prescription. I feel the need."

He went to his piano, and for an hour Dan was under the spell.

When the last sweet harmony had slipped softly away into the night, the musician sat still, his head bowed. Dan went quietly to his side, and laid a hand on the doctor's shoulder.

"Amen!" he said, reverently. "It is a wonderful, beautiful ministry, Doctor. You have given me faith and hope and peace. Thank you!"

When his friend had gone, Dr. Harry went back to

the piano. Softly, smoothly his fingers moved over the ivory keys. He had played for Dan—he played now for himself. Into the music he put all that he dared not put into words: all the longing, all the pain, all the surrender, all the sacrifice, were there. For again, when the minister had spoken of Miss Farwell the doctor had seen in his friend's face and heard in his voice that which Dan himself did not yet recognize. And Harry had spoken the conviction of his heart when he said, "You are the one to tell her, I am sure."

Of this man, too, it might be written, "He saved others; himself he could not save."

CHAPTER XXIII.

A PARABLE.

"'And do you think, Grace, that anything in all this beautiful world is of greater importance—of more value to the world—than a human life, with all its marvelous power to think and feel and love and hate and so leave its mark on all life, for all time?'"

ISS FARWELL!"

The nurse looked up from her sewing in her hands.

"What is it, Grace?"

"I—I think I will try to find a place today. Mrs. Mulhall told me last night that she had heard of two women who want help. It may be that one of them will take me. I think I ought to try."

This was the third time within a few days that the girl had expressed thoughts similar to these. Under the personal care of Miss Farwell she had rapidly recovered from her terrible experience, both physically and mentally, but the nurse felt that she was not yet strong enough to meet a possible rebuff from the community that, before, had shown itself so reluctant to treat her with any degree whatever of consideration or kindness. The girl's spirit had been cruelly hurt. She was possessed of an unhealthy, morbid fear of the world that would cripple her for life if it could not somehow be overcome.

Miss Farwell felt that Grace Conner's only chance lay in winning a place for herself in the community where she had suffered such ill-treatment. But before she faced the people again she must be prepared. The sensitive, wounded spirit must be strengthened, for it could not bear many more blows. How to do this was the problem.

Hope dropped her sewing in her lap. "Come over here by the window, dear, and let's talk about it."

The young woman seated herself on a stool at the feet of her companion who, in actual years, was but little her senior, but who, in so many ways, was to her an elder sister.

"Why are you so anxious to leave me, Grace?" asked the nurse with a smile.

The girl's eyes—eyes that would never now be wholly free from that shadow of fear and pain—filled with tears. She put out a hand impulsively, touching Miss Farwell's knee. "Oh, don't say that!" she exclaimed, with a little catch in her voice. "You know it isn't that."

The eyes of the stronger woman looked reassuringly down at her. "Well, what is it then?" The low tone was insistent. The nurse felt that it would be better for the patient to express that which was in her own mind.

The girl's face was down-cast and she picked nervously at the fold of her friend's skirt. "It's nothing, Miss Farwell; only I feel that I—I ought not to be a burden upon you a moment longer than I can help."

"I thought that was it," returned the other. Her firm, white hand slipped under the trembling chin, and the girl's face was gently lifted until Grace was forced to look straight into those deep gray eyes. "Tell me, dear, why do you feel that you are a burden upon me?"

Silence for a moment; then—and there was a wondering gladness in the girl's voice—"I—I don't know."

The nurse smiled, but there was a grave note in her voice as she said, still holding the girl's face toward her own, "I'll tell you why. It is because you have been hurt so deeply. This feeling is one of the scars of your experience, dear. All your life you will need to fight that feeling—the feeling that you are not wanted. And you must fight it—fight it with all your might. You will never overcome it entirely, for the scar of your hurt is there to stay. You will always suffer at times from the old fear; but, if you will, you can conquer it so far that it will not spoil your life. You must—for your own sake, and for my sake, and for the sake of the wounded lives you are going to help heal—help all the better because of your own hurt. Do you understand, dear?"

The other nodded; she could not speak.

"You are going out into the world to find a place for yourself, of course, for that is right," Hope continued. "And it will be best for you to find a place here in Corinth, if possible. But it is not going to be easy, Grace. It's going to be hard, very hard,

THE CALLING OF DAN MATTHEWS

and you will need to know that, no matter what
other people make you feel, you have a place in my
life, a place where you belong. Let me try, if I can,
to tell you so that you will never, never forget."

For a little the nurse looked away out of the window, up into the leafy depths of the big trees, and
into the blue sky beyond, while the girl watched her
with a look that was pathetic in its wondering, hun-
gering earnestness. When Miss Farwell spoke again
she chose her words carefully.

"Once upon a time a woman, walking in the mountains, discovered by chance a wonderful mine, of such
vast wealth that there was nothing in all the world
like it for richness. And the mine belonged to the
woman because she found it. But the wealth of the
mine went out into the world for all men to use, and
thus, in the largest sense, the riches the woman found
belonged to all mankind. But still, because she had
found it, the woman always felt that it was hers.
And so, through her discovery of this vast wealth, and
the great happiness it brought to the world, the mine
became to the woman the dearest of all her possessions.

"Tell me, Grace, do you think that anyone could
ever replace the mountains, the ocean or the stars,
or any of these wonderful, wonderful things in the
great universe, if they were to be destroyed?"

"No." The answer came in a puzzled tone.

"And do you think, Grace, that anything in all
this beautiful world is of greater importance—of
more value to the world—than a human life, with all

217

its marvelous power to think and feel and love and hate and so leave its mark on all life, for all time?"

"No, Miss Farwell."

"Then don't you see how impossible it is that anyone should ever take your place? Don't you see that you have a place in the world—a place that is yours because God put you in it, just as truly as he put the mountains, the seas, the stars in their places? And don't you see why you must feel that you have a right to your own life-place, and that you must hold it, no matter what others say, or do, or think, because of its great value to God and to the world? And Grace—look at me, child! do you think that anything in all the universe is dearer to the Father than a human life, that is so wonderful and so eternal in its power? So life should be the dearest thing in all the world to us. Not just the life of each to himself, but every life—any life, the dearest thing to all. I think this was true of Christ; I think it should be true of Christians. I believe this with all my heart."

There was silence for a little while; then Hope said again: "Now tell me, Grace, ought the mine to have felt dependent upon the woman who found it, and who valued it so highly, do you think? Then why should you feel dependent upon me? Why, you belong to me, child! Your life, the most wonderful—the dearest thing in all the world, belongs to me; just as the mine belonged to the woman and brought her great joy because it blessed the world. When others threw your life aside, when you yourself tried to throw it away, I found it. I took it. It is mine! And it is the dearest thing in all the world to me, because it is so great a thing, because no other life can take its place, and because it is of such great worth to the world. Don't you see?" The calm voice was vibrant now with deep emotion.

Looking into those gray eyes that shone with such loving kindness into her own, Grace Conner realized a mighty truth; a truth that would mould and shape her own life into a life of beauty and power.

"So, dear," the nurse continued, "when you go out into the world again, and people make you feel the old hurt—as they will—you must remember the woman who found the mine; and, feeling that you belong to me and to all life, you will not let people rob you of your place in the world. You will not let them rob me of my great wealth. And now you must try the very best you can to get work here in Corinth, but if you should fail to find it, you won't let that matter too much. You'll keep your place right here with me just the same, won't you, Grace, because you are my mine, you know?"

Long and earnestly the girl looked into the face of the nurse, and Miss Farwell understood what the other could not say. Suddenly the girl caught her friend's hand and kissed it passionately, then rushed from the room. Miss Farwell wisely let her go without a word, but her own eyes were full.

She turned to the open window to see her neighbor, the minister, coming in at the gate.

CHAPTER XXIV.

THE WAY OUT.

"'You see you will need to find a way out for yourself.'"

DEBORAH was in the rear of the house, busily engaged with a big washing. Denny had gone up town on some errand. Much to Miss Farwell's surprise Dan did not, as usual, take the path leading to the garden, but kept straight ahead to the porch, and his face was very grave as he asked if he might come in. She welcomed him with frank pleasure, and took up at once the thread of conversation which the visit of the Elders had interrupted the day before. But it was clear that her big friend's mind was busy with other thoughts, and soon they were facing an embarrassing silence. The young woman gazed thoughtfully at the monument across the street, while Dan moved uneasily. At last the man broke the silence.

"Miss Farwell I don't know what you will think of me for coming to you upon the errand that brought me, but I feel that I—I mean, I want you to believe that I am trying to do what is best."

She looked at him questioningly.

Dan went on. "I learned something yesterday, that I am sure you ought to know, and there seems to be no one else to tell you, so I—I came."

Miss Farwell's cheeks and brow grew crimson, but in a moment she was her own calm self again.

"Go on, please."

Then he told her.

While he was speaking of the Elders' visit and his talk with Dr. Abbott, she watched him closely. Two or three times she smiled. When he had finished she asked with a touch of sarcasm in her voice, "And do you wish to see my letters of recommendation? Shall I give you a list of people to whom you might write?"

"Miss Farwell!" Dan's voice brought the hot color again to her cheek.

"Forgive me! That was unkind," she said.

"Well rather. You might see that I did not come to you with this for—well for fun," he finished with a grim smile.

"You don't seem to be enjoying it greatly," she agreed critically. "I can easily understand how this talk might result in something very serious for you. You will remember, I think, that I warned you, you could not leave the preacher on the other side of the fence." She was deliberately trying him. "But of course you can easily avoid any trouble with your people, you have only to—"

She stopped, checked by the expression on his face.

His voice rang out sharply with a quality in its tone that sent a thrill to the heart of the woman. "I did not come here to discuss the possibility of trouble for me. Please believe this—even if I am a servant of the church."

He spoke the last words with a shade of bitterness, she thought, and as she looked at him—his powerful form tense for a moment, with firm-set lips and square jaw and stern eyes—she found herself wondering what would happen if this servant should ever decide to be the master.

"Don't you see how this idle, silly, wicked talk is likely to harm you?" he asked almost roughly. "You know what the same thing did for Grace Conner. It is really serious, Miss Farwell—believe me it is, or I should not have told you about it at all. Already Dr. Harry—" He checked himself. His reference to his friend was unintentional.

She finished the sentence quietly, "—has found some people who will not employ me because of the things that are being said. I knew something was wrong, for—instead of telling me of possible cases and assuring me of work, he has been saying lately, 'I will let you know if anything turns up.'"

Dan broke in eagerly, "Dr. Abbott has done everything he could, Miss Farwell. I ought not to have mentioned him at all. You must not think—"

She interrupted him with quiet dignity. "Certainly I do not think of any such thing. You and Dr. Abbott are both very kind to consider me in this way, but really you must not be troubled about this silly gossip. I am not exactly dependent upon the good people of Corinth, you know. I can go back to the city at any time. Perhaps," she added slowly, "considering everything that would be the wisest thing to do, after all. It was only for Grace Conner's sake I have remained."

Dan spoke eagerly again, "But you do not need to leave Corinth. This talk you know, is all because of your companion's reputation."

"You mean," she said quietly, "the reputation that people have given my companion."

"So far as the situation goes it amounts to the same thing," he answered. "It is your association with her. If you could arrange to board with some family now—"

Again she interrupted him. "Grace needs me, Mr. Matthews."

"But it is all so unjust," he argued lamely. "The sacrifice is too great. You can't afford to place yourself before the community in such a wrong light."

The young woman's face revealed her surprise and disappointment. She had grown to think of Dan as being big and fine in spirit as in body, and now, to hear him voice, what she believed to be the spirit and policy of his profession, was a shock that hurt. She would have flashed out at him with scornful, cutting words, but she felt, intuitively, that he was not being true to himself in this—that he was forced, as it were, into a false position by something deep down in his life. This feeling robbed her of the power to reply in stinging words, and instead gave her answer a note of sadness.

"Are you not advocating the doctrines and policy of the people who are responsible for the 'wrong light' rather than the teachings of Christ? Are you not now speaking professionally, having forgotten our agreement to leave the preacher on the other side of the fence?"

The big fellow's embarrassment was evident as he said, "Miss Farwell, you must not—you must not misunderstand me again. I did not mean—I cannot stand the thought of your being so misjudged because of this beautiful Christian service. I was only seeking a way out."

"No," she said gently, "I will not misunderstand you, but there is only one way out, as you put it."

"And that?"

"My ministry."

Dan sprang to his feet and crossed the room to her side.

"What a woman you are!" he exclaimed impulsively.

She arose, trembling; always when he came near —something about this man moved her strangely.

"But my way out will not help you," she said. "You must think of your ministry."

"I thought we agreed not to talk of that," he returned.

"But we must. You must consider what the result will be if you are seen with me—with Grace and me." She caught herself quickly. "Can the pastor of Memorial Church afford to associate with two women of such doubtful reputation? What will your church think?" She was smiling as she spoke, but beneath the smile there was much of earnestness. She was determined that he should know how well she understood his position. She wondered if he himself understood it. "You see you will need to find a way out for yourself," she insisted.

"I am not looking for a way out," he growled.

"Ah, but you should. You must consider your influence. Consider the great harm your interest in Grace Conner will do your church. You must remember your position in the community. You cannot afford to—to risk your reputation."

Under her skillfully chosen words, he again assumed an air of indignant reserve. She saw his hands clench, and the great muscles in his arms and shoulders swell.

Unconsciously—or was it unconsciously?—she had repeated almost the exact words of Elder Jordan. The stock argument sounded strange coming from her. Deliberately she went on. "Really there is no reason why you should suffer from this. It is not necessary for you to continue our little friendship. You can stay on the other side of the fence. I—we will understand. You have too much at stake. You—"

He interrupted. "Miss Farwell, I don't know what you think of me that you can say these things. I had hoped that you were beginning to look upon me as a man, not merely as a preacher. I had even dared think that our friendship was growing to be something more than just a little friendly acquaintance. If I am mistaken, I will stay on the other side of the fence. If I am right—if you do care for my friendship," he finished slowly, "I will try to serve my people faithfully, but I will not willingly shape my life by their foolish, wicked whims. Denny's garden may get along without me, and you may not need what you call 'our little friendship' but I need Denny's garden, and—I need you."

Her face shone with gladness. "Forgive me," she said. "I only wished to be sure that you understood some things clearly."

At her rather vague words, he said, "I am beginning to understand a good many things."

"And understanding, you will still come to—" she smiled, "to work in Denny's garden?"

"Yes," he answered with a boyish laugh, "just as if there were no other place in all the world where I could get a job."

She watched him as he swung down the walk, through the gate and away up the street under the big trees.

And as she watched him, she recalled his words, "I need you;—just as though there were no other place in all the world." The words repeated themselves in her mind.

How much did they mean, she wondered.

CHAPTER XXV.

A LABORER AND HIS HIRE.

"But it was a reaching out in the dark, a blind groping for something—Dan knew not exactly what: a restless but cautious feeling about for a place whereon to set his feet."

IT was the Sunday evening following the incidents just related that Dan was challenged. His sermon was on "Fellowship of Service," a theme very different from the subjects he had chosen at the beginning of his preaching in Corinth. The Doctor smiled as he listened, telling himself that the boy was already beginning to "reach out." As usual the Doctor was right. But it was a reaching out in the dark, a blind groping for something— Dan knew not exactly what: a restless but cautious feeling about for a place whereon to set his feet.

With the sublime confidence of the newly-graduated, this young shepherd had come from the denominational granary to feed his flock with a goodly armful of theological husks; and very good husks they were too. It should be remembered that—while Dan had been so raised under the teachings of his home that, to an unusual degree his ideals and ambitions were most truly Christian—he knew nothing of life other than the simple life of the country neighborhood where he was born; he knew as little of churches. So that—while it was natural and easy for him to accept the husks from his church teachers at their valuation, being wholly without the fixed prejudice that comes from family church traditions —it was just as natural and easy for him to discover quickly, when once he was face to face with his hungry flock, that the husks were husks.

From the charm of the historical glories of the church as pictured by the church historians, and from the equally captivating theories of speculative religion as presented by teachers of schools of theology, Dan had been brought suddenly in contact with actual conditions. In his experience of the past weeks there was no charm, no glory, no historical greatness, no theoretical perfection. There was meanness, shameful littleness—actual, repulsive, shocking. He was compelled to recognize the real need that his husks could not satisfy. It had been forced upon his attention by living arguments that refused to be put aside. And Big Dan was big enough to see that the husks did not suffice—consistent enough to cease giving them out. But the young minister felt pitifully empty handed.

The Doctor had foreseen that Dan would very soon reach the point in his ministerial journey where he was now standing—the point where he must decide which of the two courses open to him he should choose.

Before him, on the one hand, lay the easy, well-worn path of obedience to the traditions, policies and doctrines of Memorial Church and its denominational leaders. On the other hand lay the harder and less-frequented way of truthfulness to himself and his own convictions. Would he—lowering his individual standard of righteousness—wave the banner of his employers, preaching—not the things that he believed to be the teachings of Jesus—but the things that he knew would meet the approval of the church rulers? Or would he preach the things that his own prayerful judgment told him were needed if his church was to be, indeed, the temple of the spirit of Christ. In short Dan must now decide whether he would bow to the official board, that paid his salary, or to his God, as the supreme authority to whom he must look for an indorsement of his public teaching.

In Dan's case, it was the teaching of the four years of school against the teaching of his home. The home won. Being what he was by birth and training, this man could not do other than choose the harder way. The Doctor with a great amount of satisfaction saw him throwing down his husks, and awaited the outcome with interest.

That sermon was received by the Elders and ruling classes with silent, uneasy bewilderment. Others were puzzled no less by the new and unfamiliar note, but their faces expressed a kind of doubtful satisfaction. Thus it happened that, with one exception, not a person of the entire audience mentioned the sermon when they greeted their minister at the close of the service. The exception was a big, broad-shouldered young farmer whom Dan had never before met.

Elder Strong introduced him, "Brother Matthews, you must meet Brother John Gardner. This is the first time he has been to church for a long while."

The two young men shook hands, each measuring the other with admiring eyes.

The Judge continued, "Brother John used to be one of our most active workers, but for some reason he has dropped behind. I never could just exactly understand it." He finished with his pious, patronizing laugh, which somehow conveyed the thought that he did understand if only he chose to tell, and that the reason was anything but complimentary to Brother John.

The big farmer's face grew red at the Judge's words. He quickly faced about as if to retort, but checked himself, and, ignoring the Elder said directly to Dan, "Yes, and I may as well tell you that I wouldn't be here today, but I am caught late with my harvesting, and short of hands. I drove into town to see if I could pick up a man or two. I didn't find any so I waited over until church, thinking that I might run across someone here."

Dan smiled. The husky fellow was so uncompromisingly honest and outspoken. It was like a breath of air from the minister's own home hills. It was so refreshing Dan wished for more. "And have you found anyone?" he asked abruptly.

At the matter-of-fact tone the other looked at the minister with a curious expression in his blue eyes. The question was evidently not what he had expected.

"No," he said, "I have not, but I'm glad I came anyway. Your sermon was mighty interesting to me, sir. I couldn't help thinking though, that these sentiments about work would come a heap more forceful from someone who actually knowed what a day's work was. My experience has been that the average preacher knows about as much about the lives of the laboring people as I do about theology."

"I think you are mistaken there," declared Dan. "The fact is, that the average preacher comes from the working classes."

"If he comes from them he takes mighty good care that he stays from them," retorted the other. "But I've got something else to do besides starting an argument now. I don't mind telling you, though, that if I could see you pitch wheat once in a while when crops are going to waste for want of help, I'd feel that we was close enough together for you to preach to me." So saying he turned abruptly and pushed his way through the crowd toward a group of working-men who stood near the door.

The Doctor had never commented to Dan on his sermons. But, that night as they walked home together, something made Dan feel that his friend was pleased. The encounter with the blunt young farmer had been so refreshing that he was not so depressed in spirit as he commonly was after the perfunctory, meaningless, formal compliments, and handshaking that usually closed his services. Perhaps because of this he—for the first time—sought an expression from his old friend.

"The people did not seem to like my sermon tonight?" he ventured.

The Doctor grunted a single word, "Stunned!"

"Do you think they will like it when they recover?" asked Dan with an embarrassed laugh.

But the old man was not to be led into discussing Dan's work.

"In my own practice," he said dryly, "I never prescribe medicine to suit a patient's taste, but to cure him."

Dan understood. He tried again.

"But how did *you* like my prescription, Doctor?"

For a while the Doctor did not answer; then he said, "Well you see, Dan, I always find more religion in your talks when you are not talking religiously."

Just then a team and buggy passed, and the voice of John Gardner hailed them cheerily.

"Good night, Doctor! Good night, Mr. Matthews!"

"Good night!" they answered, and the Doctor called after him, "Did you find your man, John?"

"No," shouted the other, "I did not. If you run across anyone send 'em out will you?"

"There goes a mighty fine fellow," commented the old physician.

"Seems to be," agreed Dan thoughtfully. "Where does he live?"

The Doctor told him, adding, "I wouldn't call until harvest is over, if I were you. He really wouldn't have time to give you and he'd probably tell you so." Which advice Dan received in silence.

The sun was just up the next morning when John Gardner was hitching his team to the big hay wagon. Already the smoke was coming from the stack of the threshing engine, that stood with the machine in the center of the field, and the crew was coming from the cook-wagon. Two hired men, with another team and wagon, were already gathering a load of sheaves to haul to the threshers.

The house dog barked fiercely and the farmer paused with a trace in his hand when he saw a big man turning into the barn lot from the road.

"Good morning!" called Dan cheerily, "I feared I was going to be late." He swung up to the young fellow who stood looking at him—too astonished to speak—the unhooked trace still in his hand.

"I understand that you need a hand," said Dan briefly. And the farmer noticed that the minister was dressed in a rough suit of clothes, a worn flannel shirt and an old slouch hat—Dan's fishing rig.

With a slow smile John turned, hooked his trace, and gathered his lines. "Do you mean to say that you walked out here from town this morning to work in the harvest field—a good eight miles?"

"That is exactly what I mean," returned the other.

"What for?" asked the farmer bluntly.

"For the regular wages, with one condition."

"And the condition?"

"That no one on the place shall be told that I am a preacher, and that—for today at least—I pitch against you. If, by tonight, you are not satisfied with my work you can discharge me," he added meaningly. As Dan spoke he faced the rugged farmer with a look that made him understand that his challenge of the night before was accepted.

The blue eyes gleamed. "I'll take you," he said curtly. Calling to his wife, "Mary give this man

233

his breakfast." Then to Dan, "When you get through come out to the machine." He sprang on his wagon and Dan turned toward the kitchen.

"Hold on a minute," John shouted, as the wagon began to move, "what'll I call you?"

The other answered over his shoulder, "My name is Dan."

All that day they worked, each grimly determined to handle more grain than the other. Before noon the spirit of the contest had infected the whole force. Every hand on the place worked as if on a wager. The threshing crew were all from distant parts of the country, and no one knew who it was that had so recklessly matched his strength and staying power against John Gardner, the acknowledged champion for miles around. Bets were freely laid; rough, but good natured chaff flew from mouth to mouth; and now and then a hearty yell echoed over the field, but the two men in the contest were silent; they scarcely exchanged a word.

In the afternoon the stranger slowly but surely forged ahead. John rallied every ounce of his strength but his giant opponent gained steadily. When the last load came in the farmer threw down his fork before the whole crowd and held out his hand to Dan.

"I'll give it up," he said heartily. "You're a better man than I am, stranger, wherever you come from." Dan took the offered hand while the men cheered lustily.

But the light of battle still shone in the minister's eyes.

"Perhaps," he said, "pitching is not your game. I'll match you now, tonight, for anything you want—wrestling, running, jumping, or I'll go you at any time for any work you can name."

John slowly looked him over and shook his head, "I know when I've got enough," he said laughing. "Perhaps some of the boys here—" He turned to the group.

The men grinned as they measured the stranger with admiring glances and one drawled, "We don't know where you come from, pardner, but we sure know what you can do. Ain't nobody in this outfit hankerin' to tackle the man that can work John Gardner down."

At the barn the farmer drew the minister to one side.

"Look here, Brother Matthews," he began.

But the other interrupted sharply. "My name is Dan, Mr. Gardner. Don't go back on the bargain."

"Well then, Dan, I won't. And please remember after this that my name is John. I started to ask if you really meant to stay out here and work for me this harvest?"

"That was the bargain, unless you are dissatisfied and want me to quit tonight."

The other rubbed his tired arms. "Oh I'm satisfied all right," he said grimly. "But I can't understand it, that's all."

"No," said the other, "and I can't explain. But perhaps if you were a preacher, and were met by men as men commonly meet preachers, you would understand clearly enough."

Tired as he was, the big farmer laughed until the tears came.

"And to think," he said, "all the way home last night I was wondering how you could stand it. I understand it all right. Come on in to supper." He led the way to the house.

For three days Dan fairly reveled in the companionship of those rough men, who gave him full fellowship in their order of workers. Then he went back to town.

John drove him in and the two chatted like the good comrades they had come to be, until within sight of the village. As they drew near the town silence fell upon them; their remarks grew formal and forced.

Dan felt as if he were leaving home to return to a strange land where he would always be an alien. At his door the farmer said awkwardly, "Well, good-bye, Brother Matthews, come out whenever you can."

The minister winced but did not protest. "Thank you," he returned, "I have enjoyed my visit more than I can say." And there was something so pathetic in the brown eyes of the stalwart fellow that the other strong man could make no reply. He drove quickly away without a word or a backward look.

In his room Dan sat down by the window, thinking of the morrow and what the church called his work, of the pastoral visits, the committee meetings, the Ladies' Aid. At last he stood up and stretched his great body to its full height with a sigh. Then drawing his wages from his pocket he placed the money on the study table and stood for a long time contemplating the pieces of silver as if they could answer his thoughts. Again he went to the window and looked down at Denny's garden that throughout the summer had yielded its strength to the touch of the crippled boy's hand. Then from the other window he gazed at the cast-iron monument on the corner—gazed until the grim figure seemed to threaten him with its uplifted arm.

Slowly he turned once more to the coins on the table. Gathering them, one by one, he placed them carefully in an envelope. Then, seating himself, he wrote on the little package, "The laborer is worthy of his hire."

CHAPTER XXVI.

THE WINTER PASSES.

"And, as the weeks passed, it came to be noticed that there was often in the man's eyes, and in his voice, a great sadness —the sadness of one who toils at a hopeless task; of one who suffers for crimes of which he is innocent; of one who fights for a well-loved cause with the certainty of defeat."

HE harvest time passed, the winter came and was gone again, and another springtime was at hand, with its new life stirring in blade and twig and branch, and its mystical call to the hearts of men.

Memorial Church was looking forward to the great convention of the denomination that was to be held in a distant city.

All through the months following Dan's sermon on "The Fellowship of Service," the new note continued dominant in his preaching, and indeed in all his work. Even his manner in the pulpit changed. All those little formalities and mannerisms—tricks of the trade—disappeared, while the distinguishing garb of the clergyman was discarded for clothing such as is worn by the man in the pew.

It was impossible that the story of those three days in John Gardner's harvest field should not get out. Memorial Church was crowded at every service by those whose hearts responded, even while they

238

failed to grasp the full significance of the preaching and life of this manly fellow, who, in spite of his profession, was so much a man among men.

But the attitude of the church fathers and of the ruling class was still one of doubt and suspicion, however much they could not ignore the manifest success of their minister. In spite of their misgivings their hearts swelled with pride and satisfaction as, with his growing popularity they saw their church forging far to the front. And, try as they might, they could fix upon nothing unchristian in his teaching. They could not point to a single sentence in any one of his sermons that did not unmistakably harmonize with the teaching and spirit of Jesus.

It was not so much what Dan preached that worried these pillars of the church; but it was what he did not preach, that made them uneasy. They missed the familiar pious sayings and platitudes, the time-worn sermon-subjects that had been handled by every preacher they had ever sat under. The old path—beaten so hard and plain by the many "bearers of good tidings," the safe, sure ground of denominational doctrine and theological speculation, the familiar, long-tried type of prayer, even, were all quietly, but persistently ignored by this calm-eyed, broad-shouldered, stalwart minister, who was often so much in earnest in his preaching that he forgot to talk like a preacher.

Unquestionably, decided the fathers, this young giant was "unsafe"; and—wagging their heads wisely—they predicted dire disasters, under their breath; while openly and abroad they boasted of the size of their audiences and their minister's power.

Nor did these keepers of the faith fail to make Dan feel their dissatisfaction. By hints innumerable, by carefully withholding words of encouragement, by studied coldness, they made him understand that they were not pleased. Every plan for practical Christian work that Dan suggested (and he suggested many that winter) they coolly refused to endorse, while requesting that he give more attention to the long-established activities.

Without protest or bitterness Dan quietly gave up his plans, and, except in the matter of his sermons, yielded to their demands. Never was there a word of harshness or criticism of church or people in his talks; only firm, but gentle insistence upon the great living principles of Christ's teaching. And the people, in his presence, knew often that feeling the Doctor was conscious of—that this man was, in some way, that which they might have been. Some of his hearers this feeling saddened with regret; others it inspired with hope and filled them with a determination to realize that best part of themselves; to still others it was a rebuke, the more stinging because so unconsciously given, and they were filled with anger and envy.

Meanwhile the attitude of the people toward Hope Farwell and the girl whom she had befriended, remained unaltered. But now Deborah and Denny as well came to share in their displeasure. Dan made no change in his relation to the nurse and her friends in the little cottage on the other side of the garden. In spite of constant hints, insinuations and reflections on the part of his church masters, he calmly, deliberately threw down the gauntlet before the whole scandal-loving community. And the community respected and admired him— for this is the way with the herd—even while it abated not one whit its determination to ruin him the instant chance afforded the opportunity.

So the spirit that lives in Corinth—the Ally, waited. The power that had put the shadow of pain over the life of Grace Conner, waited for Hope and Dan, until the minister himself should furnish the motive that should call it into action. Dan felt it— felt his enemy stirring quietly in the dark, watching, waiting. And, as the weeks passed, it came to be noticed that there was often in the man's eyes, and in his voice, a great sadness—the sadness of one who toils at a hopeless task; of one who suffers for crimes of which he is innocent; of one who fights for a well-loved cause with the certainty of defeat.

Because of the very fine sense of Dan's nature the situation caused him the keenest suffering. It was all so different from the life to which he had looked forward with such feelings of joy; it was all so unjust. Many were the evenings that winter when the minister flew to Dr. Harry and his ministry of music. And in those hours the friendship between the two men grew into something fine and lasting, a friendship that was to endure always. Many times, too, Dan fled across the country to the farm of John Gardner, there to spend the day in the hardest toil, finding in the ministry of labor, something that met his need. But more than these was the friendship of Hope Farwell and the influence of her life and ministry.

It was inevitable that the very attitude of the community should force these two friends into closer companionship and sympathy. The people, in judging them so harshly for the course each had chosen—because to them it was right and the only course possible to their religious ideals—drove them to a fuller dependence upon each other.

Dan, because of his own character and his conception of Christ, understood, as perhaps no one else in the community could possibly have done, just why the nurse clung to Grace Conner and the work she had undertaken; while he felt that she grasped, as no one else, the peculiarly trying position in which he so unexpectedly found himself placed in his ministry. And Hope Farwell, feeling that Dan alone understood her, realized as clearly that the minister had come to depend upon her as the one friend in Corinth who appreciated his true situation. Thus, while she gave him strength for his fight, she drew strength for her own from him.

Since that day when he had told her of the talk of the people that matter had not been mentioned between them, though it was impossible that they should not know the attitude of the community toward them both. That subtle, un-get-at-able power —the Ally, that is so irresistible, so certain in its work, depending for results upon words with double meanings, suggestive nods, tricks of expression, sly winks and meaning smiles—while giving its victims no opportunity for defense, never leaves them in doubt as to the object of its attack.

The situation was never put into words by these two, but they knew, and each knew the other knew. And their respect, confidence and regard for each other grew steadily, as it must with all good comrades under fire. In those weeks each learned to know and depend upon the other, though neither realized to what extent. So it came to be that it was not Grace Conner alone, that kept Miss Farwell in Corinth, but the feeling that Dan Matthews, also, depended upon her—the feeling that she could not desert her comrade in the fight, or—as they had both come to feel—their fight.

Hope Farwell was not a schoolgirl. She was a strong full-blooded, perfectly developed, workwoman, matured in body and mind. She realized what the continued friendship of this man might mean to her —realized it fully and was glad. Dimly, too, she saw how this that was growing in her heart might bring great pain and suffering—life-long suffering, perhaps. For—save this—their present, common fight, the life of the nurse and the life of the churchman held nothing in common. His deepest convictions had led him into a ministry that was, to her, the sheerest folly.

Hope Farwell's profession had trained her to almost perfect self-control. There was no danger that she would let herself go. Her strong, passionate heart would never be given its freedom by her, to the wrecking of the life upon which it fixed its affections. She would suffer the more deeply for that very reason. There is no pain so poignant as that which is borne in secret. But still—still she was glad! Such a strange thing is a woman's heart!

And Dan! Dan was not given to self-analysis; few really strong men are. He felt: he did not reason. Neither did he look ahead to see whither he was bound. Such a strange thing is the heart of a man!

CHAPTER XXVII.

DEBORAH'S TROUBLE.

"'Oh, I don't know what he'd do, but I know he'd do something. He's that kind of a man.'"

WHEN the first days of the spring bass-fishing came, the Doctor coaxed Dan away for a three days trip to the river, beyond Gordon's Mills, where the roaring trout-brook enters the larger stream.

It was well on toward noon the morning that Dan and the Doctor left, that Miss Farwell found Deborah in tears, with Denny trying vainly to comfort her.

"Come, come, mother, don't be takin' on so. It'll be all right somehow," Denny was saying as the nurse paused on the threshold of the little kitchen, and the crippled lad's voice was broken, though he strove so bravely to make it strong.

The widow in her low chair, her face buried in her apron, swayed back and forth in an agony of grief, her strong form shaking with sobs. Denny looked at the young woman appealingly as—with his one good hand on his mother's shoulder—he said again, "Come, mother, look up; it's Miss Hope that's come to see you. Don't, don't mother dear. We'll make it all right—sure we will though; we've got to!"

Miss Farwell went to Denny's side and together they managed, after a little, to calm the good woman.

"It's a shame it is for me to be a-goin' on so, Miss Hope, but I—but I—" She nearly broke down again.

"Won't you tell me the trouble, Mrs. Mulhall?" urged the nurse. "Perhaps I can help you."

"Indade, dear heart, don't I know you've throuble enough of your own, without your loadin' up with Denny's an' mine beside? Ain't I seen how you been put to it the past months to make both ends meet for you an' Gracie, poor child; an' you all the time fightin' to look cheerful an' bright, so as to keep her heartened up? Many's the time, Miss Hope, I've seen the look on your own sweet face, when you thought nobody'd be noticin', an' every night Denny an' me's prayed the blessed Virgin to soften the hearts of the people in this danged town. Oh, I know! I know! But it does look like God had clean forgotten us altogether. I can't help believin' it would be different somehow if only we could go to mass somewhere like decent Christians ought."

"But you and Denny have helped me more than I can ever tell you, dear friend, and now you must let me help you, don't you see?"

"It's glad enough I'd be to let you help, an' quick enough, too, if it was anything that you could fix. But nothin' but money'll do it, an' I can see by them old shoes you're a-wearin', an' you goin' with that old last year's coat all winter, that you—that you ain't earned but just enough to keep you an' Gracie alive."

"That's all true enough, Mrs. Mulhall," returned the nurse, cheerfully, "but I am sure it will help you just to tell me about the trouble." Then, with a little more urging, the nurse drew from them the whole pitiful story.

At the time of Jack Mulhall's death, Judge Strong had held a mortgage on the little home for a small amount. By careful planning the widow and her son had managed to pay the interest promptly, and the Judge, though he coveted the place, had not dared to push the payment of the mortgage too soon after the marshal's death because of public sentiment. But now, sufficient time having elapsed for the public to forget their officer, who had been killed on duty, and Deborah, through receiving Grace Conner and Miss Farwell into her home, being included to some extent in the damaging comments of the righteous community, the crafty Judge saw his opportunity. He knew that, while the people would not themselves go to the length of putting Deborah and her crippled boy out of their little home, he had nothing to fear from the sentiment of the community should he do so under the guise of legitimate business.

The attitude of the people had kept Deborah from earning as much as usual and, for the first time, they had been unable to pay the interest. Indeed it was only by the most rigid economy that they would be able to make their bare living until Denny's garden should again begin to bring them in something.

Their failure to pay the interest gave the Judge added reason for pushing the payment of the debt. Everything had been done in regular legal form. Deborah and Denny must go the next day. The widow had exhausted every resource; promises and pleadings were useless, and it was only at the last hour that she had given up.

"But have you no relatives, Mrs. Mulhall, who could help you? No friends? Perhaps Dr. Oldham—"

Deborah shook her head. "There's only me an' Brother Mike in the family," she said. "Mike's a brick-layer an' would give the coat off his back for me, but he's movin' about so over the country, bein' single, you see, that I can't get a letter to him. I did write to him where I heard from him last, but me letter come back. He don't write often, you see, thinkin' Denny an' me is all right. I ain't seen him since he was here to help put poor Jack away."

For a few minutes the silence in the little room was broken only by poor Deborah's sobs, and by Denny's voice, as he tried to comfort his mother.

Suddenly the nurse sprang to her feet. "There is some one," she cried. "I knew there must be, of course. Why didn't we think of him before?"

Deborah raised her head, a look of doubtful hope on her tear-wet face.

"Mr. Matthews," explained the young woman.

Deborah's face fell. "But, child, the minister's away with the Doctor. An' what good could he be doin' if he was here, I'd like to know? He's that poor himself."

"Oh, I don't know what he'd do, but I know he'd do something. He's that kind of a man," declared the nurse, with such conviction that, against their judgment, Deborah and Denny took heart.

"And he's not so far away but that he can be reached," added Hope.

That afternoon the dilapidated old hack from Corinth to Gordon's Mills carried a passenger.

CHAPTER XXVIII.

A FISHERMAN.

"'Humph!' grunted the other, 'I've noticed that there's a lot of unnecessary things that have to be done.'"

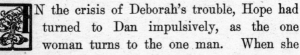

IN the crisis of Deborah's trouble, Hope had turned to Dan impulsively, as the one woman turns to the one man. When she was powerless in her own strength to meet the need she looked confidently to him.

But now that she was actually on the way to him, with Corinth behind and the long road over the hills and through the forests before, she had time to think, while the conscious object of her journey forced itself on her thinking.

The thing that the young woman had so dimly foreseen, for herself, of her friendship with this man, she saw now more clearly, as she realized how much she had grown to depend upon him—upon the strength of his companionship. How she had learned to watch for his coming, and to look often toward the corner window of the house on the other side of the garden! But, after all—she asked herself—was her regard for him more than a natural admiration for his strong character, as she had seen it revealed in the past months? Their peculiar situation had placed him more in her thoughts than any man had ever been before. Was not this all? The possibility

250

had not yet become a certainty. The revelation of Hope Farwell to herself was yet to come.

The hack, with its one passenger, arrived at Gordon's Mills about four o'clock, and Miss Farwell, climbing down from the ancient vehicle in front of the typical country hotel, inquired for Dr. Oldham.

The slouchy, slow-witted proprietor of the place passed her inquiry on to a group of natives who lounged on the porch, and one, whose horse was hitched in front of the blacksmith shop across the way, gave the information that he had seen the Doctor and the big parson at the mouth of the creek as he came past an hour before. He added that he "reckoned they wouldn't be in 'til dark, fer they was a-ketchin' a right smart of bass."

"Is it far from here?" asked the nurse.

"Somethin' less than a mile, ain't hit, Bill?"

Bill "'lowed hit war about that. Mile an' a quarter to Bud Jones', Bud called hit."

"And the road?"

"Foller the creek—can't miss it." This from the chorus. And Miss Farwell set out, watched by every eye on the place until she disappeared around the first bend.

As she drew near the river, the banks of which are marked by a high bluff on the other side, the young woman felt a growing sense of embarrassment. What would Mr. Matthews think of her coming to him in such a way? And Dr. Oldham—. Already she could feel the keen eyes of the old physician, with their knowing twinkle, fixed upon her face. The Doctor always made you feel that he knew so much more about you than you knew about your-self.

Coming to the river at the mouth of the creek, she saw them, and half hidden by the upturned roots of a fallen tree, she stood still. They were on the down-stream side of the creek; Dan, with rubber boots that came to his hips, standing far out on the sandy bar, braced against the current, that tugged and pulled at his great legs; the Doctor farther down, on the bank.

Miss Farwell watched Dan with the curious inter-est a woman always feels when watching a man who, while engaged in a man's work or play, is uncon-scious of her presence.

She saw the fisherman as he threw the line far out, with a strong, high swing of his long arm. And as she looked, a lusty bass—heavy, full of fight—took the hook, and she saw the man stand motionless, intent, alert, at the instant he first felt the fish. Then she caught the skillful turn of his wrist as he struck —quick and sure; watched, with breathless interest as—bracing himself—the fisherman's powerful figure became instinct with life. With the boiling water grasping his legs, clinging to him like a tireless wrestler seeking the first unguarded moment; and with the plunging, tugging, rushing giant at the other end of the silken line—fighting with every inch of his spring-steel body for freedom, Dan made a picture to bring the light of admiration to any woman's eyes. And Hope Farwell was very much a woman.

Slowly, but surely, the strength and skill of the fisherman prevailed. The master of the waters came nearer the hand of his conqueror. The young woman held her breath while the fish made its last, mad attempt, and then—when Dan held up his prize for the Doctor, who—on the bank—had been in the fight with his whole soul, she forgot her embarrassment, and—springing into full view upon the trunk of the fallen tree—shouted and waved her congratulations.

Dan almost dropped the fish.

The Doctor, whose old eyes were not so quick to recognize the woman on the log, was amazed to see his companion go splashing, stumbling, ploughing through the water toward the shore.

"Hope—Miss Farwell!" gasped Dan, floundering up the bank, the big fish still in his hand, the shining water streaming from his high boots, his face glowing with healthful exercise—a something else, perhaps. "What good fortune brings you here?"

At his impetuous manner, and the eagerness that shone in his eyes, and sounded in his voice, the woman's face had grown rosy red, but by the time the fisherman had gained a place by her side the memory of her mission had driven every other thought from her mind. Briefly she told him of Deborah's trouble, and a few moments later the Doctor—crossing the creek higher up—joined them. As they talked Hope saw all the light and joy go from Dan's face, and in its place came a look of sadness and determination that made her wonder.

"Doctor," he said, "I am going back to Corinth with Miss Farwell tonight. We'll get a team and buggy at the Mills."

The old man swore heartily. Why had not the foolish Irishwoman let them know her situation before? Still swearing he drew from his pocket a book and hastily signed a check. "Here, Dan," he said, "use this if you have to. You understand— don't hesitate if you need it."

Reluctantly the younger man took the slip of paper. "I don't think it will be needed," he responded. "It ought not to be necessary for you to do this, Doctor."

"Humph!" grunted the other, "I've noticed that there's a lot of unnecessary things that have to be done. Hustle along, you two. I'm going back after the mate to that last one of yours."

On the way back to the hotel Dan told the nurse that the check would mean much to the Doctor if it were used at this particular time. "But," he added thoughtfully, again, "I don't think it will be used."

They stopped long enough at the hotel for a hurried lunch, then—with a half-broken team and a stout buggy—started, in the gathering dusk for Corinth.

As the light went out of the sky and the mysterious stillness of the night came upon them, they, too, grew quiet, as if no words were needed. They seemed to be passing into another world—a strange dream-world where they were alone. The things of everyday, the common-place incidents and happenings of their lives, seemed to drift far away. They talked but little. There was so little to say. Once Dan leaned over to tuck the lap robe carefully about his companion, for the early spring air was chill when the sun went down.

So they rode until they saw the lights of the town; then it all came back to them with a rush. The woman drew a long breath.

"Tired?" asked Dan, and there was that in his voice that brought the tears to the gray eyes—tears that he could not see, because of the dark.

"Not a bit," she answered cheerfully, in spite of the hidden tears. "Will you see Judge Strong tonight?" She had not asked him what he was going to do.

"Yes," he said, and when they reached the big brown house he drew the horses to a walk. "I think, if you are not too tired, I had better stop now. I will not be long."

There was now something in his voice that made her heart jump with sudden fear, such as she had felt at times when Dr. Miles, at the hospital, had told her to prepare to assist him in an operation. But in her voice no fear showed itself.

He hitched the team, and—leaving her waiting in the buggy—went up to the house. She heard him knock. The door opened, sending out a flood of light. He entered. The door closed.

She waited in the dark.

CHAPTER XXIX.

A MATTER OF BUSINESS.

"'You say, sir, that some things are inevitable. You are right.'"

AT the church prayer meeting, that evening, Judge Strong prayed with a fervor unusual even for him, and in church circles the Elder was rated mighty in prayer. In fact the Judge's religious capital was mostly invested in good, safe, public petitions to the Almighty—such investments being rightly considered by the Judge as "gilt-edged," for—whatever the returns—it was all profit.

Theoretically the Judge's God noted "even the sparrow's fall," and in all of his public religious exercises, the Judge stated that fact with clearness and force. Making practical application of his favorite text the Judge never killed sparrows. His everyday energies were spent in collecting mortgages, acquiring real estate, and in like harmless pursuits, that were—so far as he had observed—not mentioned in the Word, and presumably, therefore, were passed over by the God of the sparrow.

So the Judge prayed that night, with pious intonations asking his God for everything he could think of for himself, his church, his town and the whole world. And when he could think of no more blessings, he unblushingly asked God to think of them for him, and to give them all abundantly—more than they could ask or desire. Reminding God of his care for the sparrow, he pleaded with him to watch over their beloved pastor, "who is absent from his flock in search of—ah, enjoying—ah, the beauties of Nature —ah, and bring him speedily back to his needy people, that they may all grow strong in the Lord."

Supplementing his prayer with a few solemn reflections, as was expected from an Elder of the church, the Judge commented on the smallness of the company present; lamented the decline of spirituality in the churches; declared the need for the old Jerusalem gospel, and the preaching of the truth as it is in Christ Jesus; scored roundly those who were absent, seeking their own pleasure, neglecting their duties while the world was perishing; and finished with a plea to the faithful to assist their worthy pastor—who, unfortunately, was not present with them that evening—in every way possible. Then the Judge went home to occupy the rest of the evening with some matters of business.

In the Strong mansion the room known as the library is on the ground floor in a wing of the main building. As rooms have a way of doing, it expresses unmistakably the character of its tenant. There is a book-case, with a few spick-and-span books standing in prim, cold rows behind the glass doors—which are always locked. The key is somewhere, no doubt. There are no pictures on the walls, save a fancy calendar—presented with the compliments of the Judge's banker, a crayon portrait of the Judge's father—in a cheap gilt frame, and another calendar, compliments of the Judge's grocer.

The furniture and appointments are in harmony; a table, with a teachers' Bible and a Sunday school quarterly, a big safe wherein the Judge kept his various mortgages and papers of value, and the Judge's desk, being most conspicuous. It is a significant comment on the Elder's business methods that, in the top right-hand drawer of his desk, he keeps a weapon ready for instant use, and that the window shades are always drawn when the lamps are lighted.

Sitting at his desk the Judge heard the front doorbell ring and his wife direct someone to the library. A moment later he looked up from his papers to see Dan standing before him.

The Judge was startled. He had thought the young man far away. Then, too, the Judge had never seen the minister dressed in rough trousers, belted at the waist; a flannel shirt under a torn and mud-stained coat; and mud-spattered boots that came nearly to his hips. The slouch hat in the visitor's hand completed the picture. Dan looked big in any garb. As the Judge saw him that night he seemed a giant, and this giant had the look of one come in haste on business of moment.

What was it that made the Judge reach out impulsively toward that top right-hand drawer.

Forcing his usual dry, mirthless laugh, he greeted Dan with forced effusiveness, urging him to take a chair, declaring that he hardly knew him, that he thought he was at Gordon's Mills fishing. Then he entered at once into a glowing description of the splendid prayer meeting they had held that evening, in the minister's absence.

Ignoring the invitation to be seated, Dan walked slowly to the center of the room, and standing by the table, looked intently at the man at the desk. The patter of the Judge's talk died away. The presence of the man by the table seemed to fill the whole room. The very furniture became suddenly cheap and small. The Judge himself seemed to shrink, and he had a sense of something about to happen. Swiftly he reviewed in his mind several recent deals. What was it?

"Well," he said at last, when Dan did not speak, "won't you sit down?"

"Thank you, no," answered Dan. "I can stop only a minute. I called to see you about that mortgage on Widow Mulhall's home."

"Ah! Well?"

"I want to ask you, sir, if it is not possible for you to reconsider the matter and grant her a little more time."

The man at the desk answered curtly, "Possibly, sir, but it would not be business. Do you—ah, consider this matter as coming under the head of your—ah, pastoral duties?"

Dan ignored the question, as he earnestly replied, "I will undertake to see that the mortgage is paid, sir, if you will give me a little time."

To which the other answered coldly, "My experience with ministers' promises to pay has not been reassuring, and, as an Elder in the church, I may say that we do not employ you to undertake the payment of other people's debts. The people might not understand your interest in the Widow's affairs."

Again Dan ignored the other's answer, though his face went white, and his big hands crushed the slouch hat with a mighty grip. He urged what it would mean to Deborah and her crippled son to lose their little home and the garden—almost their only means of support. But the face of the Judge expressed no kindly feeling. He was acting in a manner that was fully legitimate. He had considered it carefully. As for the hardship, some things in connection with business were inevitable.

As the Elder answered Dan's arguments and pleadings, the minister's face grew very sad, and his low, slow voice trembled at times. When the uselessness of his efforts were too evident for him to continue the conversation he turned sadly toward the door.

Something caused the Judge to say, "Don't go yet, Brother Matthews. You see, being a minister, there are some things that you don't understand. You are making a mistake in—" He caught his breath. Instead of leaving the room, Dan was closing and locking the door.

He came back in three quick strides. This time he placed his hat on the table. When he spoke his voice was still low—intense—shaken with feeling.

"You say, sir, that some things are inevitable. You are right."

There was that in his manner now that made the man in the chair tremble. He started to speak, but Dan silenced him.

"You have said quite enough, sir. Don't think that I have not fully considered this matter. I have. It is inevitable. Turn to your desk there and write a letter to Mrs. Mulhall granting her another year of time."

The Judge tried to laugh, but his dry lips made a strange sound. With a quick movement he jerked open the top right-hand drawer, but before he could lay hand on the weapon, Dan leaped to within easy striking distance.

"Shut that drawer!"

The Judge obeyed.

"Now write!"

"I'll have the law on you! I'll put you out of the Christian ministry! I'll have you arrested if you assault me. I'll—"

"I have considered all that, too," said Dan. "Try it, and you will stir up such a feeling that the people of this community will drive you out of the country. You can't do it and live in Corinth, Judge Strong. You have too much at stake in this town to risk it. You won't have me arrested for this; you can't afford it, sir. Write that letter and no one but you and I will ever know of this incident. Refuse, or fail to keep the promise of your letter, and no power on earth shall prevent me from administering justice! You who would rob that crippled boy of his garden—"

The man shuddered. Suddenly he opened his mouth to call. But Dan, reading his purpose in his eyes, had him by the throat before he could utter a sound.

This was enough.

With the letter in his pocket Dan stood silently regarding his now cowering victim, and his deep voice was full of pain as he said, in that slow way, "I regret this incident, Brother Strong, more than I can say. I have no apology to make. It *was* inevitable. You have my word that no one shall know, from me, what has occurred here this evening. When you think it all over you will not carry the matter further. You cannot afford it. You will see that you cannot afford it."

When the Judge lifted his head he was alone.

"Did I keep you waiting too long?" asked Dan, when he had again taken his place by Miss Farwell's side.

"Oh no! But tell me: is it all right?"

"Yes, it's all right. Judge Strong has kindly granted our friends another year. That will give us time to do something."

Arriving at the house he gave Hope the letter for Deborah. "And here," he said, "is something for you." From under the buggy seat he drew the big bass.

When Dan returned to Gordon's Mills with the team the next morning, he gave back the Doctor's check, saying simply, "The Judge listened to reason and decided that he would not press the case." And that was all the explanation he ever made though it was by no means the end of the matter.

Dan himself did not realize what he had done. He did not realize how potent were the arguments that he had used to convince the Judge.

The young minister had at last furnished the motive for which the Ally waited!

CHAPTER XXX.

THE DAUGHTER OF THE CHURCH.

"Thus the Ally has something for everybody."

DAN was right. Judge Strong could not afford to make public the facts connected with the young man's visit to him that evening. He could not afford it for more reasons than Dan knew. The arguments with which the minister had backed up his personal influence were stronger than he realized. The more the Judge thought about the whole matter the more he was inclined to congratulate himself that he had been saved from a step far more dangerous than he had ever before ventured. He saw where, in his desire to possess all, he had come perilously near losing everything. But these reflections did not make the Elder feel one whit kindlier towards Dan.

While the Judge was held both by his fear of Dan and by his own best interests, from moving openly against the man who had so effectually blocked his well-laid plans for acquiring another choice bit of Corinth real estate, there were other ways, perfectly safe, by which he might make the minister suffer.

Judge Strong had not been a ruling elder in the church for so many years without learning the full value of the spirit that makes Corinth its home.

While the Elder himself feared the Ally as he feared nothing else, he was a past master in the art of directing its strength to the gaining of his own ends. His method was extremely simple: the results certain.

When he learned of Hope's trip to Gordon's Mills and the long ride in the night alone with Dan, the Judge fairly hugged himself. It was all so easy!

In the two days preceding the next weekly meeting of the Ladies' Aid Society, it happened, quite incidentally, that the Elder had quiet, confidential talks with several of the most active workers in the congregation. The Judge in these talks did not openly charge the minister with wrong conduct, with any neglect of his duties, or with any unfaithfulness to the doctrines. No indeed! The Judge was not such a bungler in the art of directing the strength of the Ally in serving his own ends. But nevertheless, each good sister, when the interview was ended, felt that she had been trusted with the confidence of the very inside of the innermost circle; felt her heart swell with the responsibility of a state secret of vast importance; and her soul grow big with a righteous determination to be worthy.

That was a Ladies' Aid meeting to be remembered. There had been nothing like it since the last meeting of its kind. For of course, every sister who had talked with the Judge was determined that every other sister should understand that *she* was on the innermost inside; and every other sister who had talked with the Judge was equally fired with the same purpose; and the sisters who had not talked quietly with the Judge were extraordinarily active in creating the impression that they knew even more than those who had. So that altogether things were hinted, half revealed and fully told about Dan and Miss Farwell that would have astonished even Judge Strong himself, had he not known just how it would be.

The Sunday following it seemed almost as if Dan had wished to help the Judge in his campaign, for while there was much in his sermon about widows and orphans, there was not a word of the old Jerusalem gospel.

Monday evening Judge Strong and his wife called upon Elder Jordan and his family, and the two church fathers held a long and important conference, with the church mothers and the church daughter assisting.

The Judge said very little. Indeed he seemed reluctant to discuss the grave things that were being said in the community about their pastor. But it was easy to see that he was earnestly concerned for the welfare of the church and the upbuilding of the cause in Corinth. Nathan himself was led to introduce the subject. The Judge very skillfully and politely gave the women opportunities. He agreed most heartily with Elder Jordan that Dan's Christian character was above reproach, and that it was very unfortunate that there should be any criticism by the public. Such things so weakened the church influence in the community! He regretted, however, that their pastor in his sermons did not dwell more upon first principles and the fundamental doctrines of the church. His sermons were good, but the people needed to be taught the true way of salvation. Dan was young: perhaps he would learn the foolishness of taking up these new ideas of the church's mission and work, that were sapping the very foundations of Christianity.

Nathaniel Jordan, because of the very goodness of his heart and his deeply religious nature, had learned to love Dan, and to believe in him, even while he was forced—by his whole life's training—to question the wisdom of the young man's preaching. And while he was deeply pained by the things the sisters reported, he found, as the Judge intended, that Elder Strong's attitude was in close harmony with his own.

Thus the Ally has something for everybody. Those who did not doubt Dan's character questioned his preaching; and those who cared but little what he preached found much to question in his conduct.

But there was one in the company that evening who contributed nothing to the discussion, save now and then a word in defense of Dan. And everything that Charity said was instantly and warmly endorsed by the Judge.

When Judge and Mrs. Strong at last bade their friends good night and left Nathaniel and his wife to cultivate the seed the Ally had so skilfully planted, Charity retired at once to her room, but not to sleep. Not for nothing had this young woman been reared in such close touch with the inner circle of the ruling classes in Memorial Church. This was by no means the first conference of its kind that she had been permitted to attend. Her whole life experience enabled her to judge to a day, almost, the length of any minister's stay in Corinth. Few had stayed more than a year.

There was Rev. Swanson—who was too old; and Rev. Wilson—it was his daughter; and Rev. Jones —it was his wife; and Rev. George—it was his son; and it was Rev. Kern—who did not get on with the young 'people; and Rev. Holmes—who was too young, and got on with the young people too well. Charity always thought that she might have—. If he had only been permitted to stay another three months! And Rev. Colby—it was because he had neither wife nor sons nor daughters. Charity was sure she might have—. If only he had been given more time! And now—Dan!

The poor girl cried bitterly in the dark and in her tears determined upon desperate measures.

CHAPTER XXXI.

THE REALITY.

"'Faith,' said Deborah, who, in the kitchen, heard their merry talk and laughter. 'It must be the garden as does it.'"

"Who shall say that the Irishwoman had not the truth of the whole matter?"

THE incident of Deborah's trouble brought Hope to a fuller dependence upon Dan than she had ever before known. The long ride alone in the hack, with her mind so filled with thoughts of her big friend, his greeting of her and his quick response to her appeal in Deborah's behalf, with the drive home in the night by his side, and the immediate success of his call upon the Judge had all led the young woman much nearer a full realization of herself and a complete understanding of her feeling for Dan than she knew. But one touch more was needed to make the possibility which she had long foreseen a reality.

The touch needed came early in the afternoon of the day following the Judge's call upon Elder Jordan. Miss Farwell, with Grace and Denny, was in the garden, making ready for the first early seed. At Dan's urgent request a much larger space had been prepared this year and they were all intensely interested in what was to be, they declared, the best and largest garden that Denny had ever grown.

Denny with his useless, twisted arm swinging at his side, and his poor, dragging leg, was marking off the beds and rows, the while he kept up a ceaseless, merry chatter with the two young women who assisted him by carrying the stakes and lines.

Any one would have thought they were the happiest people in all Corinth, and perhaps they were, though from all usual standards they had little enough to be joyous over. Denny with his poor, crippled body, forever barred from the life his whole soul craved, yearning for books and study with all his heart, but forced to give the last atom of his poor strength in digging in the soil for the bare necessities of life, denied even a pittance to spend for the volumes he loved; Grace Conner marred in spirit and mind, as was Denny in body, by the cruel, unjust treatment of those to whom she had a right to look first for sympathy and help; and the nurse, who was sacrificing a successful and remunerative career in the profession she loved, to carry the burden of this one, who in the eyes of the world, had no claim whatever upon her. What had they to be joyous over that sunny afternoon in the garden?

"Faith," said Deborah, who, in the kitchen, heard their merry talk and laughter. "It must be the garden as does it."

Who shall say that the Irishwoman had not the truth of the whole matter?

The three merry workers were expecting Dan. But Dan did not come. And it may have been because Hope turned her eyes so often toward the corner window, that she failed to see the young woman who turned in at their own gate. Then Deborah's voice called from the kitchen for Miss Hope, and the nurse went into the house.

"It's someone to see you," said the widow with an air of great mystery. "I tuck her into your room, where she's waitin' for you. Dear heart, but the day has brung the roses to your cheeks, and the sunshine is in your two eyes. Sure, I can't think what she'd be wantin'. I hope 'tis nothin' to make ye the less happy than ye are."

"Oh you, with your blarney!" returned the young woman playfully, and then, with a note of eagerness in her voice, "Who is it, do you know her?"

"Sure I do, and so will you when you see her. Go on in child; don't be standin' here, maybe it's the job you've been lookin' for come at last. I can't think that any of them would be sendin' for you, though the good Lord knows the poor creature herself looks to need a nurse or somethin'."

She pushed Hope from the kitchen, and a moment later the young woman entered her own room to find Miss Charity Jordan.

Hope Farwell was a beautiful woman—beautiful with the beauty of a womanhood unspoiled by vain idleness, empty pleasures or purposeless activity. Perhaps because of her interest and care for the girl, to whom she was filling the place of both mother and elder sister, perhaps because of something else that had come into her life—the past few months, in spite of her trials, had added much to that sweet atmosphere of womanliness that enveloped her always. The deep, gray eyes seemed deeper still and a light was in their depths that had not been there before. In her voice, too, there was a new note—a richer, fuller tone, and she moved and laughed as one whose soul was filled with the best joys of living.

Charity arose to her feet when Miss Farwell entered. The nurse greeted her, but the poor girl who had spent an almost sleepless night, stood regarding the woman before her with a kind of envying wonder. What right had this creature to be so happy while she a Christian was so miserable?

To Charity there were only two kinds of people— those who belonged to the church and those who belonged to the world. Those of the world were strangers—aliens. The life they lived, their pleasures, their ambitions, their loves, were all matters of conjecture to this daughter of the church. They were, to her, people to save—never people to be intimate with; nor were they to be regarded without grave suspicion until they were saved. She wondered, sometimes, what they were like if one were to really know them. As she had thought about it the night before in the dark, it was a monstrous thing that a woman of this other world should have ensnared their minister—her minister.

Charity was a judge of preachers. She saw in Dan the ability to go far. She felt that no position in the church was too high for him to reach, no honor too great for him to attain, if only he might be steadied and inspired and assisted by a competent helper—one thoroughly familiar with every detail of the denominational machinery, and acquainted with every denominational engineer.

Thus to be robbed of the high place in life for which she had fitted herself, and to which she had aspired for years, by an alien to the church was maddening—if only Charity had possessed the capacity for being maddened. What right had this creature who never entered a church—what right had she even to the friendship of a minister—a minister such as Dan? And to ruin his reputation! To cause him to be sent away from Corinth! To wreck his career! To deprive him of a companion so fitly qualified to help him realize to the full his splendid ambition! Small wonder that the daughter of the church had determined upon a desperate measure.

Left alone when Deborah had gone to call Miss Farwell, Charity had examined the nurse's room with interest and surprise. The apartment bore no testimony to an unholy life. Save that it was in every way a poorer place than any room in the Jordan house, it might have been Charity's own. There was even a Bible, well worn at that, lying on a table by which a chair was drawn as if the reader had but just laid the book aside.

And now this woman stood before her. This woman with the deep, kind eyes, the soft, calm voice, her cheeks glowing with healthful outdoor exercise, and her air of sweet womanliness.

The nurse spoke the second time.

"I am Miss Farwell. You are Miss Jordan, I believe. I see you pass the house frequently. Won't you be seated, please, you seem to be in trouble."

Poor Charity! Dropping weakly into a chair she burst into bitter tears. Then before Miss Farwell could recover from her surprise, the caller exclaimed, "I came to see you about our minister, Reverend Matthews."

The color in the nurse's cheeks deepened.

"But why should you come to me about Mr. Matthews? I know nothing of your church affairs, Miss Jordan."

"I know that you do not," the other returned bitterly. "You have never been to hear him preach. You know nothing—nothing of what it means to him—to me, to all of us, I mean. How could you know anything about it?"

This passionate outburst and the sight of Charity's crimson face and embarrassed manner caused the color to disappear from the nurse's cheeks. After a moment she said coolly, "Do you not think it would be well for you to explain clearly just what you mean and why you come to me?"

In her effort to explain Charity's words came tumbling recklessly, impetuously out, in all sorts of disorder. She charged the nurse with ruining the minister's work, with alienating him from his people, with injuring the Memorial Church and the cause of Christ in Corinth, with making him the talk of the town.

"What is he to you," she finished. "What can he ever be to you? You would not dare to think of marrying a minister of the gospel—you a woman of the world. He belongs to us, he does not belong to you, and you have no right to take him from us." Then she pleaded with her to—as she put it—let their pastor alone, to permit him to stay in Corinth and go on to the great future that she was so sure awaited him.

As the girl talked the other woman sat very still with downcast face, save now and then when Charity's disordered words seemed to carry a deeper meaning than appeared upon the surface. Then the gray eyes were lifted to study the speaker's face, doubtfully, wonderingly, questioningly.

In her painful excitement Charity was telling much more than she realized. And more, Charity was not only laying bare her own heart to the nurse, but she was revealing Hope Farwell to herself. That young woman was stirred as she had never been before.

When her visitor had talked herself out the nurse said quietly, "Miss Jordan, it is not at all necessary that I should reply to the things you have said, but you must answer me one question. Has Mr. Matthews ever, either by word or by his manner towards you, given you reason to feel that you, personally, have any right whatever to say these things to me?"

It was so frank, so direct, and withal so womanly and kind, and so unexpected—that Charity hung her head.

"Tell me please, Miss Jordan. After all that you have said, you must."

The answer came in a whisper. "No."

"Thank you." There was that in the nurse's voice that left the other's heart hopeless, and robbed her of power to say more. She rose and moved toward the door.

The nurse accompanied her to the porch. "Miss Jordan." Charity paused. "I am very sorry. I fear you will never understand how—how mistaken you are. I—I shall not harm either your church or —your minister. Believe me, I am very, very sorry."

Miss Farwell could not return to the garden. He would be there. She could not meet him just yet. She must be alone. She must go somewhere to think this thing out.

Stealing from the house, she slipped away down the street. Without her conscious will, her feet led her toward the open country, to Academy Hill, to the grassy knoll under the oak in the old Academy yard.

The possibility had become a reality, and all the pain that she had foreseen, was hers. But with the pain was a great gladness.

Miss Farwell need not have fled from meeting Dan in the garden that afternoon. Dan was not in the garden. While the nurse, in her room, was greeting Miss Charity, Elder Jordan, who had stopped on his way home from the post office was knocking at the door of the minister's study.

CHAPTER XXXII.

THE BARRIER.

"As he looked at the figure so immovable, so hideously rigid and fixed in the act of proclaiming an issue that belonged to a dead age, he felt as if his heart would burst with wild rage at the whole community, people and church."

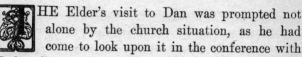

THE Elder's visit to Dan was prompted not alone by the church situation, as he had come to look upon it in the conference with Judge Strong the evening before, but by the old man's regard for the young minister himself. Because of this he had said nothing to his brother official of his purpose, wishing to make his visit something more than an official call in the interest of the church. Nathaniel felt that alone he could talk to Dan in a way that would have been impossible in the presence of Judge Strong, and in this he was not mistaken.

In the months of his work in Corinth, Dan had learned to love this old church father, whose faithfulness to the dead past and to the obsolete doctrines of his denomination, was so large an element in his religion. It was impossible not to recognize that, so far as the claims of his creed would permit, Elder Jordan was a true Christian man—gentle, tolerant, kind in all things, outside the peculiar doctrine of the founders of his sect.

It was impossible for the minister and his Elder to see life from the same point of view. They belonged to different ages. The younger man, recognizing this, honored his elder brother for his fidelity to the faith of his fathers, and saw in this very faith, a virtue to admire. But the older man saw in Dan's broader views and neglect of the issues that belonged to the past age, a weakness of Christian character—to be overcome if possible, but on no ground to be tolerated, lest the very foundation of the church be sapped.

Elder Jordan's regard for Dan was wholly personal, entirely aside from the things of the church. The Elder was capable of sacrificing his own daughter if, in his judgment, it was necessary for the good of the cause, but he would not have loved her the less. There was that inhuman something in his religion that has always made religion a thing of schools and churches, rather than a thing of farms and shops; a thing of set days, of forms, rites, ceremonies, beliefs —rather than a thing of everyday living and the commonplace, individual duties, pleasures and drudgeries of life.

The old churchman did not spare Dan that afternoon. Very clearly he forced the minister to see the situation, making him understand the significance of the gossip that had been revived, and the growing dissatisfaction of the church leaders with his sermons. Dan listened quietly, with no lack of respect for the man who talked to him so plainly—for, under the sometimes harsh words, he felt always the true spirit of the speaker and his kindly regard.

Touching his preaching Dan could make no reply, for he realized how impossible it was for the Elder to change his point of view. The young minister had, indeed, neglected the things that, to the Elder and his kind, were the vital things. That he had taught the truths that to him seemed most vital made no difference in the situation. The fact remained that he was the hired servant of Memorial Church and was not employed by that body to preach what he considered the most vital truths.

But touching his friendship with the nurse, Dan spoke warmly in defense of the young woman—of himself he said nothing. As the Elder listened, he thought he saw how Dan had been influenced in his ministry by this woman who was not of the church, and the idea that had sent Charity to Miss Farwell took possession of him. Even as his daughter pleaded with the nurse to set the minister free, Nathaniel pleaded with Dan to free himself. Inevitably the results were exactly the same.

"Think of your ministry, my boy," urged the old man, "of the sacred duties of your office. Your attitude towards this woman has been, in every way, just what the people expect the conduct of a man to be toward the one he is seeking to make his wife. Yet no one for a moment thinks you expect to marry this woman, who is known to be an alien to the church. What success could you hope to have as a minister if you take to wife one who would have nothing to do with your church? What right have you, then, to be so intimate with her, to seek her company so constantly? Granting all that you say of her character, and all that Dr. Miles has written, why does she stay in Corinth, where no one will employ her, when she could so easily return to her work in the city, taking that Conner girl with her?"

Dan could find no words to answer the Elder. He was stunned by the situation to which he had been so suddenly awakened by the old man's plain words. But there were elements in the problem unknown to Nathaniel Jordan, though the old man felt that somehow his lance had gone deeper than he intended.

When the Elder was gone Dan's mind and heart clutched those words, "No one believes for a moment that you expect to marry this woman."

"To marry this woman—to marry—to marry!" He thought of his father and mother, and their perfect companionship. "What right have you in this case, to be so intimate with her, to seek her company so constantly?"

He started to go to the window that looks down on the garden, thinking to see her there, but checked himself. He knew now why the garden had grown to mean so much to him. He tried to realize what his life would be without this woman who had so grown into it.

Dan Matthews was no weakling who could amuse himself with a hundred imitation love affairs. In his veins ran the fierce, red blood of a strong race that had ruled by the simple strength of manhood their half-wild mountain wilderness. As the tiny stream, flowing quietly through peaceful meadow, still woodland, and sunny pasture—growing always broader and deeper as it runs—is unconscious of its quiet power until checked by some barrier, and rising, swelling to a mighty flood—seeks to clear its path; so Dan's love had grown. In the fields of friendship it had gained always depth and power until now—coming to the barrier—it rose in all its strength—a flood of passion that shook every nerve and fibre of the man's being, a mighty force that would not be denied.

Going to the other window he saw the cast-iron monument. And as he looked at the figure so immovable, so hideously rigid and fixed in the act of proclaiming an issue that belonged to a dead age, he felt as if his heart would burst with wild rage at the whole community, people and church.

"What right had he to the companionship of this woman?"

"The right that God has given to every man—nay to every beast and bird—the right to seek his mate: the right of the future. What right, indeed, had anyone to challenge him, to say that he should not win her if he could? If he could—"

As suddenly as the rage had come it left him, and he shrank hopeless within himself, cowering before the thought of his position in life, and of her attitude toward the church and its ministers.

"The Elder and his people need give themselves no uneasiness," he thought. "The barrier was too well-built to be swept aside by love of man and woman."

He saw that now, even the old friendship between them would be impossible. He wondered if his going out of her life would make any ripple in its calm, even current; if she would care very much?

The Elder had asked, "Why has she remained in Corinth?"

"Could it be—No, no! That would be too much. It was her interest in Grace Conner alone that held her."

So Big Dan faced this thing against which the very strength of his manhood was his greatest weakness, and facing it he, too, was afraid to go into the garden—as he thought—to meet her. He must gain a little self-control first. He must grow better acquainted with this thing that had come upon him so quickly.

Following the instinct of his ancestors to face trouble in the open, he, too, set out, bound for a long tramp across the country. Perhaps he would go as far even as John Gardner's, and spend the night there. He went up the street for a block before turning north, lest his friends in the garden hail him. Then walking quickly he pushed on towards the outskirts of town, on the old Academy Hill road.

CHAPTER XXXIII.

HEARTS' TRAGEDIES.

"So she sent him away to fight his battle alone, knowing it was the only way such a battle could be rightly fought."

HEN Miss Farwell, under the oak tree in the Academy yard, turned her eyes from the far blue roll of hills to see Dan Matthews coming through the gap in the tumble-down fence, it was as if he had appeared in answer to her thoughts, and the intensity of her emotions at the moment, frightened her.

Her first impulse was to escape. Then she sat still, watching him as if fascinated, while her trembling fingers picked at the young grass by her side. With his face turned toward the valley below, Dan came slowly across the weed-grown yard, unconscious of the presence of the young woman on the knoll. Then he looked in her direction. With her face turned quickly half-aside, she saw him stop suddenly as if halted by the same feeling that had so moved her.

For a full minute he stood there as if questioning his senses. The girl sat very still. Once she thought he would turn back—then he came on eagerly, as he had come that day from the water when he had looked up to see her on the river bank. And then he stood before her as he had stood that other day long weeks ago, with the sunlight on his red-brown hair.

There was now no word of formal greeting. None was needed. Each seemingly knew the travail of soul of the other.

Dropping down on the grass by her side he said quietly, as if it were unnecessary that he should speak at all, "I thought you were in the garden this afternoon."

"And I thought you were in the garden," she returned.

He looked at her in wondering gladness, saying, "I had a caller. After that I could not go."

"And I—I too had a caller; and after that I—I could not go." The words were spoken almost in a whisper. Her trembling fingers were picking again at the short young grass; she was looking far away beyond the sweeping line of blue. One foot had slipped a little from under the protecting shelter of the blue skirt. He saw with a flush of anger that the shoe was very shabby. The skirt, too, showed unmistakable signs of wear. He controlled himself with difficulty, saying, "Your caller was—?"

"Miss Charity Jordan. And yours?"

"Elder Jordan." Dan looked away, and when he spoke again he said bitterly, "Then I suppose you know?"

At his tone and manner she turned her face quickly to his, permitting him for the first time to search her eyes. It was as if she wanted to comfort him, to reassure him.

"Yes!" she said softly, gladly, triumphantly, "Yes, I know!"

Something in her confident reply caused the minister to forget all his half-formed resolutions. His work, his life, the possible outcome, the world itself— were lost in the overpowering rush of the passion-flood that swept his being. His deep voice trembled. "Then you know that I love you—love you!"

He repeated the simple words as if laying his whole self—body, soul and spirit, at her feet.

And the woman, in very wonder at the fullness of the offering, was as one transfixed and could find no word fit to express her acceptance of the gift.

"It is my right to tell you this," he said proudly— defiantly almost, as though challenging some unseen spirit or power. "And it is your right to answer me."

"Yes," she said, "it is our right."

"Then you do care for me, Hope? I am not mistaken—you do?"

"Can you doubt it?" she asked.

He moved quickly toward her but she checked him, and while the love in her eyes answered to the mastering passion in his, she seemed in some subtle manner to build up a protecting wall between them, a wall to guard them both.

"I do not understand," he faltered.

"You must think," she bade him quietly, firmly. "Don't you see that, while it is right for you to tell me what you have, and right for me to tell you how proud—how glad your words have made me, and how

with all my heart and life I—I—love you, this—,"
her voice faltered now, "don't you see that this must
be all?"

"All?" he questioned.

"All," she answered. "Everything that I said to
you the first day that we met here is still true. Don't
you see that I can never, never be more to you than
I am now?"

As one who hears himself sentenced to life-exile
Big Dan dropped his head, burying his face in his
hands.

And seeing him so, such a figure of helpless
strength, the woman's gray eyes filled with tears,
that were not yet permitted to fall. In his presence
she would be strong—afterwards her own heart
should have its way.

Once her hand went out slowly towards the shaggy
red-brown hair, but was silently withdrawn, and the
trembling white fingers again plucked the young
blades of grass.

So they sat, these two—face to face with their
hearts' tragedy, each—for the other's sake—striving
to be strong.

"Tell me," he said at last, raising his head but not
looking her in the face, and speaking in tones that
were strained and hard, "if I were anything else, if
I were engaged in any other work, would you be my
wife?"

"Why do you ask that?"

"Because I must *know*," he answered almost
harshly.

"If you were a common laborer, a business or professional man, if your work was anything honorable and right, save what it is—yes, gladly; oh, how gladly!"

"Then," he burst forth hotly, "I will give up my work. I will be something else!"

"You would give up your ministry for me?" she questioned doubtfully; "your chosen life work?"

His voice sank to a hoarse whisper. "Yes, and if it need be—my religion, my God."

As he finished speaking she laid her hand on his arm. "Hush, oh hush! That is not worthy of you; it is not true to our love. You are beside yourself."

He continued eagerly, "But I have learned that other work is just as holy, just as sacred, as the work of the preacher and the church. You do not know how in the past months I have been teaching this. Why should I not give my life to some of these other ministries?"

"Because it is not some other work that calls you now. These other ministries are not yours," she answered gently. "I have learned to love you because you are so truly yourself, because you are so true to yourself. You must not disappoint me now. And you will not," she continued confidently, "I know that you will not."

At last when he had argued, protested and pleaded until she was so beset by both his passion and her own that she felt her strength going, she said: "Don't, oh please don't! I cannot listen to more of this now. It is not fair to either of us. You must have time to think alone. I believe I know you even better than you know yourself. You must leave me now. You must promise that you will not try to see me again until tomorrow afternoon at this same hour. I will be in the garden with the others until four o'clock, when I will go to the house alone. If then you have decided that you can, with all truthfulness to yourself and me, give up your ministry, come to me and I will be your wife. But whether you come or not you must always believe that I love you, that I shall always love you, as my other self, and that I shall never, never doubt your love for me."

So she sent him away to fight his battle alone, knowing it was the only way such a battle could be rightly fought, and because she wanted him, for his own sake, to have the certainty of a self-won victory, never doubting in her own heart what that victory would be or what it would mean to her. She indeed knew him better than he knew himself.

CHAPTER XXXIV.

SACRIFICED.

"Standing in the midst of these things, so much a part of his chosen life that they seemed a vital part of himself, he heard the voices in the garden."

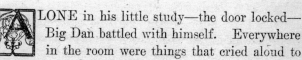

ALONE in his little study—the door locked—Big Dan battled with himself. Everywhere in the room were things that cried aloud to him of his ministry; his library—books of peculiar interest to ministers, papers and pamphlets filled with matters of the church, written for church men, his sermons—one lying half-finished on the study table, the very pictures on the walls and the un-answered letters on his desk. Standing in the midst of these things, so much a part of his chosen life that they seemed a vital part of himself, he heard the voices in the garden. He knew that she was there.

Since the beginning men like Dan Matthews have fought for women like Hope Farwell. For such women such men have committed every crime, en-dured every hardship, braved every danger, made every sacrifice, accomplished every great thing. Few of the race today are strong enough to feel such pas-sion. It was primitive—but it was more. For there had been bred into this man something stronger than his giant physical strength—a spirit, a purpose, fitting such a body.

The little clock on the mantel struck the hour. Softly, slowly, the sweet-toned notes rang out:

One! Two! Three! Four!

With face white and drawn Dan went to the window. All that afternoon, knowing that she was there, he had denied himself even the sight of her. Now he would see her.

He watched as, without a glance toward his window, the young woman left her friends and went slowly into the house. Five—ten—fifteen—twenty minutes! The ticking of the little clock seemed to beat on Dan's brain with sledge-hammer blows.

Then he saw her come out on the front porch of the cottage. Slowly she walked out into the yard, until screened from the street by the big lilac bush. Turning she faced toward his window. She waved a greeting. She even beckoned to him to come. The man swayed and put out his hand to grip the window casing. Again she beckoned him—come. When he did not leave his place and only waved a hand in return, she went slowly back into the house.

Then Dan Matthews, minister—man, staggered back from the window to fall on his knees in prayer.

It was perhaps two hours before sunrise when Dr. Harry's horse stopped suddenly in a dark stretch of timber six miles from town. Dimly the man in the buggy saw a figure coming toward him.

"Hello!" he said sharply; "what do you want?"

The man in the road laughed a strange, hoarse, mirthless laugh, saying as he continued to advance, "I thought it must be you. You nearly ran me down." And Dan climbed in by the physician's side.

The minister made no explanation, nor did his friend, after the first few surprised questions, press him. But when they were turning in towards Dan's gate the big fellow burst forth, "Don't stop, Harry— not here! For God's sake, if you love me, take me on to your house for a little while!"

Then did Dr. Harry guess the truth that later he came to know.

CHAPTER XXXV.

THE TIE THAT BINDS.

"The Ally was there in power. The day of the rack, the thumbscrew and the stake, is long past: in place of these instruments of religious discipline we have—the Ally."

ALL the next day Dan remained at Dr. Harry's home, returning to his own rooms in the evening. Early the following morning he was to take the train for the annual gathering of the denomination, that was to be held in a distant city. He would be away from Corinth three days at least.

The minister's little study, when he had lighted the lamp that night, seemed filled with a spirit that was never there before. It was as if, during his absence, some unseen presence had moved in to share the apartment with him. The very books and papers impressed him as intimate companions, as if, in thus witnessing and—in truth—taking part in the soul-struggle of the man, they had entered into a closer relation to him, a relation sacred and holy. He was conscious, too, of an atmosphere of privacy there that he had never sensed before, and, for the first time in his life, he drew the window shades.

In the battle that Hope Farwell had set for him to fight Dan had sought to be frankly honest with himself, and to judge himself coldly, without regard to the demands of his heart. If he had erred at all it was in an over-sensitiveness to conscience, for conscience has ever been a tricky master, often betraying its too-willing slaves to their own self-injury. It is a large question whether one has a greater right to injure himself than to harm another.

Dan could not admit, even to himself, that he had in any way neglected the church, or fallen short of his duties as a hired shepherd. But after all, was he not to some degree in error in his judgment of his people? Had he not, perhaps, misunderstood the spirit that moved them? He had come to Corinth from his school with the thought fixed in his mind that the church was *all* right. Had he not, by the unexpected and brutal directness of his experience, been swung to the other extreme, conceiving conditions as all wrong?

Groping in the dark of his ministry he had come to feel more and more keenly his inexperience. After all, was he right in taking the hard, seldom-traveled path, or was not the safe way of the church fathers the true way? Was not his failure to put himself in tune with things as he found them, only his own inability to grasp the deeper meanings of those things? He had come to doubt those leaders whom he had been taught to follow, but he had come to doubt more his own ability to lead, or even to find the way for himself. It was this doubt that had led him to decide as Hope Farwell knew he would.

For Big Dan could not turn from the church and his chosen work without the same certainty that had led him to it.

Least of all could he, after that which Hope had

made so clear, go to her with a shadow of doubt in his mind.

His convictions were not, as yet, convincing. His new-born love for the woman bulked too large in his life for him to trust his own motives. So it came that he had chosen at such cost to himself, and—making the greatest sacrifice possible to one of his nature—turned to give himself wholly to that which he still felt to be his ministry.

He looked forward now with eagerness to the gathering of church men to which he was going on the morrow. There he would meet the great leaders of his church, those with life-long experience in the work to which he had given himself; those whose names were household names in the homes of his people. There he would come into touch with the spirit of the church as a whole, not merely the spirit of his own local congregation, and in the deliberations of the convention, in their reports of work accomplished, of conditions throughout the country, and in the plans for work to be done, he would find—he must find—the key that would put him in full harmony with those who were his fellow-workers.

Dan's thoughts were interrupted by a familiar knock at the door. The old Doctor entered.

Of the recently-renewed talk of the community regarding Dan and Hope, and of the growing sentiment of Memorial Church the Doctor knew all that Dan knew—with this more. From long observation he understood, as Dan did not, the real significance of this revival of activities by the Ally, and the part that Judge Strong had in its inspiration. Concerning Dan and Hope he could only conjecture, but the Doctor's conjectures amounted almost to certainties. That the lad so dear to him was passing through some tremendous crisis he knew, for he had talked with Dr. Harry that afternoon. Seeing by the light in the window that Dan had returned, he had run across the way to see if all was well with the boy. It was characteristic of the Doctor that, while he did not make known the object of his visit in words, he made the minister feel his sympathy and interest, and his readiness, as he himself would have said, "to stand by."

Grasping his young friend's hand in greeting and placing his other hand on Dan's shoulder, he studied his face as he would have studied a patient. "Come boy," he said, "don't you think we better go fishing?"

The minister smiled back at him. "I wish I could, Doctor; I need it, all right. But you see there's that convention tomorrow."

"Humph!" grunted the Doctor, as he seated himself. "Heard who's going?"

Dan named a few of his church people. The Doctor grunted again. They were nearly all of the inner circle, the Judge's confidantes in matters of the church.

"Judge Strong is going too," offered the Doctor.

Dan said nothing.

"Uh-huh; told me this evening." The old man chuckled. "I rather thought I'd go myself."

"You!" Dan said in surprise.

The other's eyes twinkled. "Yes, me; why not? I've never been to one of these affairs, but for that matter neither have you. I don't suppose they would put me out. Anyway I have some business in the city and I thought it would be fine for us to go up together. Martha's tickled to death! Thinks I'll get it sure if I can only hear some of the really *big* preachers."

Dan laughed, well-pleased. He could not know of the real motive that prompted the Doctor's strange interest in this great meeting of church men.

The next morning at an early hour they were off: Dan, the old Doctor, some six or eight of the active women leaders of the congregation, Charity, and Judge Strong. The Ally went also. There was no little surprise expressed, in a half-jesting manner, by the company, at the presence of Dr. Oldham, and there was much putting together of heads in whispered consultation as to what it might mean. The Judge and his competent associates, with the Ally, kept very much together and left Dan and his friend as much to themselves. Whenever the young minister, prompted by his thoughts of the last few hours, approached the group there was a significant hush, while his pleasantries were met by very formal, and as evidently forced, monosyllables, which very soon sent him back to his seat again with a face that made the old Doctor say things under his breath.

"Look here, Dan," said the old physician, as they neared their destination, "I understand that at these meetings the visiting delegates are always entertained at the homes of the local church people. I'm not a delegate, so I go to a hotel. You come with me; be my guest. Tell 'em you have already accepted an invitation to stop with a friend. Don't worry, they'll be glad enough to have one less to care for, and I want you."

The young man eagerly accepted.

At the meeting was the usual gathering of the usual types. There were the leaders, regularly appointed by the denomination, who were determined to keep that which had been committed to them, at any cost; and to this end glorified, in the Lord's service, the common, political methods of distributing the places of conspicuous honor and power, upon program and committee, among those friends and favorites who could be depended upon to respond most emphatically, or who were—in the vernacular —"safe." Equally active, with methods as familiar but not equally in evidence—for one must be careful —were the would-be leaders, who—"for the glory of Christ"—sought these same seats of the mighty, and who were assisted by those who aspired to become their friends and favorites—joint heirs in their success should they succeed. Then there were the self-constituted leaders who pushed and pulled and scrambled to the front; content if they could, only for the moment, be thought by the multitude to be something more than they were; who were on their feet instantly to speak upon every question with ponderous weight of words, and were most happy if they could fill some vacant chair on the platform. There were the heresy hunters who sniffed with hound-like eagerness for the scent of doctrinal weakness in the speeches of their brothers; and upon every proposed movement of the body, guarded with bulldog fidelity, the faith of their fathers. There were also the young preachers who came to look with awe on the doings of the great ones, to learn how it was done and to watch for a possible opening whereby they might snatch their bit of glory here on earth.

Many there were of this latter class who, from the highest religious motives, had answered the call to the ministry as to something sacred and holy, even as had Dan. These young men, though they knew it not, were there to learn how their leaders—while theoretically depending upon God for their strength and guidance in managing the affairs of the church—depended actually upon the very methods which, when used by the world in its affairs, they stamped ungodly.

The Ally was there in power. The day of the rack, the thumbscrew and the stake, is long past: in place of these instruments of religious discipline we have—the Ally.

Mostly those on the firing line were ministers, though here and there a prominent woman leader pushed to the front. The rest were brothers and sisters, mainly sisters; who like other mortals, always backed their favorites in the race that was set before them all. These prayed sincerely and devoutly that somehow, in ways beyond their bewildered ken, the good God would bless the efforts that were being made for righteousness and truth, hoping thus for heavenly results from very worldly methods.

Judge Strong was an old campaigner. A heavy contributor to the general work and missionary funds to which the leaders looked for the practical solution of their modest bread and butter problems, he had the ears of them all. Nor was the Elder slow to use his advantage. He could speak his mind with frankness here, for these great men of the church lived far from Corinth and, while knowing much of the Elder—the church man, knew nothing of the Judge —the citizen and neighbor. More than this such reports as the Elder had to make must, in the very nature of things, for the good of the cause, be strictly private.

While the Judge was holding these little confidential chats with the leaders, and the leaders were holding equally confidential chats with their friends and favorites, and these in turn were doing as they had been done by, the Elder's assistants, assigned to various church homes in the city, were confidentially exchanging confidences with their hostesses. And this is the simple truth of the whole matter, and the way it all came about.

Dan was introduced to the secretary. "Ah—yes, Brother Matthews of Corinth! Glad to meet you. Ah, excuse me I—ah, see a brother over there with whom I must speak."

Dan was presented to the treasurer. "Oh yes, I have heard of you—at Corinth. Why, hello, Brother Simpkins"—catching a passing preacher by the arm —"glad to see you! How are you and how is the work?"

Dan introduced himself to one or two of those whom he had hungered to see, those who were noted in the church papers for their broad wisdom and saintly character, and somehow Dan felt rebuked for his forwardness when each, from his pedestal, looked at him and said, "Oh yes; Brother Matthews! I have heard of you, Brother Matthews!"

During the forenoon session of the second day the order of business was reports of the churches. In response to roll call, one after the other, the representatives of the various congregations would tell what they had done and what they were going to do. Dr. Oldham remarked later, "No one told what they had failed to do, or what they were not going to do."

As a rule the ministers reported for their own churches, save when some delegate whom the pastor knew to be peculiarly qualified, was present. Generally speaking the ministers consider the value of such a report to be greatly increased if it can be given by some such member. The minister himself always sees that the report is properly prepared.

Judge Strong, without consulting Dan, responded to the call for the Memorial Church. There was a distinct hush, and heads went forward in interest. The Elder regretted to report that, while they had held their regular services every Sabbath, and their preacher was the most popular preacher in Corinth, the conversions for some reason had not been as numerous as in some previous years. But Memorial Church could be depended upon to remedy that very soon, for they were contemplating a great revival meeting to begin as soon as a competent evangelist could be secured. [Loud applause from the professional evangelists present.] They felt that a series of good old Jerusalem gospel sermons would put them again to the front in the matter of additions. [Loud applause from the defenders of the faith.]

Dan listened in silent amazement. This was the first he had heard of a meeting in Corinth. The Doctor saw the boy's face grow burning red.

The Elder continued his report, touching every department of the church in like vein, and finished by "regretting exceedingly that their offering for the missionary, and for the general work for the present year, had fallen short of previous years." The Judge did not explain that he had subtracted from his part in the church offering an amount exceeding the shortage, which amount he had added to his usual personal subscription. As for the regular expenses of the congregation, he went on, they had been cared for.

"And," remarked the state secretary in a loud voice, rising instantly as the Judge sat down, "I want you all to know that Judge Strong's personal contribution to our funds is larger this year than ever before. We who know Brother Strong's splendid Christian generosity will understand how the regular expenses of Memorial Church have been paid." Whereupon the leaders-who-were and the leaders-who-would-like-to-be joined with one accord in loud applause.

Not a preacher there but understood exactly what the Elder's report signified.

Following the reports of the churches came the introductions of the new pastors. Skilfully the preachers were marshaled upon the platform, Big Dan towering at the foot of the line. Stunned and embarrassed as he was by the Judge's report, the boy would not have gone forward at all, had not the Doctor fairly pushed him into the aisle. The old philosopher told himself grimly that the lad might as well get all that was coming to him. In the ceremony that followed Dan got it.

One after the other the ministers were introduced by the secretary, who had a glowing word for each. "Brother Williams who has done such marvelous work at Baxter." [Loud applause for Brother Williams.] "Brother Hardy who is going to do a wonderful work at Wheeler." [Louder applause for Brother Hardy.] And so on down the line. Not one, from big church or little, from city pulpit or country district, but secured the boosting comment and the applause; for this was Christian enthusiasm.

Dan's turn came at last. His face was now white.

"And this," shouted the secretary, "is Brother Matthews, the present pastor of our church at Corinth." There was a hush still and significant; for this was church policy.

After a moment's silence the secretary continued, "Please sing hymn three-hundred and one:

'Blest be the tie that binds
Our hearts in Christian love.'

Everybody sing!" And the denominational papers agreed that they made a joyful noise unto the Lord.

Were the high officials and their mates on this ship of salvation to be blamed? Not a bit of it! The Elder's report made Dan "unsafe"—and he was. They were right. More than this, the Lord needed the Judge's influence—and money.

When the young minister came back to his seat his old friend thought his face the saddest he had ever seen.

At lunch the Doctor told Dan that he was going to call upon several friends that afternoon, and among them mentioned the superintendent of a famous steel plant in the city. Agreeing to meet at dinner in the evening they parted, Dan going alone to the convention building. At the door he paused.

Several ministers, chatting gaily with friends passing in for the opening of the afternoon session, looked curiously at the stalwart, irresolute figure standing there alone. Two or three greeted him with a word. All were sorry for him; for not one but understood the meaning of the incidents of the morning.

An hour later the superintendent of the great steel works greeted, with admiring eyes, the big clean-looking fellow and wondered at the look of sadness on his face.

"I am in the city with my friend, Dr. Oldham," explained Dan. "I expected to find him here. He told me at lunch that he was coming."

"Oldham in town? Good!" exclaimed the man of affairs. "Of course he would look me up, but he hasn't been here yet. Glad to meet any friend of the Doctor's. Sit down, Mr. Matthews; he'll be in presently, no doubt. Or perhaps while you're waiting, you would care to look about." At Dan's eager reply he touched a bell and, to the man who appeared, he said, "Jack, show Mr. Matthews around. A friend of my friend, Dr. Oldham."

And so the Doctor found the boy standing in the very heart of the great plant, where the brawny workmen, naked to the waist—their bodies shining with sweat and streaked with grime, wrestled with the grim realities of life.

For a little while the Doctor watched him; then, tapping him on the shoulder, shouted in his ear, above the roar of the furnace, the hissing of steam and the crash and clank of iron and steel. "Almost as good as a fishing trip, heh Dan?"

Back in the office again the superintendent introduced them to a gray-haired, smooth faced, portly gentleman—the president of the steel company, a well-known capitalist. The great man repeated Dan's name, looking him over the while.

"Matthews. By your name and your build, sir, you are related to the Grant Matthews who owns Dewey Bald."

"He is my father, sir," returned Dan, delighted.

"Ah yes. Through my interests in the lead and zinc industry, I am familiar with your part of the country, sir. I have met your father several times. It is not easy to forget such a man."

Dan now remembered the president's name, having heard it in connection with the mines on Jake creek, near his home.

The capitalist continued, "I have tried several times to persuade your father to open up that hill of his. He has a fortune in that mountain, sir, a fortune! Are you interested in mining, Mr. Matthews?"

"Not directly, sir."

"No? Well, if your people should ever decide to develop that property come to me; I know what it is. We would be glad to talk it over with you. Good-bye, sir; glad to have met you. Good day, Doctor." And he was gone.

The Doctor and Dan dined with the genial superintendent and his family that evening and the next morning set out for Corinth.

CHAPTER XXXVI.

GOOD-BYE.

"But the big house for Dr. Harry is still empty when he returns from his long drives; empty save for his dreams."

WHEN Hope Farwell dismissed Dan that afternoon in the old Academy yard, because she feared both for her lover and for herself, she had not for a moment questioned what Dan's decision would be. With all the gladness that their love had brought, there was in her heart no hope; for she exacted of herself the same fidelity to her religious convictions that she demanded of Dan. It would be as wrong for her to accept the church as for him to reject it. So she had gone to the limit of her strength for his sake. But when she reached again the privacy of her room, her woman nature had its way. With the morning, strength returned again— strength and calmness. Quietly she went about; for, while she had left the whole burden of decision upon Dan, her heart was with her lover in his fight.

At the appointed hour she left her friends in the garden and went into the house as she had planned. She did not expect him but she had said that she would wait his coming. Her heart beat painfully as the slow minutes passed, bringing by his absence, proof that she had not misjudged him. Then she went outside and looking up saw him standing at his window; smiling, she even beckoned to him. She wished to make the victory certain, final and complete. Very quietly she returned to her room. She did not again enter the garden.

And now the young woman was conscious that she also had a part to do. For every reason she must not remain in Corinth. She explained her plans to Grace, for she could not leave the girl, and the two commenced to make their simple preparations for the journey. Feeling that her strength was not equal to the strain which another meeting with Dan would occasion, there was no one left to bid good-bye save Deborah and Denny and—Dr. Abbott.

Dr. Abbott's faithful Jim was waiting, ready for a long trip into the country, when Miss Farwell reached the physician's home. Harry himself, dressed for the drive, met her at the door.

"You were just answering a call," said the nurse. "I will not keep you, Doctor."

"Not answering a call, just making a visit," he said, "and there is no need at all for me to hurry, Miss Farwell." He led her to the library.

"I came to tell you good-bye," she said. "I could not go away without thanking you, Dr. Abbott, for all your kindness to me."

The strong hands of the physician, so firm and sure in their professional duties, trembled, as the man placed his hat and gloves on the table.

"To tell me 'good-bye,'" he repeated blankly.

"Yes," she answered, "I cannot remain longer in Corinth."

Harry's face flushed.

"Miss Farwell you do not know how sorry I am for my failure to—"

She interrupted, "Please don't Doctor. I know how you have tried," her eyes filled, "and I know all that you have done. You understand it has been for Grace—" she paused. "Grace will go with me. I am sure Dr. Miles will find her a place in the hospital."

"Yes," he said, "I understand. I will—will see you again some day, Miss Farwell."

"I shall never return to Corinth, Doctor," she answered with a shudder. "If you come to the city, though, I shall always be glad to see you." The words were as frank as from one man to another.

Harry was thinking of his friend, the minister, of the meeting in the night, and Dan's plea to be taken to the doctor's home, where he had remained until late the evening before he left for the church convention. Why was she leaving Corinth while Dan was away attending the convention? Did she know that he was gone? What did it all mean? Could it be—! He started from his chair.

"I may see you again, then? You will be glad to see me, Miss Farwell? Hope—tell me, surely you know what I would say! I would have said it long ago but you would not let me. Tell me if there is any chance for me—ever?"

She had risen to her feet and into her face there came a look of tender sadness. She did not turn away, and the man, looking into those gray eyes, knew that she spoke truly when she said, "I am sorry, Dr. Abbott, oh so sorry! No, there can never be, for you more than my regard and friendship." Her voice trembled. "I know how it hurts because for me—for us—too, there is no chance."

Then Harry Abbott understood.

She left him in the library. Outside she paused a moment to bestow a good-bye caress upon the doctor's horse and then she quickly went away.

Other helpers have now taken the place of the faithful old Mam Liz and Uncle George, for these true souls have gone to the Master of all who truly serve. But the big house for Dr. Harry is still empty when he returns from his long drives; empty save for his dreams.

Dr. Harry will never leave Corinth. When the old Doctor berates him roughly for wearing himself out for those who never express their appreciation, and from whom he can never hope to receive a fee, he laughingly retorts in kind, charging the Doctor himself with having consigned to him such unprofitable patients. He will never give up his patients; neither will he give up his dreams.

Miss Farwell's plans for the girl, whose life she had reclaimed, did not fail. Dr. Miles, when he heard her story, gladly helped Grace to a place in the school where she might fit herself for her chosen ministry; for, said the famous physician, "The best nurses in the world are those who have themselves suffered. No amount of professional skill can make up for a lack of human sympathy and love."

As Dan, home from the convention, was turning

wearily in at his gate, Deborah, from the garden, called to him. By her manner as she came slowly to the fence, Dan knew the good soul was troubled.

"It's a heavy heart I have, Mr. Matthews," she said; "for she's clean gone, an' Denny an' me's that lonesome we don't know what to do."

Dan's big hand gripped the fence.

"Gone," he repeated blankly. He did not need to ask who was gone.

"Yes sir, gone—yesterday evenin' be the train, leavin' her kindest regards and best wishes to you."

CHAPTER XXXVII.

RESULTS.

"When he had finished his letter, he bowed his face in his hands and wept."

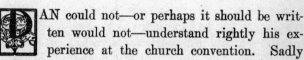AN could not—or perhaps it should be written would not—understand rightly his experience at the church convention. Sadly puzzled and surprised by the spirit and atmosphere of that meeting to which he had gone with such confidence, and sorely hurt by his reception, he had no thought of the real reason for it all. He only blamed himself the more for being so out of harmony—for failing so grievously to find the key that should put him in tune.

In the great steel works among the sweating, toiling men; with the superintendent of the plant, under whose hand men and machinery were made to serve a great world's need; and with the president whose brain and genius was such a power in the financial and industrial world Dan had felt a spirit of kinship. Amid those surroundings he had been as much at home as if he were again in his native hills, and for the hour had forgotten his fellow churchmen and their ministries. But as their train drew nearer and nearer Corinth, the Doctor saw by his companion's face, and by his fits of brooding silence, that the minister was feeling again the weight of his troublesome burden.

By this and by what he had seen at the convention, the old physician knew that the hour in Dan's life for which he watched with such careful, anxious interest, was drawing near.

With Hope gone out of his life he turned to his work with grim, desperate, determination. What, indeed, had he now to which he might turn but his work? He realized that now he must find in this work for which he had made the supreme sacrifice of his life, the only thing that would, to him, justify his choice—the choice that had cost both him and the woman he loved so much suffering. His ministry had now become something more to him than a chosen life work. To those high motives that had led him to the service of the church, he added now the price he had paid in giving up the woman who had grown so much into his life. He *must* find that in his ministry which would make the great price paid, not in vain.

So, with all the strength of his great nature, he threw himself with feverish energy into what had, in spite of himself, come to be a too-empty ministry. Crushing every feeling of being misunderstood, and unjustly criticized; permitting himself no thought that there were under the surface treacherous currents working for his overthrow; blaming himself always and others never, when he felt a lack of warmth or sympathy in his people; yielding for the time even his own conviction as to his teaching, and striving to shape his sermons to the established lines of the Elders, he fought to put himself into his work.

And always, at the beck and call of Dan's real masters, that other servant of the church—that spirit that lives in Corinth—wrought the will of those whose ally it is.

That last meeting of Dan and Hope in the Academy yard, as if by appointment; the sudden departure of the nurse so soon after; and Dan's too-evident state of mind, were all skilfully used to give color to the ugly whispered reasons for the nurse's leaving town so hurriedly.

The old Doctor knowing, watching, waited for the hour he knew would come; understanding Dan as he had always understood him; wisely recognizing the uselessness of doing aught but let him go his own strong, hard, way. And Dr. Harry also, knowing the malignant power that was forcing the end, and conscious what the end would be, watched silently, hopelessly, helplessly, as many a time he had watched the grim drawing near of that one whose certain coming his professional knowledge enabled him to recognize, while giving him no power to stay.

Memorial Church was all astir, and on the tiptoe of expectancy, preparing—they said—for the greatest revival ever held in Corinth. The professional evangelist selected by the Elder, whose choice was, as a matter of course, approved by his fellow officials and congregation, had sent full instructions for the proper advertising of himself, and—as his instructions stated—"the working up of the meeting." Dan ignoring the slight to himself in the matter of calling the evangelist, did everything in his power to carry out his part of the instructions.

The evangelist arrived. Royally received by the Elders and the inner circle, he was escorted in triumph to the Strong mansion, which was to be his home during the meeting, and within the hour began his professional duty of "setting the church in order, and gathering a mighty harvest of souls."

This evangelist was a good one, of his kind. His kind is that type of professional soul-winner evolved by the system whereby the church pays for the increase of its flock at so much per head, inasmuch as the number of his calls, and the amount of his hire depend upon the number of additions per meeting to the evangelist's credit. A soul-winner with small meetings to his credit receives a very modest compensation for his services, and short notices in the church papers. But the big fellows—those who have hundreds of souls per meeting, come higher, much higher; also they have more space given them in the papers, which helps them to come higher still. Souls may have depreciated in value since Calvary, but one thing is sure, the price of soul-winners has gone away up since the days of Paul and his fellow ministers.

Preaching every night and conducting afternoon meetings, calling at the homes of the people, directing the efforts of the members of the inner circle, sometimes with Dan—oftener without him—fully informed and instructed by the Judge, whose guest he was and to whom he looked for a larger part of his generous salary, the evangelist made himself no small power in the church of Corinth. Assisted always by the skill and strength of the Ally, the effectiveness of his work from the standpoint of Elder Strong and the inner circle at least, was assured.

That was a great meeting; a mighty revival, far reaching in its influence and results! So the denominational papers had it from Judge Strong's report, written while the services were still in progress, and edited by the evangelist. And the papers published a greater truth than they knew. There were influences of which they were ignorant, and the results reached ends they dreamed not of.

Night after night—Dan heard the evangelist with harsh words and startling roughness of expression, declare the awful, eternal disaster that would befall every soul that did not accept the peculiar brand of salvation which he and his church alone offered. He listened to the long arguments planned to prove the rightness, and therefore righteousness, of the evangelist himself and his denominational way, and the equal wrongness, and therefore unrighteousness, of every other minister and church not of his way. Then as he heard these utterances most emphatically and enthusiastically indorsed by his Elders and people as the old Jerusalem gospel, the conviction grew upon him that his preaching would never be acceptable to Memorial Church.

And what place is there in the scheme of things as they are for the unacceptable preaching of any gospel? What gospel can a preacher deliver in order to be acceptable to his peculiar church save that church's peculiar gospel? Dan was not one to ask the oft repeated question of the ministry, "What must I preach in order that I may be saved?"

In the semi-secret workers meetings; in the still more private planning of the committees; in the jubilant reports of the uneasiness of the other churches; and in the satisfying accounts of the awakened opposition and answering sermons of the other preachers; in the evidence of the general stirring up of the community; and in the schemes for further advertising and boosting the evangelist and the cause, Dan felt himself growing ever more and more out of harmony—felt himself more and more alone.

In those days the sadness of his face grew fixed; his color lost its healthy freshness; strange lines, that did not belong to his young manhood, appeared; and the brown eyes that were wont to look at you so openly, hopefully, expectantly, with laughter half-hidden in their depths, were now doubting, questioning, fearful, full of pain.

The Doctor saw, and silently "stood by." Dr. Harry saw and wished that it was all over.

Then came a letter from the officials of the Chicago church of which Dr. Miles was a member. The letter asked if Dan would consider a call to that congregation. Again and again Dan read the letter. What should he do? He could not stay in Corinth. The sense of failure haunted him, while he was unable to fix upon the reason for it. He condemned himself for committing unknown offenses. Could he honestly go to another church? How should he answer the letter? He could not answer it at once—perhaps in a few days!

While he hesitated the meeting drew to its triumphant close. After one last, mighty, farewell effort, the evangelist departed to some other grand harvest of souls, to some other church that needed "setting in order." His work was well done! So well done that he was justified, perhaps, in making another substantial increase in his stated weekly "terms."

That night when the farewell meeting was over, and the last "good-bye" and "God bless you" had been said to the evangelist, Dan stood alone in his study, by the window that looked out upon Denny's garden. He was very tired. Never before in his life had he known such weariness. He felt that in the past few weeks he had neglected the garden down there. For Denny and Deborah he had planned that the little plot of ground should be more profitable that year than it had ever been before. He would not neglect it longer. There at least were visible, actual returns for his labor. Tomorrow he would spend in the garden.

But to-night—

Seating himself at his writing table he wrote the Chicago church that he could not consider their call. And then in that little room where he had made for his ministry the supreme sacrifice of his life; surrounded by the silent witnesses of his struggle and victory, he penned his resignation as the pastor of Memorial Church.

Dan Matthews will never outlive the suffering of that hour. He had lost the woman he loved with all the might of his strong passionate manhood. When she had waited and beckoned him to come, he had chosen his ministry. And now—God pity him!—now he had lost that for which he had sacrificed both himself and the woman he loved.

When he had finished his letter, he bowed his face in his hands and wept.

CHAPTER XXXVIII.

A HANDFUL OF GOLD.

" 'I fear it is more his church than mine, sir.' "

ISING early the next morning Dan looked from his window to see a stranger already at work in the garden. He was tall, raw-boned, having the figure and dress of a laborer. A few minutes later Dan was introduced by the delighted Deborah to her brother Mike McGowan, who had arrived the afternoon before from somewhere in the west. All the morning the two men worked side by side with crippled Denny.

Returning to his self-appointed task in the afternoon, Dan was met by the brawny Irishman who in a towering rage, was just leaving the house.

"Parson," he roared, " 'tis a good man ye are, if ye be only a protestant preacher—a damn good man sir, beggin' your pardon! But you've got a danged poor kind of a boss, thot'll be lookin' more like he ought to when I git through with him."

"Why, what's the matter?" asked Dan stopping with his back to the gate, thus blocking the way, for he saw that the stranger was bent on violence to someone. "Whom do you mean, by my boss?"

"Who do I mane? And who should I mane, but him that runs the thing yonder they call a church, beggin' your pardon, sir. 'Tis the Elder, as you

319

call him—Judge Strong. I'll judge him, if I can coax him widin reach of my two hands." He shook his huge, hairy fists in the air. "It's not strong but wake he'll be when I git through wid him. Leave me pass, if you please, sir."

Dan held his place. "Come, come McGowan," he said, "let's go into the house and you tell me about this."

Deborah, who with Denny was standing in the doorway, called out to them, "That's right Mr. Matthews. Come on in Mike, and talk it over quiet like; let the minister tell ye what to do. It's him that'll save us a sight o' trouble that nobody wants. Come in sir! Come on Mike, come with the minister."

The wrathful Irishman hesitated. Dan laid a hand on his arm and together they went into the cottage.

" 'Twas this way sir," said McGowan, "I was sayin' to Debby and Denny here at dinner what a danged fine man I took ye for after workin' wid ye all mornin' in the garden, an' then she up an' tells me 'bout you fixin' up the mortgage fer them an' how they niver could find out how you fixed it with the Judge. 'The mortgage' says I, 'what mortgage is that, Debby?' 'The mortgage on the place, of course,' says she. 'Don't you mind, I was tellin' you 'bout it when ye was here before?' 'Do I mind' says I, 'I should think I did,' and wid that it all come out sir, and this is the way of it.

"When I come from Colorado that time Jack was killed I found Debby here, widout even money enough to pay for a mass, to say nothin' of the buryin', bein' as they had put iverythin' into the little place here, d'ye see? Well I had a run o' luck the week before, which is neither here nor there, but I had money. I knowed from experience that it wouldn't shtay by me long anyway, an' so I thought I'd kinda fix things up fer Debby an' the kid here, while I could, d'ye see?

"Well when 'twas all over, I paid the undertaker's bills an' iverythin' like that, an' then the very day I left I went to that damn thief, beggin' your pardon, an' paid off that mortgage in good, hard cash. Explainin' to him, d'ye see, that I wanted the papers all fixed up straight and clear and turned over to Debby here, as a kind of a surprise, d'ye see, after I was gone an' she would be feelin' down-hearted bein' left by her man and me besides. The Judge bein', as I knew, the main guy in the big church, I niver thought but that'd be all right, d'ye see? Well sir, I went away that very day as tickled as a boy over the thing an' niver thought nothin' about not gettin' a letter about it from her, 'cause ye see wid me on the move so, most of the letters I git from Debby niver find me at all. An' here she's tillin' me now that she's niver heard nothin' 'bout it from the Judge an' she's been payin' the interest right along, an' would a been turned out by him if it han't a bin fer you, sir. An' me wid no writin' nor nothin' to show for the good money I paid him. Now, ain't that a hell of a thing, sir? What kin I do save bate the face off him onless he fixes it up right an' gives back ivery cint he's had off her besides?"

As he listened to the Irishman's story, the new,

drawn lines in Dan's face deepened. He sat with bowed head as though he himself were being charged with theft. When the tale was finished there was silence in the little room for several minutes. Then Dan raised his head and the others saw that in his eyes, as though he had received a mortal hurt.

"Tell me, Mr. McGowan," he said. "Are you sure there is not some mistake somewhere? It is very hard for me to believe, that an Elder of the church—would—" his voice broke.

The Irishman's rough tones were softened as he answered, "An' how could there be any mistake, sir, wid me givin' him the hard cash out of me own pocket after his tellin' me how much it was, an' his promise to fix it up all right fer Debby when I'd explained the surprise I'd meant fer her?"

"You paid him the money, you say?"

"That I did sir—gold. Ye see I happened to have that draft—jest a thousand an' I turned it in here at the bank. I remember how the feller at the winder tried to make me take thim dirty bills an' I would not, as neither would you if you lived as long in the west as I have, sir, an' got used to the good, clean gold. 'It's the gold or nothin' I'll have' says I to him, 'clean money to pay a clean debt' an' we had some words over it—his bein' on the other side o' the winder, ye see, where he could talk to me. An even eight hundred and fifty I gave the Judge, one hundred and forty I paid the undertaker and the other tin I gave to Denny here as I was leavin'. The priest I paid out of some I had in me belt."

"Come," said Dan, "we must go to the bank."

In the rear room of the little country bank, Dan introduced the Irishman to the cashier, Colonel Dunwood.

"I think I have met Mr. McGowan before," said the Colonel with a smile. "Mrs. Mulhall's brother are you not? You were here when Jack was killed."

"I was, sir. Glad to meet you again, sir."

"Do you remember cashing a draft for Mr. McGowan, Colonel?" asked Dan.

The banker laughed heartily. "I should say I did—a thousand dollars in gold. I was glad the counter was between us, when I tried to persuade him to take paper. Why sir, not in twenty years in this state would you find a man who would even accept the gold, let alone fighting for it!"

Then Dan explained briefly the situation.

When he had finished the Colonel sprang to his feet with an oath. "And that explains something that puzzled us here in the bank, for many a day. Wait a minute."

He left the room to return with a slip of paper. "Can you tell me the exact date on which you cashed the draft?" he said to McGowan.

"It was the day after the funeral. I disremember the date, but 'twould be easy to find."

The banker nodded, "Our books show that I paid you the money the sixteenth. And here," he laid the slip of paper before them, "is a deposit slip made out and signed by Judge Strong dated the seventeenth, showing that on that date he deposited eight hundred and fifty dollars in gold. That is what puzzled us, Mr. Matthews—that the Judge should deposit that amount of gold, there being, you see so little gold handled here. It makes it very easy to trace. I'll illustrate." He turned to Mike. "Did you spend any more of the gold in Corinth?"

McGowan told him about paying the undertaker. After a moment the Colonel triumphantly laid before them a deposit slip made out by the undertaker dated a day later, showing an item of one hundred and forty dollars in gold.

"You see," he said, "how easy it is."

"Colonel Dunwood," said Dan, "would this be sufficient evidence before a jury to—" He hesitated.

The Colonel let fly another oath, "Yes sir, and before any jury you could get together in this county it wouldn't take half this to send that damned, long-faced, sniveling, hypocrite where he belongs. He is one of our best customers, too, but I reckon this bank can get along without his dirty money. I beg your pardon, sir; I forgot he is an Elder in your church."

Dan smiled sadly, "I fear it is more his church than mine, sir." And they left the banker to puzzle over the minister's remark.

That evening Dan went again to the home of Judge Strong. He had persuaded McGowan to let him act in the matter, for he feared that the Irishman's temper would complicate things and make it more difficult to secure Deborah's rights by creating some feeling in the community against the little family.

Dan found the Judge in his library. Very quietly, sadly indeed, he told the story. The Elder, righteously indignant, stormed at the minister, denying everything; accusing Dan of being an impudent meddler; threatening him with dismissal from the church and the denomination; accusing him even, with unlawful interest in the affairs of the widow, and taunting him with the common reports as to his relations with Miss Farwell and her companion.

Dan with a look of sadness growing deeper on his face listened, without a word until the final insinuation; then he checked the other sharply, and his voice had the ring of metal in it as he said slowly, "Judge Strong you shall answer to me later for this insult to these good women. Just now you will not mention them again. I am here in the interests of Mr. McGowan. Confine your remarks to that subject."

Then he laid before the Judge the evidence he had obtained at the bank and pointed out its damaging strength. The man was frightened now, but still he obstinately denied having received any money in payment of the mortgage. Dan pleaded with him, urging even the cause of the church, telling also how McGowan had agreed to do nothing further if the Judge would simply make restitution.

The Judge answered arrogantly that he had been a faithful member, and an Elder in the Memorial Church, too long to be harmed by the charges of a stranger, a wandering ruffian, who had nothing but his word to show that he had paid him a sum of money. "And as for you, young man," he added, "I may as well tell you now that your time is about up in Corinth, and I'll take mighty good care that you don't get another church in our brotherhood either. I'll show you that preachers get along better when they attend to their own affairs."

Dan's final words, as he stood by the door, were, "I cannot believe Judge Strong, that you will force my friends to take this matter into the courts. But we will certainly do so if I do not receive from you by tomorrow noon the proper papers and a check for every cent you have taken from Mrs. Mulhall."

Until late in the night after Dan's departure, Judge Strong still sat at his desk, deep in thought. Occasionally he rose to walk the floor.

When the Judge had received that money from McGowan he had had no thought but regret at losing the property he coveted. With Deborah and Denny left alone in the world, he knew that in time the place would be sure to come to him. He had only to wait. This wild Irish brick-layer—and who knows what beside—who was he to block the Elder's plans with his handful of gold?

The gold! How well the Judge remembered that day, and how when Mike was gone, he had sat contemplating the shining pieces! What a fool the man was to carry such stuff on his person! The careful Judge never dreamed that the money had come from his own bank. The Irishman was going away on the morrow. Planning gleefully to surprise his sister, he had told no one. He would wander far. It would be years before he would return, if he ever came back. By that time the property would be—

It was seemingly all too easy. The Judge's character was not a character to resist such an opportunity. The gold alone perhaps would not have won, but the gold and the place—the place he had planned for and felt so certain of owning—that was too much!

And now this big sad-faced preacher—the Irishman again, and the bank! The more the Judge thought over Dan's quiet words, the more he saw the danger.

So it came about, that the next morning Dan, waiting in his study, received a visitor—the good old Elder—Nathaniel Jordan.

CHAPTER XXXIX.

THE VICTORY OF THE ALLY.

"So the old Doctor found him in the late afternoon—his great strength shaken by rage and doubt; found him struggling like a beast in the trap."

NATHANIEL was greatly agitated as he faced the minister in the doorway. He moved unsteadily across the room, stumbling toward the chair Dan offered, and his hand shook so violently that his cane rattled against the window ledge, where he attempted to lay it—rattled and fell to the floor. He jumped in his seat at the sound. Dan picked up the cane and placed it on the table. Then the Elder found his voice—thin and trembling —and said, "I came about—about Brother Strong, you know."

"Yes," said Dan, a great pity for this good old man in his heart. "Did Judge Strong send anything?"

The Elder fumbled in his pocket and drew out an envelope. He extended it with shaking fingers to Dan, who opened it and examined the contents. Slowly he replaced them in the envelope and, looking at his visitor, waited.

Again the Elder found his voice and said with a little more self-control, "A bad business, Brother Matthews; too bad, too bad; poor Brother Strong!"

He shook his head sadly. Dan looked at him curiously, but made no reply.

"Poor Brother Strong," the Elder repeated. "Brother Matthews, I want to ask you to use your influence with these people to keep this sad affair from getting out. Do you think they will insist on —ah, on bringing action against Brother Strong now—now that he has—ah, complied with your request?"

"And why," asked Dan, "should you wish the matter kept secret?"

The Elder gazed at him blankly. "Why? Why, on account of the church, of course. Judge Strong is one of our leading members—an Elder. He has been for years. It would ruin us—ruin us!"

"But," said Dan coolly, "he is a thief. You must know that he stole this money. Here—," he stretched forth his hand, holding the envelope, "here is his confession of guilt."

The Elder's voice trembled again. "Brother Matthews! Brother Matthews! I—I protest! Such language, applied to an Elder is unchristian; you know the scripture?"

"Is it not true?" persisted Dan.

"Ahem! Brother Strong may have made a mistake, may—ah, have done wrong, but the church— the church; we must think of the good name of the cause! Coming so soon after the revival, too!"

"Am I to understand, then, that the church will keep this man in his place as an Elder; that you will protect him when you know his true character?"

At the question the other stared blankly. "Why—why how could we get along without him?"

"How can you get along with him?" asked Dan.

"But there isn't a man in Corinth who has done so much for us and for the missionary cause! No, no, we must be more careful, Brother Matthews."

"Then for the sake of his contributions and his position in the community the church will shield him from the results of his crime?"

The Elder squirmed uneasily in his chair.

"Is that what you mean?" insisted Dan.

"Why—I—I don't think, Brother Matthews, for the good of our cause in Corinth, that it would be good policy to make this matter public and so create a great stir. Brother Strong has made restitution. We must be charitable, brother, and forgiving. You must not think too—too hard of him. Are these people determined to push this matter?"

"Oh, no," said Dan, "not at all. They want only that which belongs to them. You may rest easy; as I told the Judge last night, this will end the matter. It was under that promise that he made restitution, as you call it. I was simply asking to know how the church would look upon such a thing when it touches an Elder. You have explained it clearly —*policy!*"

The Elder stiffened. It was remarkable how quickly he revived under Dan's assurance that the danger was past! Very dignified now, as became one in his position, he said, "Ahem, ahem! I fear, Brother Matthews, that you are not—ah—not entirely in harmony with our brotherhood in many things."

Dan was silent.

"Ahem! The tone of your sermons has been I may say—ah, questioned by a good many of us, and your attitude toward the board has not been quite as cordial as we feel we have a right to expect."

"Do you speak from personal experience, sir?"

"Oh, no—no indeed, Brother Matthews; but—ah, Brother Strong has felt for some time past that you have treated him rather coldly."

Dan waited.

"A lack of harmony between a pastor and his Elder is very bad—ah, very bad. Ahem! Ahem! And so, considering everything we—Brother Str— that is the board have thought best that your relations with the Memorial Church should discontinue."

"And when was this action taken?" asked Dan quietly.

"The day before the meetings closed. We wished to have the benefit of Brother Sigman's advice before he left. He met with us and we considered the whole matter quite carefully and prayerfully. I was appointed to tell you. I should add that there is no doubt but the people will concur in the board's decision. Many of the members, I may say, were seen before we took action."

Dan glanced toward his desk where, in the envelopes, lay his resignation and his answer to the Chicago church. In the excitement of McGowan's trouble he had neglected to mail them.

"Of course," he questioned, quietly curious now, "the board will give me a letter?"

"Ahem! We—ah, discussed that also," said the Elder. "Brother Strong and the Evangelist—and, I may say, the entire board feel that we cannot consistently do so."

"May I ask why?"

"Ahem! Your teaching, Brother Matthews, does not seem to be in harmony with the brotherhood. We cannot endorse it, and the talk in the community about your conduct has been very damaging; very!"

"Is it charged that my teaching has been false to the principles of Christianity as taught by Christ?"

"I cannot discuss that part, Brother Matthews. It is not such teaching as the churches of our brotherhood want."

"Does the church, sir, believe that my character is bad?"

"No, sir—no, sir! No one really believes that, but you have been—ah, injudicious. There has been so much talk, you know—"

"Who has talked?" Dan interrupted.

The Elder continued, "These things follow a minister all his life. We cannot recommend a man of bad repute to our sister churches; it would reflect upon us."

"For the same reason that you keep in a high office in the church a man who is an unrepentant thief?" said Dan.

The Elder rose. "Really, Brother Matthews, I cannot listen to such words about our Elder!"

"I beg your pardon, sir," said Dan huskily. "I

was thinking aloud. Please tell me one thing more. I have here a letter from a church in Chicago asking me to consider a call. Have the Elders received a letter from them?"

"Ahem! Yes, we considered it at that same meeting."

"And you have written them?"

"We could not recommend you. I am sorry, Brother Matthews."

"I believe you are," said Dan slowly. "Thank you."

When the Elder was gone Dan turned sadly back to his little study; the study that had come to stand so for everything to which he had devoted his life with such holy purpose, for which he had sacrificed so much.

Slowly he went to his desk and looked down upon the work scattered over it. Taking up the two letters he tore them slowly into fragments and dropped them into the waste basket. Then as slowly he turned to his books, touching many of the familiar volumes with a caressing hand. Then he went to the table where lay his church papers and the missionary pamphlets and reports. The envelope from Judge Strong caught his eye.

Mechanically he took his hat and went to carry the message to his friends on the other side of the garden. From across the street the old Doctor hailed him but he did not hear.

Delivering the envelope, with a few brief words, the minister left his friends and wandered on down the street in a bewildered, dazed fashion, scarce knowing where he went, or why; until he turned in through the gap in the tumble-down fence to the old Academy yard.

But he could not stay there. The place was haunted, he could not stay! He turned his face toward the open country, but the fields and woodlands had no call for him that day. It was his little study that called; his books, his work.

As one goes to sit beside the body of a dear friend, conscious that the friend he loved is not there, yet unable to leave the form wherein the spirit had lived, so Dan went back to his room, his desk, his books, his papers—that which had been his work.

And now the deep passions of the man stirred themselves—awoke. Wild anger, mad rage, seized and shook him. His whole sense of justice was outraged. This was not Christianity, this thing that had caught him in its foul snare. And if the church was not Christian what was Christianity? Was there, indeed, such a thing? Was it all such a hollow mockery?

So the Doctor found him in the late afternoon— his great strength shaken by rage and doubt; found him struggling like a beast in the trap.

And the Doctor saw that the hour for which he had waited had come.

Dan needed him—needed him badly!

CHAPTER XL.

THE DOCTOR'S GLASSES.

"'There is no hatred, lad, so bitter as that hatred born of
a religious love; no falsehood so vile as the lie spoken in
defense of truth; no wrong so harmful as the wrong committed in the name of righteousness; no injustice so terrible
as the injustice of those who condemn in the name of the
Saviour of the world!'"

WHEN Dan, forced into something of his
habitual self-control and calmness by the
presence of his old friend, began telling the
Doctor of the action of the church the other checked
him abruptly with, "I know all about that, lad."

"You know!" ejaculated Dan.

"Certainly I know. Isn't Martha one of the elect?
I reckon everybody in the whole town but you knew
it before noon of the day after the meeting."

Dan muttered something about being a blind fool
and the old Doctor answered, "Humph! The fools
are they who see too much, boy. Such blindness as
yours is a gift of the gods; for Heaven's sake don't
let any quack fit you out with glasses!"

Dan threw himself wearily into a chair and there
was a spirit of recklessness in his reply, as though he
were letting go of himself again. "How is a blind
man to recognize a quack? I would to God I had
your glasses!"

"Perhaps," said the Doctor deliberately, "I might lend them to you, just for once, you know."

"Well then," said the other, sitting up suddenly, "let me have them! How do you see this thing? What have I done or not done? For what shall I blame myself? What fatal error have I made that, with the best of motives, with the—," he hesitated, then—"I can say it to you, Doctor, and I will—with the sacrifice of the dearest thing in the world to me, I am cast out in this fashion? If I can find a reason for it, I can bear it."

"It is your blindness, boy. You could not help it; you were born blind. I have always known this would come."

"You have always known this would come?" repeated Dan questioningly.

"Yes, I have always known, because for half a century, boy, I have observed the spirit of this institution. Mind, I do not say the spirit of the people in the institution. Strong people, Dan, sometimes manage to live in mighty sickly climates. The best people in the world are sometimes held by evil circumstances which their own best intentions have created. The people in the church are the salt of the earth. If it were not for their goodness the system would have rotted long ago. The church, for all its talk, doesn't save the people; the people save the church. And let me tell you, Dan, the very ones in the church who have done the things you have seen and felt, at heart respect and believe in you."

Dan broke forth in such a laugh as the Doctor had never heard from his lips. "Then why?"

"Because," said the old man, "it is their religion to worship an institution, not a God; to serve a system, not the race. It is history, my boy. Every reformation begins with the persecution of the reformer and ends with the followers of that reformer persecuting those who would lead them another step toward freedom. Misguided religious people have always crucified their saviors and always will!"

Dan was silent, awed by the revelation of his old friend's mind. Presently the Doctor continued, "There is no hatred, lad, so bitter as that hatred born of a religious love; no falsehood so vile as the lie spoken in defense of truth; no wrong so harmful as the wrong committed in the name of righteousness; no injustice so terrible as the injustice of those who condemn in the name of the Saviour of the world!"

"What then, as you see it—what can I do?" demanded Dan.

The Doctor changed his tone. His reply was more a question than an answer. "There are other churches?"

Dan laughed bitterly. "They have taken care of that, too." He began to tell of the call to Chicago and the Elders' refusal to give him a letter, but again the Doctor interrupted him. "Yes, I know about that, too."

"Well," demanded Dan almost angrily.

"Well," answered the other easily, "there are still other churches."

"You mean—."

"I mean that you are not the only preacher who

337

has been talked about by his church, and branded by his official board with the mark of the devil in the name of the Lord. It's easy enough! Go farther, get a little obscure congregation somewhere, stay long enough to get a letter, not long enough to make another name; try another in the same fashion. Lay low, keep quiet, stay away from conventions, watch your chance, and—when the time is ripe—make a hit with the state workers in some other state. You know how! It's all easy enough!"

Dan leaped to his feet. "Good God, Doctor! I have done nothing wrong. Why should I skulk, and hide, and scheme to conceal something I never did, for the privilege of serving a church that doesn't want me? Is this the ministry?"

"It seems to be a large part of it," answered the other deliberately. "My boy, it's the things that preachers have not done that they try hardest to hide. As to why, I must confess that I am a little near-sighted myself sometimes."

"I can't, I can't do it, Doctor!"

"Humph! I didn't suppose you could," came dryly from the old man.

Dan did not heed but went on in a hopeless tone to tell the Doctor how he had written his resignation, and had declined to consider the call to Chicago. "Don't you see that I couldn't take a church if one were offered me now?" he asked. "Don't you understand what this has done for me? It's not the false charges. It's not that! It's—it's the thing, whatever it is, that has made this action of the church possible. I am forced to doubt, not alone the church, but everything—the people, myself, God, Christ, Christianity, life itself; everything! How can I go on with a work, in which I cannot say to myself with truth that I believe?" His voice ended in a groan.

And the old man, who knew the lad so well felt as though he were gazing upon the big, naked soul. Then, indeed, the Doctor knew that the hour had come.

There are those who, capable of giving but little to life, demand of life much in return. To such weak natures doubt means not much. But souls like this one, capable of giving themselves to the last atom of their strength, demand no small returns in convictions as to the worthiness of the cause to which they contribute. To such, doubt is destruction. It was because Dan had believed so strongly, so wholly in the ministry of the church that he had failed. Had he not accepted so unreservedly, and given himself so completely to the ministry as it was presented to him in theory, had he in some degree doubted, he would have been able to adjust himself to the actual conditions. He would have succeeded.

For while, theoretically, the strength of the church is in its fidelity to the things in which it professes to believe; practically and actually the strength of the church of today is in its tacit acceptance of its unbeliefs. Strange things would befall us if we should ever get the habit of insisting that our practice square with our preaching; if churches should make this the test of fellowship—that men must live their doctrines, rather than teach them—that they must live their beliefs rather than confess them —that they must live their faiths, rather than profess them.

Dan's was not a nature that could preach things in which he only half believed to a people whose belief he knew to be no stronger than his own. It was with these things in mind that the Doctor had waited for this moment in Dan's life, for the old man realized, as the young man could not, what such moments mean.

Rising and going to the window overlooking the garden the Doctor called to Dan, "Come here, boy!"

Together they stood looking down on the little plot of ground with its growing vegetables, where Denny, with his helpless, swinging arm, and twisted, dragging foot, was digging away, his cheery whistle floating up to them. The physician spoke with a depth of feeling he had never betrayed before, while Dan, troubled as he was, listened in wonder to his friend, who had always been so reticent in matters such as this.

"Dan," he said, "you wished for my glasses. 'Tis always a mighty dangerous thing to try to see through another man's eyes, but here are mine." He pointed below.

"Down there I see religion—Christianity—what you will, but religion; living, growing, ever-changing, through the season-ages; lying dormant sometimes, it may be, but always there; yielding to each season the things that belong to that season; depending for its strength and power upon the Great Source of all strength and power; depending as truly upon man's efforts, upon his cultivation and care. There is variety, harmony, law, freedom. There is God! Something for all—potatoes, peas, turnips, cabbage. If you do not care for lettuce, perhaps radishes will satisfy. And there, boy, in the midst of his church, ministering to the needs of his congregation, and thus ministering to men—is my minister: crippled, patient Denny, who gives his frail strength to keep the garden growing.

"And look you, boy, at the great rock in the very center of the field! How often Denny has wished it out of his way! I caught the poor lad digging, one time, to find, if he could, how deep it is in the earth, and how big. For three days I watched him. Then he gave it up. It is beyond his strength and he wisely turned to devote his energies to the productive soil around it.

"There is a rock in every garden, Dan. Religion grows always about the unknowable. But Denny's ministry has naught to do with the rock, it has to do with the growing things about it. So religion is in the knowable things not in the unknowable; there such men as you, lad, must find it. And the rock, boy, was not put in the garden by men. It belongs to the earth itself."

While the Doctor was speaking his eyes had been fixed on the crippled boy in the garden. He turned now, for the first time, to face the young man by his side. Dan's eyes had that wide, questioning look. The old physician moved to the other window.

"Now come, see what men have done." He pointed to the cast-iron monument. "These people will tell you that was erected to commemorate the life of my friend. His was a warm, tender, loving spirit—a great, ever-growing soul. What can that hard, cold, immovable mass tell of him? How can that thing—perpetuating an issue that belongs to a past age, that has nothing to do with the life of today—how can that thing speak of the great heart that loved and gave itself always to men?

"Through my glasses that is the church? How can an institution, or a system of theological beliefs —with cast-iron prejudices, cast-iron fidelity to issues long past and forgotten, cast-iron unconcern of vital issues of the life of today and cast-iron want of sympathy with the living who toil and fight and die on every side—how can such speak the great loving, sympathetic, helpful spirit of Him whose name only it bears, as that bears only the name of my friend?

"But would the people of this town, out of love for my dead friend, tear down that monument if Denny should leave his garden to argue with them about it? Why, they would tell him that it is because of their love for the statesman that they keep it there and they believe it—and it is true. Well, then, let them keep their monument and let Denny work in his garden! And don't you see, Dan, that the very ones who fight for the cast-iron monument must depend at last for their lives and strength upon the things that Denny grows in his garden. Now boy, that's the first and only time I ever preached."

CHAPTER XLI.

THE FINAL WORD.

"'This closes my ministry as you understand it. It by no means closes my ministry as I have come to understand it.'"

DAN'S farewell sermon was to be given in the evening. John Gardner, who—true to the promise he had made when he challenged the minister, after that sermon on "Fellowship of Service"—had become a regular attendant, was present in the morning.

In the afternoon the farmer called on Dan in his study.

"Look here, Dan," he said. "You are making the mistake of your life."

"You're wrong, John. I made that mistake nearly two years ago," he answered.

"I mean in leaving Corinth as you are leaving it."

"And I mean in coming to Corinth as I came to it."

"But wait a minute; let me tell you! You have done a lot of good in this town; you don't know——."

"So have you done a lot of good, John; you don't know either."

The farmer tried again. "You have helped me more than you know."

"I'm glad, John, because you have helped me more than *you* know."

343

"Oh, come; you know what I mean!"

"Well, don't you know what I mean?"

"Yes, I think I do. I've been listening pretty close to your sermons and so have a lot of others. I have managed to talk with a good many church people since it was known that you were going; just common plugs in the congregation, like me, you know." Dan smiled. "We all understand what you have been driving at in your preaching, and we know pretty well what the bosses think about it, and why they have let you out. No one takes any stock in that foul gossip, not even Strong himself. Now what I came to say is this: a lot of us want you to stay. Why can't we have another church for our people right here in Corinth? There's enough of us to back you, and we mean business."

Dan shook his head sadly.

"Thank you, John," he said simply. "It is useless for me to try to tell you how much good this does me; but I can't accept. I have thought of the possibility you mention, but I can't do it. You do not need another church in Corinth. You have more than you need now."

Nor could any argument move him.

"Well," said the farmer, when at last he gave it up and rose to say good-bye, "I suppose I'll keep right on being a church member, but I reckon I'll have to find most of my religion in my work."

"And that," said Dan, as he gripped his friend's hand, "is the best place I know of to look for it. If you cannot find God in your everyday work, John, you'll not find Him on Sunday at the church."

That farewell sermon is still talked about in Corinth or rather—it should be said—is still remembered, for it was one of those sermons of which, while little could be said, much could never be forgotten. And the picture of the big lad, whose strong, clean-looking body drooped so as if in great weariness; whose frank open countenance was marked with drawn lines; in whose clear brown eyes were shadows of trouble and pain; whose voice betrayed the sadness of a mighty soul, will also remain long in the memory of those who were there that evening.

The place was crowded. The triumphant Judge and his friends of the inner circle were there in force, striving in vain to hide, with pious expression of countenance, the satisfaction and pride they felt in their power. The other members were there, curious to hear what Dan would say; wondering how much he knew of the methods that had brought about his dismissal; a little sorry for him; a little indignant; and with a feeling of impotence withal that made their sorrow and indignation of no worth whatever. With identically the same emotions as the members, except that it felt free to express them more freely, the world was there. To a portion of the congregation Dan stood in the peculiar position of a friend whom, as an individual, they loved and trusted, but whom, as a preacher, they were forced to regard as unsafe and dangerous.

It would not do to report all he said, for much of his sermon was not fashioned for the printed page.

But his final words were: "It is not the spirit of wealth, of learning, or of culture that can make the church of value, or a power for good in the world, but the spirit of Christ only. It is not in fidelity to the past but in fidelity to the present that the church can be Christian. It is not the opinion of man, but the eternal truths of God that can make it a sacred, holy thing. It is holy to the degree that God is in it. God is as truly in the fields of grain, in the forests, in the mines, and in those laws of Nature by which men convert the product of field and forest and mine into the necessities of life. Therefore these are as truly holy as this institution. Therefore, again, the ministry of farm, and mine, and factory, and shop; of mill, and railroad, and store, and office, and wherever men toil with strength of body or strength of mind for that which makes for the best life of their kind—that ministry is sacred and holy.

"Because I believe these things I am, from this hour, no longer a professional preacher, hired by and working under the direction of any denomination or church leaders. This closes my ministry as you understand it. It by no means closes my ministry as I have come to understand it."

When he had finished they crowded around him to express regret at his going—sorry that he was leaving the ministry; the church needed men of his great ability—prayed God to bless him wherever he should go—all this and much more, with hand-shaking and many tears from the very people who had made it impossible for him to stay. For this is the way of us all!

As quickly as he could Dan left the church, and with the Doctor walked toward home. The two made no exchange of words, until they reached the monument, where they paused to stand silently contemplating the cast-iron figure. At last Dan turned with a smile. "It is very good cast-iron, I suppose, Doctor."

Then, as if dismissing the whole matter, he took his old friend's arm and, with a joyous ring in his voice that had not been there for many months, said, "Doctor, you'll do me one favor before I leave, won't you?"

"What?"

"Go fishing with me tomorrow. There is something, still, before I can leave Corinth—. I do not know how— Will you go?"

CHAPTER XLII.

JUSTICE.

"The last shadow of his Corinthian ministry had been
lifted from his soul."

ARLY the next morning Dan and the old
Doctor set out for Wheeler's Ford. It was
the nearest point, and while the fishing was
not so good as at other places they knew the spot was
what they wanted. This was one of the days when
they would go fishing—but not for fish.

Leaving their rig by the roadside near the fence,
the two friends wandered away up the stream; cast-
ing their hooks now and then at the likely places;
taking a few fish; pausing often to enjoy the views
of silver water, over-hanging trees, wooded bluffs,
rocky bank or grassy slope, that changed always with
the winding of the creek.

Returning to the rig for their lunch and to give the
old horse his generous allowance, they went down-
stream in the afternoon, this time leaving their rods
behind.

"Really, you know," said the Doctor, "the tackle
is such a bother on this kind of a fishing trip." At
which sage remark Dan's laugh rang out so freely
that the woods on the other side of the little valley
gave back the merry sound.

Dan felt strangely light-hearted and free that day.

348

The Doctor thought the lad was more like himself than he had been for months. The truth is that Dan's gladness was akin to the gladness of home-coming. He felt as one who, having been for long years in a foreign land, returns to his own country and his own people. He was again a man among his fellow-men, with no barrier between him and his kind. Once more he was in the world to which he belonged, and it was a good world.

There was, too, a strange, delightful feeling of nearness to her—the woman he loved. He had had no word since she left Corinth, nor did he know where she was. He would never find her again, per-haps, but he no longer belonged to a world separate and apart from her world. He felt nearer to her even than when they were together that last time in the old Academy yard.

Dan was conscious, too, of a sense of freedom—of a broader, fuller life than he had ever known. Through the old Doctor's timely words, setting his thoughts into new channels, he had come out of his painful experience with a certain largeness of vision that made him stronger. He had found himself. He did not know yet what he would do; he had plans dimly formed, but nothing fixed. What did it matter? Somewhere he felt his garden waited for him; he would find his work. He was free from the deadening influence of the cast-iron monument and that, for the moment, was enough. So far as his Corinthian ministry was concerned only one shadow, out of all the dark cloud of his troubled experience remained. When that was lifted he would turn his back upon Corinth forever, but until then he did not feel free to go.

They were lying on the grassy bank of a woodland pasture, where a herd of cattle grazed or lay contentedly in the shade of the scattered trees.

"Heigh-ho," said the Doctor, "I believe I will go with you, lad."

For some time they had been silent and it was almost as though the old man had spoken to his companion's thoughts.

"Go where?" asked Dan, turning over on his side and half-raising himself on his elbow.

"Why home to Mutton Hollow, of course. You'll be leaving pretty soon now, I reckon."

"I suppose so," mused Dan vaguely. "But I'm not going home."

The old Doctor sat up. "Not going home!"

Dan smiled. "Not just yet," he answered. "I want to run about a little first."

"Uh-huh," the Doctor nodded. "Want to get your hair dry and your shirt on right side out before you face the folks."

Dan laughed. "Perhaps I want to look for my garden," he said.

"Good!" ejaculated the other, now very much in earnest. "Let me help you, lad. You know what I have always hoped for you. My profession needs—."

Dan interrupted gently, "No. No Doctor, not that. I have a notion—but there—it's all too vague yet to even discuss. When I am ready to go home I'll write you and you can meet me there. Will you?"

The old man hid his disappointment, answering heartily. "Sure I will! I'll be there when you arrive, to help kill the fatted calf." He did not tell Dan of a letter from his mother urging him, for certain reasons, to visit them, or that he had already promised her to be with them when Dan should return.

The shadows were beginning to stretch toward the river, and the cattle were moving slowly in the direction of the farmyard, hidden somewhere beyond the fringe of timber, when the two friends went leisurely back to the road to find their rig and start for home.

Climbing the fence they paused and—seated on the top rail—watched a team and buggy just coming down the opposite bank of the stream to cross the ford. Midway the horses stopped to drink.

"By George," muttered the Doctor, "it's our friend the Judge!"

The same instant, Dan recognized the man in the buggy. With the recognition all the brightness went out of his face—as a cloud, all the sadness returned.

"Doctor," Dan said, slipping down from the fence as he spoke, "excuse me a minute. I must speak to that man."

The Doctor kept his place on the fence, while Dan stepped into the road. The team, when they had left the ford, stopped as they reached him.

"How do you do, Doctor?" called the man in the buggy in a loud voice; then to Dan, "Well, sir, what do you want now?"

Dan stood near the horses' heads, his eyes fixed

on their driver, and the Judge, seeing the sorrow in his face, misunderstood, as always.

"Judge Strong," said Dan. "You are the only man in the world with whom I am not at peace. I cannot be content to leave Corinth, sir, with anything between us."

The crafty Judge thought he understood. He took Dan's words, with his manner, as an acknowledgment of defeat; an act of submission. The Elder had not believed that the young man had really wished to leave the ministry. He was quite sure now that the preacher, recognizing at last the power that had thrust him from his position and place in the church, wished to sue for peace, that the same power might help him to another position. So this big upstart was tamed at last, was he?

The Doctor, sitting on the fence and hearing every low-spoken word, held a different view of the situation.

"Well," said the Judge haughtily.

Dan hesitated. "I—I wished to ask a favor, sir; one that I feel sure a Christian could not refuse."

Now the Judge was confident of his position and power. He grew still more dignified and looked at Dan with the eye of a master.

"Well, out with it. It is growing late and I must be going."

"You will remember, sir, that the last time I called on you in your home, you made certain grave charges against three women who are my friends."

"I repeated only the common—"

"Wait, please," interrupted Dan. "This is a matter between you and me. I understand that you were angry and spoke hastily. Won't you please retract those words now?" Dan's voice was almost pleading in its sad slowness; his eyes were on the Judge with an anxious, appealing look. Disappointed at the request so different from that which he had expected, the Judge angrily answered, "Stand out of my way; I have no time for this, sir!"

But quietly, carelessly it seemed, Dan laid one hand on the back of the nearest horse, almost touching the rein, and moved a step or two closer to the buggy.

"Sir, I am sure you do not understand. Miss Farwell and I—I had hoped to make her my wife. We—we parted because of the church."

The Doctor on the fence felt a lump in his throat at the pain in the boy's voice. Dan continued, "I am telling you, sir, so that you will understand. Surely you cannot refuse to take back your words under the circumstances."

"Oh, I see," sneered the Judge. "You lost the girl because of the church and then you lost the church! A fine mess you made of your pious interference with other people's business, didn't you?" And then he laughed. Looking straight into those sad, pleading eyes—he laughed.

"The damned fool," muttered the old Doctor on the fence.

"Am I to understand that you refuse to retract your words after my explanation?" Dan's tone was mildly doubtful.

The Judge was well pleased at what he had heard.

"I have absolutely nothing to take back, sir." He laughed again. "Now if that is all, stand aside!"

But suddenly the light in Dan's eyes flashed red.

"No!" he cried, "that is not all!" With a long step he reached the side of the buggy.

The next moment the Judge found himself on the ground.

"Wh—what do you mean sir?" he roared. "Take your hands off of me!"

Dan's voice was trembling with rage, but he spoke deliberately.

"You unspeakable cur, I have felt sorry for you because of your warped and twisted nature; because you seemed so incapable of being anything more than you are. I have given you a chance to act like a man, and—you—you laugh at me! You escaped punishment for your theft from that poor widow. You have escaped from God knows how many such crimes. But now, in the name of the people you have tricked and robbed under the cover of business, in the name of the people you have slandered and ruined under cover of the church, I'm going to give you what such a contemptible rascal as you are, deserves."

The Judge was a large man, in the prime of life, but his natural weapons of warfare were those of the fox, the coyote and their kin. Cornered, he made a show of resistance, but he was as a child in the hands of the young giant, who thrashed him until he lay half-senseless, moaning and groaning in pain, on the ground.

When Dan at last drew back the Doctor, who

through it all had remained quietly seated on the fence—an interested spectator—climbed down from his position and came slowly forward. Looking the Judge over with a professional eye he turned to Dan with a chuckle.

"You made a mighty good job of it, lad; a mighty good job. Lord, how I envied you! Chuck him into his buggy now, and I'll take him home. You can follow in our rig."

So they went home in the dusk of the evening. And the old Doctor told around town a tale of how the Judge had met with an accident at Wheeler's Ford that would keep him in the house for quite a spell.

Dan spent his last evening in Corinth with Dr. Harry and the next morning he left. The last shadow of his Corinthian ministry had been lifted from his soul.

Corinth still talks of the great days that are gone, and the greater days that are to come, while still the days that are, are dead days—shadowed by the cast-iron monument which yet holds its place in the heart of the town, and makes of the community a fit home for the Ally.

Judge Strong has gathered to himself additional glory and honor by his continued activity and prominence in Memorial Church and in his denomination, together with his contributions to the various funds for state and national work.

Elder Jordan has been gathered to his fathers. But Nathaniel came to feel first, the supreme joy of seeing his daughter Charity proudly installed as the assistant pastor to the last of Dan's successors. They live at the old Jordan home and it is said he is the most successful preacher that the Memorial Church has ever employed, and the prospects are he will serve for many years to come.

Denny, through his minister friend, has received his education and—surrounded now by the books he craved—cultivates another garden, wherein he bids fair to grow food for men quite as necessary as cabbages or potatoes. Deborah is proud and happy with her boy; who, though he be crippled in body, has a heart and mind stronger than given to many.

The Doctor seldom goes fishing now, though he still cultivates his roses and, as he says, meddles in the affairs of his neighbors. And still he sits in his chair on the porch and watches the world go by. Martha says that, more and more, the world, to the Doctor, means the doings of that minister Dan Matthews.

It was a full month after Dan left Corinth when he wrote his old friend that he was going home. The Doctor carefully packed his fishing tackle and started for Mutton Hollow.

CHAPTER XLIII.

THE HOME COMING.

"Some things, thank God, are beyond the damning power of our improvements."

AND now this story goes back again to the mountains to end where it began: back to where the tree-clad ridges roll, like mighty green billows into the far distant sky; where the vast forests lie all a-quiver in the breeze, shimmering in the sun, and the soft, blue haze of the late summer lies lazily over the land.

Beyond Wolf ridge, all up and down Jake and Indian creeks, and even as near as Fall creek, are the great lead and zinc mines. Over on Garber the heavily loaded trains, with engines puffing and panting on the heavy grades, and waking the echoes with wild shrieks, follow their iron way. But in the Mutton Hollow neighborhood, there are as yet no mines, with their unsightly piles of refuse, smoke-grimed buildings, and clustering shanties, to mar the picture. Dewey Bald still lifts its head in proud loneliness above the white sea of mist that still, at times, rolls over the valley below. The paths are unaltered. From the Matthews house on the ridge, you may see the same landmarks. The pines show black against the sunset sky. And from the Matthews place—past the deerlick in the big, low gap—

past Sammy's Lookout and around the shoulder of Dewey—looking away into the great world beyond, still lies the trail that is nobody knows how old.

So in life. With all the changes that time inevitably brings, with all our civilization, our inventions and improvements, some things must remain unchanged. Some things—the great landmarks in life and in religion, the hills, the valleys, the mists, must ever remain the same. Some things, thank God, are beyond the damning power of our improvements.

In minor things the Matthews home itself is altered. But Dan's father and mother are still—in spite of the years that have come—Young Matt and Sammy.

It was that best of all seasons in the Ozarks—October—the month of gold, when they were sitting on the front porch in the evening with the old Doctor, who had arrived during the afternoon.

"Now, Doctor," said the mother, "tell us all about it." There was no uneasiness in her calm voice, no shadow of worry in her quiet eyes. And the boy's father by her side was like her in serene confidence. They knew from Dan's letters something of the trials through which he had passed; they had assured him often of their sympathy. It never occurred to them to doubt him in any way or to question the final outcome.

"Yes, Doctor," came the deep voice of the father. "We have had Dan's letters of course, but the lad's not one to put all of his fight on paper. Let's have it as you saw it."

So the Doctor told them—told of the causes that had combined to put Dan on the rack, that had driven him in spite of himself to change his views of the church and its ministry; told of the forces that had been arrayed against him, how the lad had met these forces, and how he had battled with himself —all that the Doctor had seen in the months of watching; all that he knew of Dan, even to the time when Dan declared his doubt of everything, and to the chastising of Judge Strong. He omitted nothing except the declaration he had heard Dan make to the Judge.

Several times the narrator was interrupted by the deep-voiced, hearty laugh of the father, or with exclamations of satisfaction. Sometimes the Doctor was interrupted by a quick, eager question from the mother, that helped to make the story clear. Many times they uttered half-whispered exclamations of wonder, distress or indignation.

"When he left Corinth," said the Doctor in conclusion, "he told me that he had no clearly-defined plans, though he hinted at something that he had in mind."

"But, Doctor, haven't you forgotten a very important part of your story?" the mother asked.

"What have I forgotten?" he questioned.

"Why, the girl of course. What is a story without a girl?" she laughed merrily.

To which the Doctor answered, "I reckon Dan will tell you about that himself."

At this they all joined in a hearty laugh.

The next day Dan arrived and after a brief time,

given up to the joy of family reunion, he took up the story where the Doctor had left off.

From Corinth Dan had gone directly to the president of the big steel works, whom he had met at the time of the convention. With the assistance and advice of this man of affairs he had been visiting the big mines and smelters and studying zinc and lead. He had worked out his plan and had interested capital and had come home to consult with his parents concerning the opening and development of the mine on Dewey Bald.

Then he talked to them of the power of wealth for good, of the sacredness of such a trust— talked as they had never heard him talk before of the Grace Conners, and the crippled Dennys, who needed elder brothers willing to acknowledge the kinship.

When he had finished his mother kissed him and his father said, "It is for this, son, that mother and I have held the old hill yonder. It is a part of our religious belief that God put the wealth in the mountains, not for us alone, but for all men. So it has been to us a sacred trust, which we have never felt that we were fitted to administer. We have always hoped that our first born would accept it as his life work—his ministry."

So Dan found his garden—and entered the ministry that has made his life such a blessing to men.

The next morning he saddled his mother's horse early. At breakfast she announced that she was going over to the Jones ranch on the other side of Dewey. "And what are you planning to do today?" she said to Dan as he followed her out of the house.

"I was going over to old Dewey myself," he answered. "I thought I would like to look the ground over." He smiled down at her. "But now I'm going with you. Just wait a minute until I saddle a horse."

She laughed at him. "Oh no, you're not."

"But, mother, I want to talk to you. I—I have something to tell you."

"Yes, I know," she nodded. "You have already told me—"

"Has Doctor—" he burst forth.

"No indeed! For shame, Dan. You know Doctor wouldn't. It was in your letters, and—— But I have planned for you to tell me the rest this evening. Go with your father and Doctor to look at the stock this morning and write your business letters while I attend to *my* affairs. Then, the first thing after dinner, you slip away alone over to Dewey and do your planning. Perhaps I'll meet you on the old trail as you come back. You see I have it all fixed."

"Yes," he said slowly, "you always have things fixed, don't you? What a mother you are! There's only one other woman in all the world like you."

And at this she answered bravely, "Yes, I know dear. I have always known it would come, and I am glad, glad my boy—but—I—I think you'd better kiss me now." So she left him standing at the fence and rode away alone down the old familiar path.

After dinner Dan set out.

CHAPTER XLIV.

THE OLD TRAIL.

" . . . Those whose hearts and souls are big enough
to follow the trail that is nobody knows how old."

LEAVING the ridge just beyond the low gap,
Dan made his way down the mountain side
into the deep ravine, below Sammy's Lookout, that opens into the hollow.

For an hour he roamed about, his mind upon his
plans for the development of the wealth that lay in
the heart of the mountain. After a time, still intent
upon his work, he scrambled up the end of the little
canyon, regained the ridge near the mouth of the
cave, then climbed up on the steep slope of Dewey to
the top. From here he could follow with his eye a
possible route for the spur that should leave the
railroad on Garber to the east, round the base of the
mountain and reach the mine through the little
ravine on the west.

From the top he made his way slowly toward the
Lookout, thinking from there to gain still another
view of the scene of his proposed operations and to
watch the trail for the coming of his mother.

Drawing near the great ledge of rock that hangs
so like a cornice on the mountain side, he caught a
glimpse—through the screen of trees and bushes—of
a figure seated on the old familiar spot. His mother
must have come sooner than she intended, he

thought, or else he had been longer than he realized. He looked at his watch; it was early yet. Then going on a little, he suddenly stopped—that was not his mother! He drew nearer and pushed aside a bush for a better view.

His heart leaped at sight of the familiar blue dress and its white trimming! The figure turned slightly as if to look up the trail. The big fellow on the mountain side trembled.

"How like," he whispered half aloud, "God, how like—"

Softly as one fearing to dispel a welcome illusion he drew nearer—nearer—nearer. Suddenly a dry bush on the ground snapped under his foot. She turned her face quickly toward him.

Then, springing to her feet Hope Farwell stood waiting with joy-lighted face, as Dan went stumbling in wondering haste down the hill.

"I thought you were never coming," she said. "I have been waiting so long." And then for a little while there was nothing more said that we have any right whatever to hear.

When he insisted upon an explanation of the miracle, she laughed merrily.

"Why it's like most miracles, I fancy, if only one knew about them—the most natural thing that could happen after all. Dr. Miles came to me some two months ago, and said that he had a patient whom he was sending into the mountains with a nurse, and asked me if I would take the case. He said he thought that I would like to see the Mutton Hollow country, and—and that he thought that I needed the trip. You can imagine how quickly I said that I would go. I am living down at the Jones place."

"Where my mother went this morning?" Dan broke in eagerly.

She nodded, "Your mother and I are—are very good friends," she said demurely.

"Does she—"

Hope blushed. "I couldn't help telling her. You see she had your letters and she already knew a great deal. She—"

"I suppose she told you all about it—my finish at Corinth—I mean, and my plans?" interrupted Dan.

"Yes," Hope replied.

"Then there's nothing more to do but— How is your patient?" he finished abruptly. "How long must you stay with the case?"

She turned her head away. "My patient went home three days ago."

When the sun was touching the fringe of trees on the distant ridge, and the varying tints of brown and gold, under the softening tone of the gray-blue haze that lies always over hollow and hill, were most clearly revealed in the evening light—Dan and Hope followed the same path that Young Matt and Sammy walked years before.

In the edge of the timber beyond the deerlick, the two young lovers found those other older lovers, and were welcomed by them with the welcome that can only be given or received by those whose hearts and souls are big enough to follow the trail that is nobody knows how old.

THE END.

PELICAN POUCH SERIES

VOODOO IN NEW ORLEANS
by Robert Tallant

THE VOODOO QUEEN
by Robert Tallant

THE DEVIL'S BACKBONE
by Jonathan Daniels

OLD CREOLE DAYS
by George W. Cable

STRANGE TRUE STORIES OF LOUISIANA
by George W. Cable

THE CREOLES OF LOUISIANA
by George W. Cable

THE GRANDISSIMES
by George W. Cable

THE SHEPHERD OF THE HILLS
by Harold Bell Wright

THE CALLING OF DAN MATTHEWS
by Harold Bell Wright

THAT PRINTER OF UDELL'S
by Harold Bell Wright

THE WINNING OF BARBARA WORTH
by Harold Bell Wright

LEGENDS OF TEXAS VOLUMES I AND II
edited by J. Frank Dobie

PILGRIMAGE: A TALE OF OLD NATCHEZ
by Louise Wilbourn Collier

EVANGELINE
by Henry Wadsworth Longfellow

EVANGELINE: A NOVEL
by Finis Fox

THE NEUTRAL FRENCH:
THE EXILES OF NOVA SCOTIA
by Mrs. Williams

SOUTHERN LIBRARY SERIES

HUEY LONG'S LOUISIANA HAYRIDE
by Harnett T. Kane

GUMBO YA-YA: FOLK TALES OF LOUISIANA
by Lyle Saxon, Edward Dreyer, and Robert Tallant

OLD LOUISIANA
by Lyle Saxon

FABULOUS NEW ORLEANS
by Lyle Saxon

LAFITTE THE PIRATE
by Lyle Saxon

CHILDREN OF STRANGERS
by Lyle Saxon

MARDI GRAS . . . AS IT WAS
by Robert Tallant

**THE PIRATE LAFITTE AND
THE BATTLE OF NEW ORLEANS**
by Robert Tallant

EVANGELINE AND THE ACADIANS
by Robert Tallant

NEW ORLEANS: AS IT WAS
by Henry C. Castellanos

**OLD NEW ORLEANS:
WALKING TOURS OF THE FRENCH QUARTER**
by Stanley Clisby Arthur

MARDI GRAS: A PICTORIAL HISTORY OF
CARNIVAL IN NEW ORLEANS
by Leonard V. Huber

END OF AN ERA: NEW ORLEANS, 1850-1860
by Robert C. Reinders